BITTER HEAT

SINGED SERIES
BOOK ONE

MIA KNIGHT

COPYRIGHT

CHAPTER 1

"*J*asmine?"

She turned from her contemplation of the snowy world outside to see Kaia was finally awake. The older woman lay in a hospital bed. The gray hair at her temples was damp with sweat, and her stout figure seemed to have shrunk in the span of six hours. A thick bandage peeked out of the top of her hospital gown, covering a fresh incision down the middle of her chest. She went to Kaia's side and grasped her hand.

"How are you feeling?"

Kaia grimaced. "Like I got kicked in the chest by a horse."

Her mouth curved in a wan smile. "You pulled through the surgery like a champ. Everything's going to be okay now."

Kaia's eyes glistened with tears. "What are the chances that after all these years of asking you to visit, the first time you come, I have a heart attack?"

She blocked out the mental image of how she had found Kaia this morning. "It was meant to be that I was here, so I could help."

Kaia searched her face. "Are you okay?"

She let out a choked laugh. "You're asking me that? You're the one who had open-heart surgery."

1

"Jasmine."

Kaia's sympathetic voice made her eyes sting. She averted her gaze and cleared her throat. "I'm fine. I'm just glad you're all right."

"I know you're supposed to head back to New York, but can you stay a little longer?"

The panic that had dogged her all day threatened to choke her. "I would, but..." She met Kaia's pleading gaze. "They called him."

Kaia's brows drew together.

"I can't be here when he arrives." Despite her effort to keep her shit together, her words started tripping over each other. "It's been five years. I can't... If he sees me, I don't know what he'll—"

Kaia gripped her hand with surprising strength. "He won't come."

She blinked. "What are you talking about? Of course, he will."

"He won't." Kaia closed her eyes as if she couldn't keep them open a second longer. "You know we've never been close."

She did know. It was the only reason she decided to come in the first place. "I'm sure once he hears you had a heart attack..."

"He's visited once since he left for college. He won't come back, even for an emergency. Promise me you'll stay, at least until I get back on my feet."

She couldn't deny Kaia when she looked so frightened and fragile. "Okay, I'll stay."

Kaia's relief was obvious as she shifted on the pillows and let out a pained gasp.

"Do you need a nurse?" she demanded as she leaped for the call button.

"No, no," Kaia mumbled. "I'm fine. You should leave now before the snow gets any worse."

Automatically, her gaze went back to the window. White flakes flirted with the frosted glass before drifting innocently down. Two hours ago, she called the only inn in town, but all the rooms were filled. Either she had to make the trek back to Kaia's remote mountain cabin or sleep in the hospital. She didn't like either option.

"Ma'am?" A nurse appeared in the doorway. "Visiting hours are over. You can come back tomorrow."

She nodded and looked back at Kaia to see that she had fallen asleep. When she leaned down and kissed Kaia's weathered cheek, the older woman made an urgent sound and reached for her.

"She'll be fine," the nurse said when she hesitated. "It's been a long day for both of you. You should get some rest."

Jasmine left the room on quaking legs that carried her just beyond the doors of the ICU. She leaned against the wall, closed her eyes, and let out a shaky breath. It had been a long, exhausting day, but it was over. Kaia was going to be all right. That's all that mattered.

She was so drained, she could barely think. As she stood there, trying to figure out what to do next, the sound of a stifled sob captured her attention. Several doors down, a doctor tried to console a man who had tears running down his face. The man's helpless despair was easy to read. Her emotions surged, but she ruthlessly tamped them down and switched her attention to a nurse pushing a cackling old man in a wheelchair down the corridor. The nurse altered her course to avoid a large man standing in the middle of the hall. Jasmine's gaze idly flicked to the man and slid back to the nurse before all her senses went on high alert. Her attention snapped back to the newcomer. She was too far away to make out his features, but her sixth sense told her who he was—her worst nightmare in the flesh. She pushed off the wall and headed in the opposite direction. Even as her mind told her that she was overreacting, she rounded the corner and broke into a run.

A cluster of nurses around a desk looked up as she blitzed past. One of them called out to her, but she didn't stop. She dodged around the medical staff, raced down deserted hallways, and shoved through double doors. She didn't stop until she came upon an unlit corridor.

As she skidded to a stop, the lights flickered on, revealing a wing under construction with plastic sheets on the ground, a scaffold, and paint buckets lined up against the wall. She bent over and placed her hands on her knees as she panted. Maybe it wasn't him. The only details she could discern from that distance was a large man with dark hair. That had been enough to make her bolt. God wouldn't be cruel enough to add him on top of everything else, would he?

"Still running from me, Jasmine?"

That all-too-familiar voice reverberated in her ears. God was fucking cruel. In all the different scenarios where they faced one another, a deserted hospital corridor never crossed her mind. In the best scenarios, she was at a party looking like a million dollars on the arm of a man who couldn't take his eyes off her. Instead, she was dressed in an old college T-shirt and jeans, didn't have on a lick of makeup, and hadn't brushed her hair before she rushed Kaia to the hospital.

"Pretending I don't exist isn't going to work."

The taunt made her whip around. He was standing closer than she anticipated. She had to stop herself from backing up at the sheer size of him. Before, his size had made her feel feminine, dainty, and protected, but those days were long gone. If it wasn't for the suit beneath his open overcoat, he could be mistaken for a football player, ranch hand, or construction worker. His tailored clothes were an indication of how far he'd come in life, if she'd been living under a rock and failed to see his face plastered on magazines or on the news. James Roth's success was well-documented by the media, who couldn't get enough of his rags-to-riches story.

Her eyes flicked up and collided with his, a stunning liquid black that had fascinated her from the start. He was racially ambiguous, with strong features from Kaia's American Indian background and his German and Danish father. The full beard was new, as was the faintest hint of silver in his hair, even though he hadn't hit forty. Despite his refined appearance, something about him was still rough around the edges. Once upon a time, that raw power had drawn her to him, but now, she examined her ex-husband through a jaded lens. He was downright frightening. What the hell was her twenty-three-year-old self thinking? Roth wasn't the type of man she wanted to meet in a dark alley... or a deserted corridor.

"You're the last person I expected to see here."

His dispassionate tone snapped her out of her dazed horror. It had been five years since she laid eyes on him, and that was all he could say? Her chest burned, but she banked her anger and donned the mask she had cultivated in the public eye when she was a child. If he wanted to play cool and unaffected, then she would do the same.

"I could say the same about you." It took considerable effort to sound as blasé as him, but she managed.

"What are you doing here, Jasmine?"

"Visiting."

His eyes narrowed. "Since when are you and my mom so close?"

"I always kept in touch with her even after..." She trailed off and gave a one-shoulder shrug. "I call her occasionally to check on her. She always invites me to visit, but this was the first time I took her up on it. I'm glad I was here for her today."

He didn't respond. He just stood there, staring at her. She knew the tactics. Her father was a master manipulator, after all. Roth was trying to intimidate her with his silence. Not going to happen. The initial shock of seeing him made her lose her head, but she was in control now, and she could handle him.

"As much as I'd like to engage in a staring contest, I have places to be," she said airily. "The only reason I'm still here is because Kaia didn't think you would come, but you're here now, so I'll..."

She took a step to the side and froze when he shifted with her. She stared at him for a moment before she took another step. Again, he moved to block her.

"Roth," she said in a warning tone.

"Do you know how long I've waited for this moment?"

His crooning tone raked over her taut nerves like sandpaper.

She edged backward. "I'm not playing this game with you."

She desperately raked her mind for an exit strategy as he invaded her space.

"Who said I'm playing a game?"

"You're always playing a game. Everything you do is calculated. You're a chess master, herding people where you want them before you take them out."

"Some people think life is a game. I've always known it's war."

Her control snapped as she stumbled on the dirty plastic covered in paint splatters. "Fuck you, Roth! Get out of my way."

"Your face has been all over the news since your father died."

She stopped dead in her tracks, hands balling into fists at her side. "Don't talk about my father."

He cocked his head to the side, scenting blood like the predator he was.

"Patched things up with him, did you?" he asked softly.

"None of your fucking business," she said through clenched teeth.

"Oh, I think it is."

She wasn't prepared for the hand that wrapped around her throat, or the way he pulled, so she was forced onto her tiptoes. Her heart careened into her throat as she gripped his massive wrist with both hands.

"You think I forgot what he did to me?"

His clinical tone made the hairs on her nape stand up.

"That was a long time ago," she said hoarsely.

His impassive expression melted into one of savage fury. "He kept at it until the day he fucking died."

She didn't want to believe it. "No, he—"

His fingers tightened around her throat, stopping her denial. He leaned in, so close that their lips were mere inches apart.

"Are you calling me a liar, princess?"

The vicious energy pouring from him made her temples throb.

"If you don't let me go, I'm going to scream."

"Do it," he invited with a cold smile that didn't reach his eyes. "I'm sure your sisters would love to see our names linked together in the media." He leaned in and pressed his lips against her ear. "You're not in New York with your bodyguards or your family to hide behind. You're in Colorado in the middle of a snowstorm with nowhere to go. Don't push me."

The threat combined with his hot breath gusting over the shell of her ear made her shiver. His beard scraped against her cheek as he pulled back. His proximity, the firm hold on her throat, and the resolve in his expression scrambled her thoughts. She was no match for him, and the satisfied gleam in his eyes told her he knew it. As she tried to think of a way out of this, her eyes dropped from his and landed on the scar on his upper lip. The beard covered another scar on his jaw, but she could see the tail end of it on his neck.

"Did he bribe you to leave me?"

Her gaze flew back to his. "What?"

A muscle clenched in his jaw. "Did he promise to give you your inheritance if you left me?"

She was so stunned, she couldn't answer. She watched turbulent emotions play over his face and saw the flash of impatience before his fingers tightened around her throat.

"Answer me," he said, words laced with menace.

Her nails dug into his wrist. His hold on her throat was just shy of bruising. He wasn't hurting her. Yet.

"Fuck you, Roth." He played her so badly that even now, the shame of knowing how gullible she had been ate at her. He wanted to rehash old times? Screw him.

"I'm not playing, Jasmine. Answer me."

She punched him in the chest. There wasn't much power behind it, but she still expected some reaction. He didn't give her one. He just watched her with eyes that belonged to the Grim Reaper. She wanted to scream in his face and knee him in the balls, but it was impossible with the way he was holding her.

"No, he didn't bribe me," she said through clenched teeth.

"Then why?"

"I left you because I refused to be a pawn!"

"Is that what you think?" he asked as his eyes moved over her face.

"It's what I know."

"You know nothing."

"If you don't let me go, I swear to God I'll—"

He propelled her backward. She landed against the wall hard enough to make her grunt. Her mind went blank with shock as he plastered his rock-hard body against hers. Her puffy jacket stopped her from discovering if he still had abs, but her jeans and thermal underwear did nothing to protect her from his bottom half. He dropped his hold on her throat and slid his hand into her tangled hair. Gripping it, he forced her head to tip sideways, baring her throat to him. One thick thigh pressed between her legs, forcing them to part.

"Roth, stop!"

He bit her. Her shrill scream echoed down the hallway. She raised her hand to claw his face, but he grabbed her wrist and yanked it down as he sucked hard enough to make her buck against him. Her neck was an erogenous zone he had discovered early on in their relationship. He reclaimed the spot as if they hadn't been separated for years. Her free hand twisted in his suit as her eyes closed, and her body went up in flames.

"Don't," she whispered hoarsely.

He cupped her ass and dragged her up his thigh, creating a friction that made her hiss.

"If you hadn't run to your father, you'd still be mine."

The rage and resentment she felt for him crumbled beneath a tidal wave of lust. She shuddered against him like a junkie, alternately wanting to draw blood while also aching to feel him inside her. He would give it to her right here, right now—rough, dirty, raw—just the way she needed it. She came to Colorado to leave everything behind and forget, just for a little while. Roth could do that for her. He would leave her so sated, she would feel nothing. Their chemistry had been explosive right from the start, but she had been too innocent to know how to combat what was happening between them. He used her curiosity to introduce her to dark, erotic fantasies that no self-respecting Hennessy should have, and now she was stuck with them.

Strands of Roth's hair brushed against her jaw. He was wearing cologne, something familiar she had gotten a whiff of at the funeral. Roth never used to wear cologne or tailored suits, and had been more likely to wear work boots with jeans and a button up. At first, her father had been amused by Roth's refusal to conform. That was before he learned of their affair. She thought she was going against the grain by marrying a man who hadn't been born into her father's circles, but she was wrong. Roth was every bit as ruthless. It just took a few years for him to afford to dress and smell like men of her father's caliber.

When she went boneless, he growled in approval. She wanted him so badly, she could taste him in her mouth. Body and mind clashed. She had to stop this before she made a monumental mistake she'd regret. What would her father think if he could see her now? That killed her buzz and brought back all the shit she had been trying to forget.

"You have to stop," she whispered.

He ignored her and pressed in closer. She was losing the fight. In a last-ditch effort to hold on to a shred of her self-respect, she uttered the one thing she knew would get a reaction from him.

"Jamie, please."

He went rigid against her and lifted his mouth from her skin. Uttering his nickname evoked memories she had buried long ago. No one was allowed to call him by his first name, so she gave him a ludicrous nickname and teased him unmercifully about it. That seemed like a lifetime ago.

"I want to go home," she whispered, voice thick with tears as her emotions got the better of her. Weeks of stress caught up to her, leaving her depleted and fighting to keep her composure. It was all too much.

The thigh between her legs disappeared so abruptly, she stumbled like a newborn foal. Before she could find her balance, a beefy hand manacled her wrist and began to drag her back the way she'd come.

"What are you doing?"

"We have to leave now before we get snowed in."

She dragged her boots against the tiles in an effort to slow him down. "I'm not going anywhere with you!"

"Airport's closed until tomorrow, there's nowhere to stay in town, and the snow's coming down thick and heavy. We're going to the cabin."

"*You* can go to the cabin. I'm staying here."

"They'll kick you out."

"I'll sleep in the waiting room."

"And chance being recognized? A picture like that could end up on tomorrow's front page. I can see the headline now: Homeless Hennessy Heiress."

"I don't care!" She blamed her pitiful tone on the fact that it had been the day from hell. "Who do you think you are? You can't—"

"I can do whatever the fuck I want."

"Not with me!"

"We'll see about that."

She had the crazy urge to leap on his back and pound him on the head. "Why are you here? Kaia said you wouldn't come."

"I wasn't going to, but I decided to be a good son for once in my life." He shot her an unreadable glance. "I never thought I'd run into my elusive ex-wife. I guess this trip wasn't for nothing."

"How can you be so cold?" He didn't even bother to act concerned for Kaia. "Your mother had a heart attack! You haven't even asked me how she is!"

"I was informed that she pulled through surgery."

"And that's enough information for you?"

"Yes."

"You should be grateful you have a mother who cares about you."

"You think so?"

"Yes! She's a sweet woman living up in the mountains all by herself. You never visit her."

"For good reason."

He turned the corner, shamelessly lugging her behind him. A nurse came out of a room with a chart in hand and stopped dead when she caught sight of them.

"Married squabble," Roth said with an ease that shocked her.

"We're divorced!" Jasmine retorted and finally picked up her feet because the awful squeaking her shoes were making on the tile would wake every patient on the floor.

"Roth, let me go!"

"Are you afraid of me?"

Yes. "No!"

"Then what do you have to worry about? Tomorrow, we'll come back to town, and you can leave."

One night. A couple of hours… She could do that, right?

Roth stopped at the ICU counter. The nurse who told her visiting hours were over looked up with a scowl, but her expression altered once she got a good look at him.

"Can I help you?"

"My mom's Kaia Roth," he stated.

The nurse glanced at Jasmine before she said, "She's resting. You can come back tomorrow. We'll discuss the care she's going to need for the next couple of weeks."

He nodded and continued down the hallway. She tried to come up with a plan, but her mind was alarmingly blank. He pulled her into the elevator. When the doors closed, she stared at their reflection. He towered over her, richly dressed and intimidating in his fine clothes, while she looked like a grubby teenager.

"I can't do this," she said.

"You can."

"Fine. I don't *want* to do this."

"Suck it up."

The elevator stopped, allowing a doctor to get on. She debated whether she should reach out for help. As if Roth could read her mind, he tightened his hold on her, a clear warning not to test him. She wanted to push, but she was too damn tired.

The elevator opened on the first floor. He tugged her out and stopped in front of the double doors that led out to the parking lot.

"Keys," he said curtly.

"What?"

He slipped his hand beneath her jacket and into her jeans pocket.

"What the hell?" she screeched and clawed his wrist.

He held her irate gaze as he fished. Her nerves were shot by the time he retracted his hand and held up the keys to his mother's truck. He knew exactly what he was doing. Touch was a powerful tool, and he was wielding it unmercifully against her, pushing her to her limit.

"Fuck you. I'm staying here," she said and turned away.

He wrapped an arm around her waist and lifted her off the ground. She howled as he carried her through the double doors into the snow. The frigid temperature took her breath away. Fluffy white flakes fell into her gaping mouth. He trudged through the snow until he found Kaia's truck, which was quite a feat since it was nearly unrecognizable coated in white. He unlocked the driver's door and shoved her in. She crawled across the bench seat as he climbed in behind her.

"I-I'm not going a-anywhere with-with—" she chattered.

"Shut it," he said as he turned the key in the ignition and adjusted the seat to fit behind the steering wheel.

When she reached for the door handle on the passenger side, he grabbed her jacket and jerked her around to face him. Their breaths came out in white clouds and clashed in the air between them.

"You owe me, Jasmine."

Something inside her snapped, and a moment later, he jerked back. Belatedly, she registered that her palm was stinging and realized what she'd done. His dark skin wouldn't show her handprint, but the promise of retribution in his eyes confirmed that she had struck him. She didn't fucking care. After a hellish day of fear and worry, his bullying had pushed her over the edge.

"I owe you?" She was so furious, she could barely speak. "I-I broke off my engagement for you! I got disowned and didn't speak to m-my family for years because of you! I gave up *everything* for you!"

She wasn't aware that she grabbed fistfuls of his coat or that she tried to shake him as she unraveled.

"You married me for my name. You *used* me."

Her voice broke as the past filled her with mortification and pain. A tear spilled down her cheek, but she was too pissed off to care that she was revealing a hole in her shield to a man who preyed on weakness.

"The only reason you held on to me was to spite my dad. You two were caught up in this battle that had nothing to do with me, so I left. You got everything you wanted. You skyrocketed after the divorce. You're the mogul you always wanted to be."

She looked at her hands bunched in the rich fabric of his overcoat and dropped them.

"I don't owe you shit, Roth. You cost me everything."

She brushed her sleeve over her cheek and, once again, reached for the door handle. A firm tug on her jacket told her he wasn't giving up.

"We'll finish this at the cabin," he said without inflection.

"There's nothing to finish," she told the frosted window.

"Your tears say different."

"It's been a long day."

"You can rest when we get there."

She turned her head and glared at him through her tears. "I don't want to be around you."

"Tough shit." He put the truck in gear. "Buckle up."

CHAPTER 2

The small Colorado town was closed up for the night. The streets were deserted, and there were hazy orange halos around the streetlights as the storm attempted to swallow everything in its path. She adjusted the vents, even though the air wouldn't get warm enough to take away the chill in her bones. Kaia's old truck might have an engine that was still going strong, but that was all it had in its favor. The vehicle sorely lacked the creature comforts like heat and comfortable seats. She pulled up her hood and angled her body away from Roth as they left behind all signs of civilization and headed out on the open highway.

She rested her forehead against the chilly window and closed her eyes. Her impulsive trip to Colorado was turning into a disaster. She couldn't say it was a complete flop since she had saved Kaia's life, but any hope of gaining a scrap of inner peace about her father's untimely death had vanished. Roth's proximity riled her, reminding her how gullible and naïve she'd been.

Did he bribe you to leave me?

As his question echoed through her mind, she wondered what game he was playing. He knew exactly what made her leave. That night in London had played over and over in her mind on an endless loop for the past five years. She could quote every word he had uttered that night. It was inked on her soul. That night, he didn't destroy just their marriage, but her as well. She walked away disillusioned, humiliated, a shell of a human being. She spent the years since meticulously piecing herself back together and fortifying her shields, so no man would be able to use her as he had. It took him minutes to wreck years of progress.

She had always wondered how he would react to seeing her again. Never in a million years had she entertained a scenario where he pinned her against the wall and bit her. She shuddered, and this time, it wasn't from the cold. He still had the power to turn her body against her. He could make her forget her common sense and morals and make her desire him despite all that had transpired. How was that possible?

Seven years ago, Roth shook her perfect world to its core when he convinced her to take a gamble on him. When their eyes locked for the first time, something lit up inside her, recognizing him as someone special and once in a lifetime. What a load of bullshit. She'd been so insanely in love with him that she gave up everything—her family, birthright, and fiancé. Roth was a tornado, appearing out of nowhere and dragging her into his world before he disappeared, leaving her scattered in pieces. Their marriage was short-lived and filled with public scandal and emotional trauma. Thanks to the fact that Roth had recently reached the coveted billionaire status, their names linked together in any capacity would make headlines. She wanted to avoid media scrutiny at all costs and keep the scandal where it belonged—in the past.

The truck lurched to the right, jolting her out of her thoughts, and slamming her against the door. She hissed and sat up. At some point, Roth had left the highway and was now navigating a steep mountain road. The headlights reflected off the snow falling steadily around them, limiting their visibility. She had sweated bullets navigating the treacherous road in broad daylight, so how he could do so in the dead of night was unfathomable to her. She clutched her seat belt as the sound of snow crunching beneath the tires filled the cab.

She leaned forward, desperately trying to see through the swirling white.

"We should turn around," she said.

"We're fine."

"Roth, it's getting heavier. I can't even see the guardrail!"

"I've been driving this road all my life. I know every turn."

"You haven't been home in years," she said through clenched teeth as the truck plowed through the deepening snow.

"Hush."

"Roth—" Her teeth snapped together as the truck rocked violently to the left.

He shifted gears and slowed the truck to a crawl. She could feel him flexing his impenetrable will as they crept up the mountain, determined to reach their destination. In a distant part of her mind, she knew turning back wasn't an option. She sat very still, leery of distracting him. The narrow, winding road was barely big enough for two cars to pass one another and filled with hairpin turns and stretches where nothing protected them from going over the side. The few guardrails that existed were mangled or missing chunks from cars that had careened into them.

When the truck began to slide, she bit back a scream and held on for dear life. Roth turned into the slide and, when the tires found traction, shifted gears again and soldiered on.

"We'll be there soon."

He sounded unruffled and completely in control. She hoped he wasn't faking it. She mentally helped him steer as they climbed. Her anxiety rose as the snow got heavier.

"I'm surprised you're here alone," she said, unable to take the silence. She was about to lose her shit.

"What did you expect?"

"Personal assistant, bodyguards."

"Depends on the nature of my business."

"No need to bring them when you're coming to see your sick mother?"

"No."

She cast him a fuming glare and ground her teeth as he shifted gears again.

"Do your sisters know you're here?" When she didn't answer, he said, "I didn't think so."

"It was supposed to be a quick trip. I didn't anticipate any of this," she said, voice shaking as tendrils of frigid air seeped from the vents. She wrapped her arms around herself as a gust of wind battered the truck.

"You shouldn't have come here alone."

"Why?"

He glanced at her, the lights from the dashboard turning his eyes an eerie green. "Now you have no one to save you."

"I'm not afraid of you."

His attention went back to the road. "Says the woman who ran through a hospital to avoid me."

"You're the last person I wanted to see."

"I realized that when you ran to your father instead of talking to me."

She opened her mouth to defend herself.

"We made it."

She could barely make out the cabin through the snow coming down in heavy sheets.

"Thank God," she said.

"Be careful. The snow's deep."

He wasn't wrong. When she swung out of the cab, her boots disappeared into the white powder. She braced herself against the icy wind and followed the path Roth made to the porch. She gave her feet a cursory stomp to get off as much snow as possible before she dashed inside. Her hand smacked the light switch. Nothing happened.

"Power's out," he said.

This was a straight-up nightmare. "W-what are we going to d-d-do?"

"I'll turn on the generator."

He pulled up the collar of his stylish overcoat, which definitely hadn't been made to brave these brutal elements, and slammed the door on his way out. She pulled her phone out of her pocket and turned on the flashlight. The cabin felt like a freezer. Her thick jacket and thermal underwear were no help against the arctic temperature. Why had she thought coming to the mountains would be a peaceful experience? She staggered to the fireplace, breath materializing in a small cloud as she began to build a fire the way she had observed Kaia doing it. She knocked pinecones into the fireplace and tried to crumple up newspapers, but her stiff hands weren't working right. She grabbed the lighter and clicked it a few times before the paper took the flame. By the time Roth returned, she was huddled so close to the fire, she was in danger of being singed.

Roth shook off a considerable amount of snow and flipped on the lights, which made the cabin feel more like a home and less like a drafty cave.

"She doesn't have much fuel for the generator," he said. "We have enough to run the heat, but not much else. We'll have to pick up more when we drive into town tomorrow."

Instead of warming himself by the fire, he disappeared into his mother's room. She was too cold to be curious about what he was up to. When the ice melted on her front, she stood and turned her back to the fire. Kaia's home was a one-bedroom A frame with a loft. The cabin was old, but Kaia was quite the handy-woman and did a good job of keeping it up. A wall of glass let in the maximum amount of light, and showed remarkable views of the mountain range. There hadn't been a speck of snow when she arrived two days ago. Now, it felt like the dead of winter instead of October. Snow pelted the glass in angry swirls while the wind howled. She was in a straight-up horror movie. Remote cabin? Check. No electricity? Check. Roads blocked? Check. Scary male with sketchy intentions? Fucking double check. She should have taken her chances at the hospital.

Roth emerged from his mother's bedroom with a duffel over one shoulder. He tossed it on the ground before he opened the door to a storage closet under the stairs. He emerged with an armful of supplies —a rifle, candles, flashlights, and blankets. He threw everything on the couch before he approached the fireplace. She scooched to the side so she wouldn't brush shoulders with him and stomped her feet because her legs were numb.

"You should change," he said.

Even though she didn't want to leave the warmth of the fire, she understood changing out of her damp clothes was imperative. "Any chance of hot water?" she asked and was pleased her teeth were no longer chattering.

"Yes."

She was so relieved, she would have hugged him if he wasn't such a bastard. She went up to the loft, which had a bed and tiny sitting area, grabbed fresh clothes, and locked herself in the tiny bathroom. She ran the water until it was hot and moaned in relief when she stepped under the sizzling spray. A hot bath after this hectic day was just what she needed, though as soon as she turned off the water and the steam dispersed, the cold began to set in again. Before she finished slathering her arms with lotion, she was already back to shivering. Kaia's old heating system would take hours to warm the cabin. She whimpered as she dressed in three layers of clothing and left the bathroom.

Roth sat in front of the fire with his phone. From his disgusted expression, it was obvious he didn't have service. Not good news. She went up to the loft and pulled on her beanie cap and gloves before she dove under the covers. They were damp from the cold. She buried her face in her frosty pillowcase as a door closed downstairs. Roth probably needed a shower more than she did after being out in the snow.

She curled into a ball and willed the sheets to accept her body heat, but it wasn't happening. She would risk getting hypothermia rather than sit by the fire with her ex-husband. As the minutes passed, she realized her thermal underwear wasn't doing shit. If anything, any warmth she regained from changing into dry clothes was evaporating. By the time he emerged from the bathroom, her teeth were clacking together.

"Jasmine, get down here!"

"I-I'm—" She tried to get out 'fine', but that was beyond her. She was miserable. The sound of the whistling wind only added to her belief that she was going to freeze to death.

There was no door to the loft, just a railing that overlooked the first floor, so she didn't get a warning. One minute, she was trembling beneath the covers, and the next, she was being lifted into the air. She shrieked and kicked before her stomach landed on his shoulder.

"P-put me d-down!"

"I spent winters sleeping in front of the fire," he said as he carried her downstairs and plopped her on the couch he had moved in front of the fireplace. "You'll freeze up there."

"I-I was okay the other n-nights," she stammered, even as she held her hands out to the flames.

"On the other nights, the cabin was already warm, and the temperature wasn't in the single digits."

She whipped her head around to blast him and blinked. The fancy suit and overcoat were gone. In its place were stained, worn jeans and a battered khaki-colored wool-lined jacket with a plaid flannel beneath. Roth went from mogul to mountain man so fast, she was struck speechless. The practical, no-frills clothing was worlds away from the polished veneer he cultivated, but somehow, it fit. It shouldn't have. He was made for the business world and had carved a path that many could only dream of. It was easy to forget his roots, since he hadn't shown signs of it until now. As she examined the outfit, which included well-worn snow boots, she had to admit that he had never looked better. She had grown up around wealthy businessmen. She knew what cologne they wore, the women they married, the cars they were chauffeured in, and what made them tick. None of that interested her, but this outfit captivated her attention more effectively than a ten-thousand-dollar suit.

"Where did you get those clothes?" she asked.

"They were my father's."

"I thought you said he passed when you were a kid."

"He did," he said as he sat on the couch beside her.

"Kaia kept his clothes all these years?"

"Yes."

She edged away so they weren't touching. Nevertheless, she caught a whiff of him and felt a strange stirring. He used her black orchid body wash. Why hadn't he used his mother's Irish Spring soap? Despite the fact he used a girly product, an undercurrent of cedar and evergreen changed the scent into something masculine and alluring.

When the sound of the wind rose to a roar, she hunched her shoulders as if that could protect her from the storm. Two days ago, she watched the snow fall with a smile on her face. At the time, she took it as a sign that everything was going to be okay. Bad shit happened, but the seasons were still going to change, and she had to move with it. Now, the relentless white made her shudder. If she had tried to come back to the cabin by herself, she would have frozen to death. She didn't know anything about generators and would have huddled in front of the fireplace, praying she didn't get frostbite.

"Tell me what happened today."

She wrapped an old quilt around her shoulders as she said, "This morning, she was making cornbread. I took a shower, and when I came out, she was face down on the floor."

The memory of the terror she felt when she had found Kaia made her shift restlessly. It was how she had found her father mere weeks ago. She spent a hellish day pacing the waiting room, braced for the worst. The fact that Kaia pulled through was nothing short of a miracle.

"I knew it would take too long for an ambulance to come. I don't know how I did it, but I managed to pick her up and get her in the truck. It was snowing, and I couldn't see very well. I haven't driven a stick shift in years. I was worried we wouldn't get there in time…" She shivered and drew the quilt tighter around her. "Once we got there, they told me she needed open-heart surgery."

"You kept a cool head and did what you had to."

She glanced at him over the edge of the quilt and quickly averted her gaze. The clothes and warm light playing over his face made him seem more approachable and down to earth, which was a damn lie.

"It was meant to be that I was here when she needed someone," she said.

"You saved her life."

She rose, unable to take his proximity or his attempt to play the grateful son. Not even an hour ago, he had freely admitted he wasn't sure he would come to Kaia's aid even though she had a heart attack. She wasn't going to be manipulated into feeling whatever he wanted her to.

"Where are you going?" he asked.

"Food," she snapped as she headed to the kitchen with the quilt wrapped around her like a cape.

She turned on the gas stove and filled a kettle with hot water. Why hadn't she thought of making tea earlier? She opened the oven, which she had remembered to turn off after she'd gotten Kaia in the truck, thank God. She was forced to shed the quilt, so she could slice the cornbread. Roth loomed in the entry, but she ignored him and exchanged the screeching kettle for a pot of chili. She made two cups of peppermint tea, but didn't offer the second one to him. She left it on the counter and was petty enough to give him the most emasculating mug Kaia had—a goofy, grinning bear. He had to take sips between two round ears. She wasn't sure if his ego could take the hit, but that wasn't her problem. After she took her first gulp, she was suffused with warmth.

"Did you get your inheritance, or did he shaft you in the end and leave you with nothing?" he asked, interrupting her moment of tranquility.

Her eyes cut to him over the top of her glass. He leaned against the wall, composed and at ease with the bear mug in hand. She was miffed to see that, paired with his outfit, the cup didn't look as ridiculous as she had hoped. She ignored his question and stirred the chili.

"You didn't like the terms of his trust," he surmised when she didn't respond. "You didn't get a cut even though you went back and played the perfect daughter. That's why you came to Colorado. You're on the run again."

Her jaw ached from clenching her teeth. She made a monumental mistake when she confided her hopes and fears to him. She handed him every weapon he needed to dissect and manipulate her.

"Did you really think Maximus would treat you like your sisters if you left me? He's a fucking bastard."

She whirled to face him with a wooden spoon covered in chili in hand. She jabbed it in his direction and didn't care that chili splattered over the floor. "Don't talk about him like that!"

She raised the spoon as he approached. He stopped just out of swiping distance and set the empty bear mug on the counter with a finality she didn't like. When he leaned forward, she prepared to smack him, but he didn't reach for her. Instead, he skewered her with eyes that glittered with banked rage.

"Your father was no saint," he said. "He publicly disowned and humiliated you."

"My broken engagement ruined his partnership with Parker Baldwin. He lost millions."

"Don't make excuses for him."

"I'm used to business coming first." She gave him a pointed look. "I'd think you out of all people would understand that."

They stared at one another, their past pulsing in the air between them.

"My father changed," she said quietly.

"I doubt that."

"It doesn't matter whether you believe me or not. It's done. He's gone."

"It's just begun," he countered. "We'll see how Colette and Ariana handle Hennessy & Co without his guidance."

She lifted her chin. "My sisters have been handling the company for years. They'll be fine."

"Did he leave a portion of Hennessy & Co to you?"

She frowned. "Why would he? I haven't been involved in the company since I was twenty-three."

"That doesn't mean you can't contribute."

She raised a brow. "Aren't you the one who told me I was no good at business?"

"You had the right mind, not the right heart."

"What the hell does that mean?"

He pointed at her. "Right there."

"What?"

"Too much emotion."

She was surprised the wooden spoon didn't crack under the pressure she exerted. "You're not so staid yourself."

"It depends on the topic."

"Right." Business and sex were the only things that made him show his true emotions. Everything else didn't blip on his radar.

"You follow the rules and don't have the heart to take from others. Your sisters do."

She squashed the pang of resentment. It was clear he admired her sisters, who were following in their father's footsteps. He was right. She didn't have the heart to play the high stakes game her family thrived in. Roth had more in common with her family than she did. If Roth had the right pedigree, her father would have welcomed him with open arms. Instead, Roth's businesses had been destroyed when her father discovered their affair. He had been forced to go overseas to rebuild.

"What did Maximus leave you?"

She crossed her arms over her chest. "You already assumed he left me nothing."

"I doubt he changed, but there's always room for error. Am I wrong?"

"You're obsessed with his trust."

"Everyone's curious."

"You seem more curious than most."

He gave a one-shoulder shrug. "I can't help wanting to know how he divided his fortune."

"You're the last person I'd confide in."

He eyed her for a long moment before he said, "Chili's boiling."

She whirled and whipped the pot off the fire before it burned. "Get out of here! You're distracting me."

She reached for a cabinet, letting it swing open close enough to his face to make him back off. After he left the tiny kitchen, she made another cup of tea. She left the quilt on the counter, so she could carry her tea and food back into the living room. Roth had built the fire into a blaze. She basked in the heat before she dug in. She didn't realize how hungry she was until she took her first bite. She was halfway through her meal when he joined her. He sat on the opposite end of the couch and propped his boots on the raised hearth. They ate in silence. She went back for seconds and made another pot of tea. When she finished, she curled up in her corner of the couch with the quilt wrapped around her. Now that she was clean, fed, and warm, she relaxed.

The sound of the crackling fire soothed her fried nerves and blocked out the storm raging outside. She silently willed Mother Nature to calm the fuck down, so she could get out of here first thing in the morning. Women had an obligation to help each other out, right?

Roth returned from the kitchen and settled beside her. The couch was small and uncomfortable. Like everything Kaia owned, it was old and in desperate need of an update. Out of the corner of her eye, she saw Roth angled in her direction. He rested his knee on the cushion between them and draped his arm along the back of the couch.

He said nothing.

He thrived on other's discomfort. She could feel his eyes moving over her. She inwardly bristled and tried to don an indifferent expression, but she was out of practice. Roth knew how to get under people's skin and was doing a damn good job of using that skill on her now.

"Stop it," she said when she couldn't take it any longer.

"Stop what?"

"Staring at me."

"Make me."

She turned her head and locked eyes with him. She couldn't read him worth a damn. She wasted two years trying to get in his head before she realized she would never understand him. How could she when he categorized everything in terms of profit and loss? She wasn't capable of being as brutally calculating as he was. Memories of that night in London seeped into her mind, and she looked away.

"Tell me about Thalia Crane."

Her head whipped around so fast, she felt a streak of pain in her neck. She couldn't have heard right... but his calm, expectant expression said she wasn't having a nightmare. He knew. Oh. My. God. Her need to flee was so strong, her eyes moved to the door.

"You won't get far," he said quietly.

CHAPTER 3

*S*he covered her face with her hands and moaned. No, this couldn't be happening. She rocked back and forth as if she were locked in fervent prayer—and she was. If God made her vanish in a puff of smoke or just struck her dead, she would be eternally grateful. Anything to save her from this.

"You hit it big writing about our affair, the scandal, being disowned, about our sex life—"

She dropped her hands to declare, "It's *loosely* based on us."

"The virgin scene is position by position our first time."

She wrapped her hands around her throat because she could feel it closing. "Y-you *read*…?"

He tapped his fingers on the back of the couch as his mouth curved into a mocking smile. "All four."

Bile rose. "Some scenes are us but…"

"That scene in the alley was us. That's when we discovered you have a thing for doing it in public—"

"Roth!" She was torn between pummeling him to make him shut up, or locking herself in Kaia's room and freezing to death. She didn't like either option. Her head felt as if it was going to explode. "If you read the books, you know that Rex, the guy who *represents* you, has

27

been in and out of the series so," she said with heavy emphasis, leaning toward him to make her point, "it. Isn't. Us. *Obviously*."

"I think they may get back together in book five."

"They don't," she said flatly.

"Have you finished it?"

It was what she was writing before her father had died. "No."

"Do your sisters know about your pen name?"

"No."

"Does anyone know?"

"Less than five people on the planet," she said through clenched teeth.

"Now six."

"I hate you."

"In the books, you love me."

Her back went ramrod straight. "Shut the fuck up."

"I'm partial to the first book. It has the best sex scenes, if I do say so myself."

She erupted from the couch and stood, hands fisted at her sides. "Shut up, or I swear to God, I'm going to shoot you!"

The fact that Roth read the books, which documented most of their affair and then some... Her feelings for him were in black and white. So were their sexual preferences and fetishes. She hadn't held back when she wrote it. Why would she? She had the protection of a pen name, and she wasn't going to tell anyone about it. Ever. And now... Now it was all out in the open. She couldn't handle this.

"If you shoot me, you'd be killing off one of the main characters."

She let out a strangled yell as she stalked away from him. The bathroom was the only sanctuary in the cabin, aside from Kaia's bedroom. Impulsively, she ducked into the bedroom and slammed the door. She turned the old-fashioned lock and was on her way to the bed when the door opened.

She whirled, and bellowed, "Get out!"

He leaned against the doorjamb. "Just so you know, none of the locks work."

"But the doors do, so get out."

"If anyone should be upset, it's me. You never asked for my permission."

She gaped at him. "Excuse me?"

"The guy has my build, my face, my words, and my background. I'm surprised no one figured it out. Those books are everywhere. Soon, it'll be made into a movie, and then everyone will know."

"I based the characters and situations on real things, but everything else is made up. No one suspects anything."

He surveyed her through hooded eyes. "How much of it's true?"

"What do you mean?"

When he came toward her, she looked around for a weapon, but the only thing in the spartan room worth hurling at him was an old lamp or a Bible. Fuck.

He stopped two feet away. He didn't look amused any longer. He was deadly serious.

"I didn't cheat on you."

Her blood ran cold. "What?"

"In the book, you leave your husband because you found out he was cheating. I didn't cheat on you."

Oh, God. This couldn't be happening. "The books are fiction," she said through numb lips.

"But you divorced me, just like the woman in the book."

He wasn't shying away from their past, he was diving right in. Damn him for being so confrontational. This was her worst nightmare. "I didn't know when I started the series that the couple wouldn't stay together. Cheating was just a way to break them up."

"You mean us."

She ground her teeth. "The characters started out like us, but now they're their own thing."

"So, you didn't go on a fuck fest after you left me?"

Even as her stomach iced over, she raised her chin. "What happened after you is none of your business."

Her muscles locked as he crowded her, blocking out the rest of the room and intimidating her with his size.

"You'll always be my business," he growled.

"That's all I ever was to you."

"What does that mean?"

She tried to walk around him, but he grabbed her arm. When she struggled, he gave her a shake that rattled her teeth.

"Stop fucking running and talk to me!" he shouted.

She had never heard him yell before. The sound of his enraged boom freaked her out.

"Talk!" he ordered.

She shoved him as hard as she could, gaining her freedom in the process by forcing him to take a step back, before she blasted him back.

"I don't want to talk. There's no point in this! It's over."

"Yet here we are." He spread his arms wide. "And there's no one around to save you."

"I don't need anyone to save me from you. I can handle you on my own."

"Can you?" he asked softly.

"Yes." She had no choice.

The confines of the bedroom were stifling, and she was freezing. She raised a hand to her cheek and let out a disgusted sound when she couldn't feel it. She passed him and headed back to the fire. There would be no sanctuary, not tonight. If he wanted to bring up the past, she was unable to avoid it. His intimate knowledge of her Thalia Crane series was the cherry on top of this nightmare sundae. He knew everything. He had the power to destroy her professionally and skewer her emotionally, and there was nothing she could do about it.

She rewrapped herself in the quilt, tucked her feet under her, and leaned into the armrest. As he reclaimed his seat on the opposite end of the couch, she stared into the flames and wished she could be consumed by them. Daylight would come soon. The storm would pass, and this would all be over.

"You had to know this day would come," he said.

She shook her head. "No."

"You thought you could avoid me forever?"

"Why would we bump into each other? I'm not part of your world."

"You still make headlines."

"Only when my father forced me to attend functions and ..." *And during his funeral.* It had been a media circus.

As if he were following her line of thought, he said, "You were photographed with Lincoln at your father's funeral."

She gave him a disgruntled glance before she looked back at the flames.

"Matthew too."

"It's expected." She had been photographed with every prominent businessman and politician in New York.

He tugged on the quilt to gain her attention, as if she was capable of ignoring his ass.

"Anyone interested in you?"

She stared into the flames and pulled the covers tighter around herself.

"They're from the right families," he said in a deceptively even tone. "Men your family would approve of."

"Don't, Roth."

"How much of the fucking around with other guys in the books is real?"

The sensible part of her knew she shouldn't bait him, but did he expect her to live the life of a spinster after she divorced him?

She gave him a taunting smile. "What do you think?"

Roth knowing about her alter ego, Thalia Crane, could go both ways. If he read the books, he knew a fraction of the salacious exploits she'd had post-divorce. She had lived recklessly for a time and didn't regret it. She tried to keep a straight face as she imagined Roth reading the steamier sex scenes. The series had been a hit. A divorcee attempting to build a new life, find herself, and letting everyone in on the drama along the way.

"You're better than that," he said.

"No, I'm not. I may be a Hennessy by blood, but I've never lived up to their standard. After the divorce, I realized I was free. For the first time in my life, I had no one to impress and no expectations to live up to. So, I did what I wanted. I threw myself away for a while."

She peeked to see how he was taking that. He was *not* pleased. If he could be honest, then so could she. So, what if she fucked a ton of guys? She was no one's wife, and she wasn't running a billion-dollar corporation like her sisters. He said he hadn't been unfaithful during their marriage, but they had spent most of their time apart, so how could she be certain? Besides, she was sure he hadn't lived the life of a monk since the divorce, so who was he to judge her?

"How did you find out I'm Thalia Crane?" she asked.

When he didn't answer immediately, she raised her brows.

"Roth?" she prompted.

"My assistant."

She jerked. "What?"

"She read your books under Minnie Hess."

"And how would she know my other pen name?"

"I told her."

"Why?"

He shrugged. "My assistant is an avid reader. Every free moment she has, her nose is in a book. I told her to read your work."

"You were trying to promote me?" She couldn't believe it.

"She asked what you did for a living, and I told her you're a writer and gave her your pen name. When Thalia Crane became popular, she picked it up and recognized the similarities in the writing styles and our history. She gave the series to me without telling me a thing. Two months ago, I was on a flight and cracked it open. It took me less than two pages to realize it was you."

How random was that? If his assistant wasn't a reader, he would be none the wiser. "Did you ask her not to…?"

"She won't reveal your identity."

She scrubbed a hand down her face. "Oh, my God."

"The series has been gaining in popularity. It's just a matter of time before someone you know figures it out. How long do you think you can keep your identity a secret?"

"Forever."

"Why'd you stop writing as Minnie Hess?"

"They weren't selling, and I wanted to write something more..." She pursued her lips as she searched for the right word. "Adult."

"Thalia's adult, all right."

She shot him a quelling glance. "I started writing as Thalia when you moved to London, and I was still in college. I was... exploring." She had been romanticizing her life like a naïve idiot, but the series had morphed into something else. The books gave her an anchor when her life turned upside down.

She studied him surreptitiously. If her readers could see the inspiration for her anti-hero, Rex, they would understand why she risked everything for him. Roth still dripped sex appeal. His size wasn't just for looks, either. When they had sex, he used every inch of his body to drill her. He was a bastard, but he was still as sexy as fuck. Couldn't he have gotten fat or lost an eye or something? Shit.

She sighed and snuggled into the cushions and pretended they were stuffed with feathers instead of flat as pancakes. "You were right."

"About what?"

"I wasn't cut out for the business world. I would have worked under my sisters and followed their lead if you hadn't come along and told me to follow my passion. That's one good thing that came out of our marriage, so... thanks."

"You built a career from our sex life."

She gave him a saccharine smile. "I'll put you in the acknowledgments for the next book."

"You do that. I have a fan base."

Her smile melted into a glare. His eyes moved over her with an intimacy that made her want to slap him.

"You need more material?" he asked.

"I'll pass."

"Why did you come here, Jasmine?"

"Why do you keep asking me that? I wanted a change of scenery."

"That's not it. What happened in New York?"

"Nothing happened—" she began, but the lie caught in her throat, and she stopped. She took a deep breath and then another. Something trickled down her face. She raised a shaking hand to her cheek and stared at her wet fingertips.

"Jasmine."

Out of the corner of her eye, she saw him reach for her. She stumbled to her feet with the quilt wrapped around her. She put some distance between them as she tried to stuff her emotions back into the box where they belonged. She couldn't break down here. He was the last person she wanted to see her like this, but grief didn't care where she was. It wanted its pound of flesh.

"Jasmine."

When his hand closed on the back of her neck, she jerked away.

"Don't touch me!" she hissed as she swiped at the hot tears slipping down her face.

She was trembling, but it wasn't from the cold. Pain threatened to split her heart in two.

"Jasmine."

When he appeared in front of her, she backed away.

"I don't..." She swallowed hard and tried again. "I don't *want*—"

Her throat closed, and she dropped her head to hide her face as emotion took over. When he wrapped his arms around her, she fought him. He ignored her struggles and drew her against his chest. She clenched her teeth to stop herself from making a sound, but her ragged breathing was far from calm. He cupped the back of her head, fingers tunneling through her damp hair as he massaged. She grabbed fistfuls of his jacket as she battled for control.

"Just breathe."

"I-I can't," she whispered.

The loss she hadn't allowed herself to feel hit her full force. When the first sob escaped, she tried to smother the sound against his body. He picked her up and carried her back to the couch as she clutched at him, battling her emotions for supremacy. He settled on the couch with her on his lap and unzipped his jacket. Her cheek landed on his broad shoulder covered in soft flannel. She shook her head as she fought the tide threatening to pull her under. A keening sound escaped. Even to her own ears, the pitiful sound was filled with heartache and despair. He pressed her face against his throat. The familiar scent of him added more turbulence to an already potent emotional cocktail.

She tried again. "I don't want—"

"You don't know what you want."

"I do," she said, her vehemence ruined by a hiccup.

"You don't get what you want out of life. You get what you need."

"But—"

He cupped the side of her face and pressed his thumb against her quivering lips. "Hush."

"You can't—"

His hand dipped beneath her chin and tipped her face up. His mouth landed on hers, and she stopped breathing. The kiss was gentle and soothing and so unlike him. More tears slipped from her eyes. He was trying to comfort her. Did he know how many times over the years she wished he had done this? Held her on his lap and acted like he cared? Her breath hitched. He kissed the corner of her mouth, her wet cheek, and then her forehead.

"Stop," she whispered.

He ran his fingers down her cheek, tracing the progress of a tear, before he kissed her again. Soft, slow, and too short.

"Talk to me, Jasmine."

They stared at one another for a long minute before she reached out. He didn't stop her as she ran her fingertips through his beard. Sorrow churned in her chest as she stroked his harsh face. Every instinct she possessed told her to keep her cards close to her chest and not let him in, but she needed to get it out. It was eating her alive.

"He had another stroke," she whispered.

"Yes."

Her hand dropped from his face and curled into a fist.

"He fell into a coma. The doctors didn't think he would wake up." Her lip trembled, and she swallowed hard. "The lawyers came in, and he... he named me as executor."

She couldn't finish, but realized she didn't have to when he said, "Fuck."

"He said if that ever happened, he didn't want to live like that, and I… I didn't want him to suffer." She dropped her face, so guilt-ridden she couldn't even meet his eyes. "Maybe I should have waited a little longer. I don't know if—"

"You respected his wishes. You made the right call. He would be proud of you."

She swallowed hard as more tears slid down her cheeks. "I hope he knows I was there. I didn't want him to be alone."

"You were there. That's all that matters."

When she covered her face with her hands, he drew her back against him, and this time, she let him. After being ignored by her workaholic father for most of her life, she finally got one in her late twenties… and now he was gone again. The shock of not only losing her father but being forced to make the decision whether to keep him on life support traumatized her. Her sisters had turned their backs on her, leaving her to deal with his death and funeral by herself. She didn't have time to grieve, not with so many things to do. Even after the funeral, she had been locked in a shell-shocked state of denial.

Everything she had been keeping in came out in an unstoppable tide. The façade of acceptance and strength crumbled. She sobbed against his chest as sorrow and guilt built into an excruciating crescendo and then slowly ebbed, leaving her empty and drained. She listened to his steady heartbeat as she calmed.

"I called your mom. She's always been so nice to me. She invited me out here, so I said yes, and then this morning, she…" She swallowed hard. "I-I was so worried that she…"

The fear that once again, she would have to deal with a parental figure dying shattered her. The added stress of facing her ex-husband pushed her to the breaking point, leaving her with no shields to hide behind.

"She's going to be fine," he said.

"I'm sorry."

"For what?"

She sniffled and brushed her hand over damp flannel. "Wetting your shirt."

"Don't worry about it."

She wanted to sleep, wanted it so badly her head throbbed, but her mind wouldn't shut down. So many things were waiting for her in New York, things that couldn't be put off forever, and here she was in the mountains crying on her ex-husband's shoulder. The practical side of her brain told her she needed to put some much-needed distance between her and Roth, but she was finally warm. And his arms around her felt good. Good enough for her to stay right where she was.

"I haven't been able to sleep more than a few hours since he passed," she said, her voice as dazed as she felt. "I'm tired of being tired. I came here to get away…"

When her breath hitched, he stroked the side of her face.

"You're fine," he said.

"I'm not."

"You will be."

His scent tantalized her. She nuzzled his neck and then tasted his skin. Was it her imagination, or did his heartbeat stutter? That encouraged her to put her mouth on his neck. She sucked gently, taking her time, nursing the area with kisses before she sat back to examine her handiwork.

"Jasmine."

Her mind was cloudy with grief and exhaustion, but the dark hunger on his face called forth her own. This man had hurt her more than any other man on the planet. Once upon a time, she would have sacrificed everything for him, and now… Now, he was a stranger, one who she had off the chart's chemistry with. Her volatile feelings for him mixed with her grief-stricken loneliness.

She rested her forehead against his and surrendered. "Fuck me."

His eyes bored into hers. "Why?"

"Because I'm tired of thinking."

He didn't move. She cupped his face and shifted on his lap and felt the hard ridge of his penis between her legs. Her pussy clenched. She knew what it felt like to be beneath him, knew he could wring her dry and leave her so satisfied she couldn't think.

"One night," she murmured.

He looked savage and angry and not the least bit lover-like. Her mouth curved at the corner as she stroked his sinister face.

"Is that what you want?" he growled.

"What I want," she whispered as she let herself fall into the abyss, "is a night when I don't worry about what's waiting for me in New York. I want a night when I don't have to think about who I am or what's expected of me." Her hand glided down his neck, between his pecs, down his abdomen, and landed on his tented crotch. "I want one last night to work you out of my system and not feel guilty about it."

"I'm not noble," he ground out. "If you let me have you, I'll take."

"Take," she challenged as she wrapped her hand around him. "And don't you dare let me think."

CHAPTER 4

$\mathcal{H}$e grabbed her face, angled it the way he wanted it, and kissed her. This time, there was nothing sweet about it. Her mind went blank as he applied pressure on her cheeks, forcing her mouth open to accept his tongue, which invaded with a sensual thrust that made her nipples tingle. He tasted like buttery cornbread and something intrinsically him, which tickled the back of her mind and evoked memories of their past.

She fell into him. There was no need to think, no need to strategize or worry because he knew what he was doing. In this arena, no man could match him. She discovered that after the divorce. He taught her to love savagely and hold nothing back. He told her she could let go with him and be who she wanted to be... and then he abandoned her.

She wasn't paying attention to what her hand was doing to his crotch until he brushed it aside. He kept her mouth busy, drinking from her so deeply, she felt drunk. She hummed when he unzipped his pants and then wrapped her hand around him. This, too, felt innately familiar. She hadn't forgotten him at all. Not the taste of him, the size of his hands, or the cock that made her into a woman. He was the biggest she'd had, and he knew what to do with it. Roth put himself on a pedestal, and even though she begged other men to knock him off, they hadn't. It wasn't fair, but none of that mattered now.

His hand closed over hers, telling her without words exactly what he wanted, as if she could forget. When he undid her jacket, the cold draft made her stiffen, but that was forgotten a moment later when his large hand closed over her breast. He squeezed and released, making her blood run hot. When he squeezed her nipple, she let out a mewl, and his dick jumped in her hand. She smiled and knew he felt it because he knocked her hand away.

"Can't take it?" she taunted, words slurring as if she were intoxicated.

He yanked on her jacket, forcing her arms backward as he took it off, leaving her in two sweaters. Their mouths detached, so he could rip the sweaters over her head and toss them. She hunched her shoulders against the chill and wrapped her arms around herself, now clad in a lace bra, long johns, and jeans. Goosebumps popped up over her skin. She wasn't sure if they were from the cold or Roth, who yanked her forward with a tight grip on her ass and buried his face between her breasts. She braced her hands on the back of the couch and looked down at the erotic sight.

"No rules."

His voice was muffled by her skin, but she still heard it.

"What?"

He turned his head to the left and lapped at her nipple through the lace.

"You're giving me free rein. I can do whatever I want to you. No stopping, no matter what," he said between licks that made it hard to focus.

"Yeah, whatever," she said impatiently and gripped a handful of his hair.

She thought she saw a flash of white as he smiled and then closed his mouth around her nipple and sucked. She tipped her head back and closed her eyes as he sent electrical shocks through her with each pull. One of his hands slid along the seam of her jeans, between her ass, and then pressed against her aching pussy. She rocked her hips, riding his knuckles, feeling the material bunch up to give her the friction she needed.

He switched to her other nipple and began the process again. Nuzzle, kiss, suck. She ran her hands through his hair as he coaxed her mind away from anything serious and responsible and created a reality focused on carnal pleasure. This was how it had always been with him. He was the master and she, the willing slave.

Her body bowed as he sucked hard enough to bruise. "Roth!"

She pushed him into the cushions and yanked on his hair. Just when she was about to smack him, he released her. She moaned as he tongued her swollen nipple and moved to her neck. With unerring accuracy, he latched onto the same spot that he had in the hospital as his hand drifted over her quivering belly. She sucked in a breath as he undid her jeans and sank his hand into the tight space. Two fingers dipped in, and she spread her legs to give him access.

"Dripping wet for me," he said against her neck.

"What are you gonna do about it?" she asked as he played with her honey. He wasn't stimulating her, just exploring, and she wasn't pleased.

"I'm gonna eat it."

He rose without warning, effortlessly rising with her in his arms, before he tossed her on the couch and sent the whole thing skidding back with a booted foot. She watched dazedly as he tossed quilts, old comforters, and random blankets on the ground in a makeshift bed in front of the hearth before he dragged her unceremoniously off the couch. She landed on the pile, which didn't offer much cushion.

"Ouch, you ass!" she growled and yelped when he grabbed her ankles and tipped her on her back.

He shook her out of her jeans and long johns and ripped off her matching lace underwear. She opened her mouth to snap, but forgot what she was going to say when he knelt and dragged her toward him.

His eyes were trained on her pussy as he lifted her and slid a pillow under her ass. His eyes flicked up to hers as he stroked her thighs. He started at her knee and then traveled slowly up, rough hands scraping deliciously over her sensitive skin. She gave in to the compulsion to spread her thighs and saw his mouth curve in a satisfied smile. Fucker.

He leaned down and kissed one inch below her belly button. She shifted restlessly beneath him. He kissed her thigh, lapping so close to what was dripping for him.

"Fuck, Roth."

He looped his arm around her left thigh before he placed his hand on her pussy and spread her.

"So pretty," he murmured as he lowered his head. "Pretty and pink and slick for me."

The first stroke of his tongue made her toes curl.

"You taste the same." His fingers dug into her soft thigh as he went back for another taste. "God-fucking-dammit."

He had always enjoyed going down on her. It wasn't until she dated other guys that she realized not all men were into giving women oral sex, which was beyond lame. If someone thought licking her kitty was gross, no blowjob for them. Simple. Out the door they went.

Roth's free hand wandered over her body. He stroked her belly before he traveled to her breasts. He kneaded them roughly as he ate her. She planted one foot on the floor and lifted her ass off the pillow. When he growled, she looked down the length of her body. Their eyes collided, his black ones reflecting the fire and an animalistic lust that made her womb clench in anticipation. He was going to fuck her so hard. She couldn't wait. She closed her eyes and let him play. His beard created a rough friction she wasn't familiar with and discovered she was totally into.

She could feel her orgasm building. Her breathing became ragged and uneven. He pinched her nipple. She jerked and grabbed a handful of blankets in preparation.

Some days I wish I never laid eyes on you.

Her eyes flew open as the ghost of his words echoed through her head—just as they had for the past five years. Her orgasm vanished along with the carnal fog she had been floating in. What the fuck was she doing?

She immediately tried to scoot out from under his mouth. The beefy arm circling her upper thigh flexed, keeping her in place, while the hand on her breast tightened painfully. She smacked it, but he didn't ease his grip.

He raised his head and glared at her. "What the fuck?"

"I'm done."

His eyes narrowed. "You're not calling the shots."

She rolled onto her hands and knees. He rolled with her, so he was on his back beneath her. He gripped her hips and held her in place when she tried to crawl away.

"Stop, Roth!"

"You're not in control," he said as he positioned her over his face. "You gave me permission to do what I want, and that's what I'm gonna do. Now be a good girl and spread."

"Fuck you!"

He gripped her ass in a vise-like grip that made her yelp. "I'm getting my fill," he hissed as he yanked her down to his open mouth. "No thinking, no tomorrows. Just *this*."

Her mind went blank as he clamped his mouth on her clit. His fucking beard was making her crazy. She moaned and dug her nails into the pile of blankets. Fuck. He was so good and in this position... She rocked, and his bruising grip on her ass immediately began to stroke in encouragement. She buried her face in the blankets that smelled of mothballs and crooked one leg up to ride his face.

Her climax hit so suddenly, she didn't have time to prepare. Her body went taut as a bowstring. Her hand sank into his hair as she pumped her hips against his mouth until that awful tension left her. She moaned and tipped to the side. Roth refused to relinquish his position and rolled with her again, so they were in their original position, her on her back with him between her legs. She hissed when he continued to play with her throbbing clit.

"Fuck, stop, I'm finished," she huffed.

"Not even close," he said before his hands and mouth disappeared.

He stood over her as he undressed. She watched from beneath heavy eyelids as he stripped off his jacket, plaid shirt, and then his jeans. He was the definition of a man. Broad shoulders, a ridged abdomen, and defined arms and legs. He was supersized all over. He wasn't perfect, though. He had little nicks and scars over his body, but that just made him Roth. He had a hairy chest and trail that led to his cock, which was standing at attention. His body had always been beautiful, but something about seeing the firelight playing over his skin and the howling wind outside made her think he looked like a gladiator from another lifetime... and he was going to conquer her. Even though she'd had an orgasm, she was hungry for more. She wanted him inside her.

He held out his hand. Curious, she took it and allowed him to pull her up. He sat, kissed her mound, and lapped at the groove between her thigh and pelvis before he looked up.

"Come here."

As she sank onto his lap, one hand went to her ass and placed her where he wanted her, with one leg on either side of him. She hissed as his fingers slipped inside her. He coated his cock with her while he held her gaze.

"Now, give me that pussy."

Her blood thrummed in her veins as she rose with his hands gripping her ass, then lowered. She braced her hands on his shoulders and let gravity do its thing. She bared her teeth as she worked herself on him. His expression of pain and savage satisfaction rekindled her lust.

When she had worked him all the way inside her, he placed a tender kiss on her temple. She tipped her head back. He took advantage of the invitation and kissed the curve of her jaw.

"It all begins and ends here for us," he growled against her ear as his hands lifted and then lowered her on his cock.

"What?"

"The moment I saw you, I knew I'd do whatever it took to have you under me. That was before I knew you were a Hennessy."

She couldn't focus on his words, not when he was fucking her. Slow and gentle, so different from the way he had been in the past.

"Didn't expect you to be a virgin. Didn't expect you to match me so well."

She wrapped her arms around his neck and ignored his guiding hands and began to fuck him the way she needed. His hands dug into her hips hard enough to make her stop.

"What the fuck, Roth?"

"This is my show."

He licked her sweaty neck and then raised and lowered her again. The sound of her sloppy pussy made her nails dig into his skin.

"Never thought I'd get you here again, so I'm taking advantage. You won't get any sleep tonight."

She bit his shoulder. "Stop messing around!"

He shoved her. She landed on her back with him crouched over her, hands planted on either side of her body. He slid back in and pumped hard enough to make her gasp. The blankets offered no barrier between her and the floor, and he knew it. He rolled his hips, and her eyes crossed as he went deeper than he ever had.

"Do you know how many times I imagined you like this?" He leaned down and gripped her throat. "You're going to feel me tomorrow, princess."

He began to move the way she knew he could. Hard and rough. Holy shit, he was splitting her apart, but she didn't care.

"Didn't matter how long it took for me to catch up with you. I knew I would eventually."

"I hate you," she panted as he raised her thighs and shoved even deeper.

"You don't know how to hate."

She raked her nails down his back and was sure she drew blood as he sped up his thrusts. Her pussy was on fire, and she felt battered and close to tapping out when another climax hit. Her vision flashed white, and she bit into his beefy shoulder to help her through the pleasure-pain. He didn't let up on his pace. Tears streamed down her face as she looked up to find his eyes on her, lips peeled back from his teeth as he fucked her.

"My name," he demanded.

"Roth," she said hoarsely.

His eyes burned. "Your name for me."

She hesitated and then cried out when he ground against her. "Jamie!"

He pulled out, straddled her chest, and cupped her chin.

"Open," he commanded.

When she didn't comply, he gripped her cheeks, forcing her lips apart. Two strokes were all it took for him to come. Squirts of milky white flew over her face, in her mouth, and slid down her chin. They stared at one another as he continued to stroke himself. It was a dominant move he started when they were dating. Back then, it shocked the hell out of her… and then she started craving it.

His expression was softer, but still alert, and one hundred percent focused on her. His intensity was still there, just banked for the moment. The phenomenal view was complemented by the scent surrounding her. Expensive cologne, sweat, and that bite that was uniquely him. If they were in a different time in their lives, she would have teased his still-sensitive cock and sucked him until he was hard again. He stayed crouched over her. What was he waiting for?

"You're heavy," she said.

He shifted, and when she raised her hand to wipe her face, he grabbed her wrist to stop her. Their eyes held as he leaned down and placed a soft kiss on her lips. When she tried to pull back, he grabbed her hair to keep her still. She closed her eyes and gave in. When he pulled back, he wiped her face with a thin blanket before he lay on his side and tucked her against him.

Her body felt warm and heavy. He had given her exactly what she needed. There were no worries about consequences or responsibilities. There was no need to run anymore.

"Rest," he ordered.

She trembled and shifted against him. "I need my jacket."

"I'll keep you warm. Sleep."

"But—"

A hand fisted in her hair and jerked her head back. His mouth landed on hers. The gentleness was gone, as if it had never been. He kissed her hard enough to make her lips throb.

"Your body's revved up. I'm giving you a couple of hours to recover before I fuck you again."

"But—"

He started to tip her on her back.

"Okay, okay."

He tossed his heavy leg over both of hers while he trapped her against him. Though it was a suffocating hold, it was comforting nonetheless. At home, she had a weighted blanket that dulled her senses, so she could shut her overactive mind down, but this was better. With the fire at her back and her face buried in the hollow of his throat, her eyelids drooped. She was toasty warm and sticky and exhausted and content for the first time in weeks. She breathed in his musk and rubbed her face against his skin, unknowingly pressing a kiss over his heart before she sighed and let go.

HER PUSSY WAS BURNING. She struggled, but her arms were pinned, and her legs were spread wide. She had a moment of respite before she was speared. She let out a guttural scream.

"That's what I want to hear, princess."

Her eyes flew open, but nothing made sense. The walls were colored in orange light, and a large man was holding her down. He was fucking her deep, rocking her hips against an unforgiving floor, and saying things she couldn't process.

"Show me those pretty eyes."

She stared up at the man and tried to see his face, but it was cast in shadow. The pain was turning into pleasure, but she couldn't under-stand why.

"Your body knows mine. You get wet just from my voice." The

man's warm breath wafted over her face. "Fuck yeah, wrap me up tight."

"Who are you?" she whispered as she struggled to find the strength to free herself.

"Your god. Remember, Jasmine?"

She tossed her head back and forth as he pounded her burning pussy and finally climaxed, bellowing her name and holding her in place as he planted himself deep. She slapped his shoulders as he covered her like a massive sweaty blanket. She drifted back to sleep with him still inside her.

SHE WOKE flat on her stomach. A man was fucking her from behind. Her calves kicked up as he planted himself deep enough to make her squeal. Her face was turned toward the blazing fire. She knew exactly where she was, why, and who was fucking her. When she shifted beneath him, he gave her his weight to keep her in place.

"I want to be on my knees," she said.

He pressed his cheek against hers. "You awake this time, princess?"

"Stop calling me that."

He chuckled as he uncovered her nape and bit it.

"Let me up," she demanded.

"I like you how you are."

"You'll like the view better if you let me up."

His weight disappeared, and his cock slid out of her swollen pussy. She shifted gingerly, feeling every ache in her muscles as she got on her hands and knees and rested her cheek on a pillow.

He caressed her ass before his fingers brushed over her left hip. "You have tattoos now."

"Several."

"Why?"

Her mouth quirked. "Because I can."

"Why an origami paper crane?"

"Cranes are a symbol of good fortune and peace," she said as she stared at the leaping flames. "The origami represents me as a writer and my life and dreams written on the page. It's a marriage between who I am and what I want out of life."

"And this?" He palmed the vine of delicate flowers that went from hip to ribs on her right side.

"Those were just for fun."

"Never thought you'd get a tattoo."

That was the whole point. "I wanted to make sure I wasn't tempted to go back."

"Back to what?"

"Being a Hennessy."

"You are a Hennessy."

"Not a true one. I can't wear the dresses everyone would expect me to wear without showing a tattoo. I did it purposely. I don't care anymore." She sighed as he gripped her hips and pressed the head of his cock against her. "I stopped playing the game and got out. I'm a nobody now."

"You'll always be a Hennessy and therefore newsworthy."

She moaned into her pillow as he invaded. Though swollen and raw, she was still hungry for more. He awakened something greedy and uncivilized that would never be sated. No one had been able to fulfill her dark needs, so she would take as much as she could get. Once they left here, she would go back to nothing.

"Sore?" he asked against her ear.

"Yeah."

"Good."

He pushed through her inflamed folds, forcing her face into the pillow.

"Tell me you like this."

"I do," she said through clenched teeth.

"You crave it?"

"Yes," she gasped as he fucked her forward.

He hauled her back onto his cock, making her toes curl. He grabbed her by the hair and yanked as he changed position, drilling down and making her eyes cross.

"No one will ever give it to you the way you need it."

When he bit her neck again, she cried out as he pumped his hips. He released her hair and grabbed her by the shoulders to hold her in place as he fucked her. She squirmed beneath him and fell flat on her stomach when he came and used his considerable strength to lodge himself as deep as possible. He panted into her hair before he dropped his face beside hers.

Her body was a trembling, throbbing mess, but it felt damn good. It had been years since she had been so thoroughly wrecked. Her eyes drooped when he rolled off her. She moaned in sleepy complaint as he pulled her against his chest and spooned her from behind.

"You feed my demons," he rasped.

"You created mine."

He introduced her to the darker spectrum of sex, and she'd taken to it with boundless enthusiasm and ease. Being used soothed something broken and lost inside her.

His hand coasted over her body, and she arched lazily into his touch. She let her mind float in this alternate universe. There was no time here, no consequences. Only pleasure, hunger, and warmth.

"I always wondered what I'd do when I caught up with you," he said as he stroked her skin. "You never do what I expect."

"Good. I wouldn't want anyone to think they have me pegged."

His hand splayed over her stomach. "You never remarried."

"No."

He kissed the side of her neck. "I'm sure you had offers."

"Sure." Being a Hennessy, even an illegitimate one, ensured an endless supply of suitors wanting to get their hands on her father's money.

"Why didn't you?"

"They want my name, not me."

"You think so?"

"Yes."

She hovered on the edge of sleep, but didn't succumb. Her mind was cloudy but still chugging along. She enjoyed the intense heat from the fire and imagined she was lying on a beach getting a tan instead of in a remote cabin in the middle of a snowstorm.

She watched the flames devour the wood blocks. She was the wood. He was the flame. After this, they would be ash.

"Was it all worth it?" she asked quietly.

The raw fucking had its desired effect. She was drained of all emotion, which left her clearheaded enough to examine their catastrophic relationship objectively without her heart interfering.

"What?" he asked.

"The long hours, the nights of no sleep... Your face was on the cover of *Forbes* a couple of months ago and now *Business Weekly*. You made it. Are you satisfied?"

"No."

No hesitation in his response.

She rested her cheek against his bicep and sighed. "It will never be enough." She hesitated before she said, "Dad had three strokes. He almost killed himself trying to be the best."

"He's a legend."

"Is that what you're striving for?" It seemed like such an empty goal, but she had grown up around people like Roth her whole life. They were chasing something intangible. Once they reached one goal, they immediately moved onto the next. No celebrations, no breaks, no life. She saw her father suffer in the end. Despite her feelings toward Roth, she didn't want the same for him. "People become legends only when they're dead."

"But their legacies live on."

"You're just like him."

He tensed. "I'm not like Maximus."

She ignored his denial. "We were destined to fail."

"No."

"I was engaged—"

"An arranged marriage."

"It's expected. That's what my sisters have, and they're happy."

"You weren't."

She followed the path her father had laid out for her: private schools, college majors, and even who she would marry. It was expected that during her summer and holiday breaks, she would be at Hennessy & Co, observing and learning. She hadn't been unhappy until she met Roth. He made her feel brave, rebellious, and adventurous. She tossed her morals and fears into the wind and dived headlong into a torrid affair with another man's ring on her finger. She wasn't thinking about consequences, only of herself and what she wanted, and it ended in disaster for all of them. She lost her family and sense of self. Roth was forced to go overseas where he worked like a madman to rebuild what he lost. Her father took a huge financial blow when her broken engagement shattered his partnership with Parker Baldwin, who he had been friends with for decades. All of them paid a price, and for what?

"I accepted my place. Once I graduated, Ford and I would marry. I would quit Hennessy & Co once I got pregnant. That's another thing you and my dad agreed on. I wasn't performing the way he wanted me to in the company, so he thought it was best I became a mother. At least then I would be useful."

"He's a fucker."

"Like you said, it's about legacies. Marrying Ford would have strengthened Dad's ties with the Baldwins, but the broken engagement nearly crippled the company instead. Even though Dad disowned me, his relationship with Parker was never the same." She sighed. "I don't know why I am the way I am."

"There's nothing wrong with you."

She reached back and patted his bristled cheek. "You're sweet."

"I'm not."

"No, you aren't," she agreed before she withdrew her hand. "But that was nice of you to say."

"It's the truth." His arms tightened around her. "You wouldn't have been happy married to Ford."

"He's a good man."

"You'd be bored out of your mind."

Maybe, but they would never know.

"Tell me about the books."

She was too relaxed to go on the defense. "You were in London. I just graduated from college and couldn't get a job because Dad was being an ass... You told me to pursue writing full-time, so I did. I wrote about us. I published the first book under Thalia Crane, and it was a hit. I couldn't wait to tell you. I used my money from the book to go to London and..." Her voice trailed off as the memories began to surface.

I don't know if this is worth it.

The echo of his cold voice uttering those words made her stiffen. Even as she gathered herself to roll away, his hand went to her pussy. When she gripped his wrist to pull him away, his marauding fingers rubbed expertly.

"No tomorrows. Feel me," he murmured.

Her breath hitched as he sucked on her pulse.

"I ..." She tried to gather her thoughts, but they slipped away as quickly as they came.

He pushed her onto her back while he lay on his side. One large thigh slipped between hers and draped her leg over his, giving him unlimited access. She stared up at the open beam ceiling as he rubbed her clit, kissed her neck and massaged her breast. Damn, he was good. It didn't take much time for her body to ignite for him. She grabbed a handful of his hair and pulled.

"Do me," she snarled.

He obeyed, lifting her thigh and sliding his big dick inside her. He rocked slowly. The angle turned out to be more than she could handle. She begged him to hurry, but he kept his pace infuriatingly slow until she climaxed, and even after, he kept it up while she mewled and tried to go back to sleep.

"I'm tired," she grumbled.

He kissed her jaw. "I don't mind fucking you while you sleep."

"Hurry up."

"I'm taking my time. This." He pushed deep, and she gasped. "Feels too good to stop."

It seemed to go on forever. She gave herself up to it and couldn't believe it when he pushed her into another climax and finally came with her. He tossed an arm over her and tucked his face against hers.

"What time is it?" she asked in a raspy voice.

"Five."

"I should get up," she said, but made no move to do so.

"It's still snowing. I'll drive out and check the road in an hour or two. Sleep."

CHAPTER 5

*S*he woke on her side with the fire at her back. She opened one eye. Sunlight poured into the cabin, marking a brand-new day. She was alone. She used the couch for support as she slowly got to her feet and wrapped one of the stiff blankets around her. On her way to the bathroom, she paused in front of the large wall of glass to stare at the world blanketed in sparkling, untouched white. The wind had stopped, and a blue sky unmarred by any clouds stretched over the white mountain range. It was like the night from hell never happened. Looking down at her bare feet, which were toasty warm, she swore she would never take central heating for granted again.

Once in the bathroom, she stepped beneath the steaming spray and washed it all away. She was freakishly calm. Roth accomplished what time hadn't been able to do. He refocused her attention on something tangible and carnal and emptied her, so she could start anew.

Though the tiny mirror was too small to show anything but her face, she felt every mark on her body. He had used her well and made good on his promise because she could still feel him. She borrowed Kaia's fluffy robe and was on her way to the loft when she felt an unpleasant draft. Apparently, the loft still wasn't heated. Clothes weren't vital at the moment, so she detoured to the kitchen and popped an aspirin while she hunted for something to eat. She decided to make a grilled cheese sandwich and was pleased to find a stash of tomato soup as well.

As she turned on the stove to heat the pan, she glanced at the microwave, which flashed zeroes. She went searching for her purse and pulled out her phone, which she had turned off before her flight to Colorado. When she turned it on, a flood of texts, emails, and voicemails greeted her. She ignored all of that and focused on the time, 8:30. She dialed the hospital to check on Kaia and was promptly told they couldn't release any information since she wasn't a relative. She hung up and tried to call Roth before she realized she didn't have his number.

"Shit."

As butter sizzled in the pan, she nuked the tomato soup and listened to the first voicemail.

"Girl, I'm going to plant a tracking device in your ass," Sunny drawled.

Her lips twitched as she put the security coordinator she inherited from her father on speaker as she pulled dishes from the cabinets.

"You take too many risks." Sunny sighed. "I know you need time, but you can't take off like that. You ditched them at a boutique and then turned off your phone so we couldn't track you? Do you know who you are? Dammit, Jas, Lyle's been on my ass since you disappeared. He fired me, by the way, so thanks for that."

Jasmine rolled her eyes. She would deal with Lyle when she got back.

"I hope you're okay. Let me send at least one guy to you. Or better yet, let us pick you up. Call me back."

If it wasn't for her father's death tossing her back into the spotlight, there would be no need for bodyguards. Not only was she trying to cope with her father's death, but she also had security in her face asking for a daily schedule. She felt suffocated and trapped, which is why she ran to Colorado for a break.

Not surprisingly, the next voicemail was from Lyle, her brother-in-law.

"I don't know where you are, but when you come home, I'm going to beat the living daylights out of you," Lyle snapped. "Fuck, Minnie, this isn't a game, and you can't take off anymore. If you're emotional or whatever, go see a therapist or go to a fucking spa. Don't take off without telling us. You can't even shoot me a fucking text? I'm in fucking Amsterdam. I'm up to my ass in meetings. You don't think I have more important shit to worry about? Fuck."

She could hear voices and ringing phones in the background and imagined him pacing as he spoke to her.

"Colette told me about Maximus' will and how she reacted. I didn't know. We need to have a family meeting." A pause and then, "Call me back the minute you get this. I'm worried about you, you little shit. I love you."

She was a teenager when her oldest sister Colette married Lyle. He was from the right family, a tycoon in his own right, and a brasher version of her father. But, unlike her father, family meant something to Lyle. Even while they were estranged, Lyle kept in touch with her. He wasn't afraid of her father and was one of the few who knew about Thalia Crane and was proud as fuck of her. He had an appreciation for art that was lost on her sisters.

Deciding to take pity on him, she called as she bit into her sandwich. He picked up in the middle of the first ring.

"I'm going to kill you."

She munched loudly in his ear and said nothing.

"What the fuck is that?"

She grinned. Nothing like a big brother to make her want to act like a bratty younger sister. "Hello to you too."

"Where the hell are you?"

"I'm still in the States."

"You put us through hell."

She doubted her sisters cared that much, but she didn't feel like arguing. "I'm fine."

"Stop saying that. We all know you aren't."

"Well, I am now." A night of dirty sex could do miracles for one's outlook on life. "I'll be back in New York soon."

"How soon?"

"Sometime today, I think? I'm not sure yet."

"How can you not know—?" He stopped himself before he could finish the question. "Never mind. Do we need to brace ourselves for anything?"

She flipped a sandwich in the pan. "Like what?"

"Whether you shaved your head, got a face tattoo, or decided to get drunk and strip in a public place?"

"No."

Roth wasn't one to kiss and tell. No one would find out about this. Once they left here, they would cease to exist for one another. He would go back to being king of the business world, and she would go back to being an anonymous writer.

"Colette and I will host a family dinner tonight. We should talk before you run off to the country."

He knew her so well. "Fine."

"I'll see you tonight."

He never failed to close a deal. "See you."

She hung up and propped her hip on the counter as she dipped her sandwich in soup. The food settled her stomach and made her feel human again. When her father passed, she put her life on hold and hadn't picked it up since. Her desire to write had been snuffed out, along with her ability to care about anything. After making such a life-changing decision for her father, she had been terrified to make any others, so she hadn't and stayed in limbo. Sparring with Roth snapped her out of her catatonic state and roused her fighting spirit. By simply telling her she made the right call, Roth alleviated the weight she'd been carrying around for weeks. He didn't absolve her of all guilt—no one could do that—but she could accept the fact she had obeyed her father's wishes, and that was that.

She survived Roth. She had some battle wounds, but they were the delicious kind that would fade. Now, she wouldn't have to look over her shoulder or worry about running into him again in the future. If they crossed paths, she was sure that Roth would be civil.

She kicked the last sandwich out of the pan and was drinking tea when she noticed a strange glimmer in the air. She crept toward the window and looked up at the cloudless sky as silver particles drifted down like confetti onto the untouched, sparkling snow. She was so focused on the strange phenomenon that she didn't notice a figure coming toward her until he passed right in front of her face. She leaped back from the window with a stifled shriek before she recognized Roth. He was bundled up and carrying a rifle with an ease that disconcerted her. He shuffled through the deep snow and came around to the front door. She went to the kitchen entrance and watched as he entered, tracking snow into the house. She wrapped the robe tighter around herself. Just looking at him made her cold. He propped the rifle in the corner and dusted off his wool jacket.

"Everything okay?" she asked.

"Yes."

"What's with the gun?"

"A precaution. They're just starting to clear the roads. We should be able to leave in two hours."

"Did you call the hospital?"

"They said she's doing good."

"Great." She hesitated, and then asked, "Is it just me or is it snowing glitter?"

"It's called diamond dust, light reflecting off ice crystals. It happens on sunny days when the temperature dips into the negatives."

Her gaze went back to the window. She wanted to get a closer look, but she wasn't about to leave the warm cabin. "It's incredible."

"Not when you're walking around in it." He ran his hand through his damp hair. "You cooked something?"

"I made grilled cheese sandwiches and warmed up soup."

When she padded back into the kitchen, she heard the sound of his heavy footfalls behind her. As she reached for another plate, two arms caged her against the counter and a large body pressed against her back.

"Night's over, Roth," she said quietly as he buried his face in her wet hair.

"You smell clean," he murmured.

"I showered."

"I prefer you dirty."

He cupped her ass before his hand slipped beneath her robe. She jumped, knocking his head backward. He swore as she whirled around.

"Your hands are like ice! You didn't wear gloves?"

He glared at her. "If I had gloves, I'd fucking wear them."

"You need to go by the fire."

"Why don't you warm me up instead?"

He boosted her up on the counter. She shrieked when he buried his face in the crook of her neck.

"You're insane! Get off me!"

He spread her legs and moved between them. She smacked his chest as his hands moved over her flesh.

"You're freezing," she whined and covered his cheeks and ears with her arms. "You stupid man. You're going to get sick."

"I haven't been sick in years."

"Today might be your lucky day," she retorted.

"I grew up here. I know my limits."

When he pressed his cold nose against her cheek, she flinched.

"Warm me up, princess."

"Seriously, Roth, you need to—"

Two cold fingers speared into her, and she gasped at the polarizing sensation. "Oh, my God."

"I was hoping I could fuck you awake," he said against her ear. "See, my hand's already warm. Your pussy gives off more heat than the fire."

He roused her curiosity and lust. Could she warm him up? Well, if she didn't, he was going to be in trouble. She cupped his clammy neck, and he pressed against her, telling her without words to carry on. Hmm... She pushed against his chest, but he didn't budge.

She raised a brow. "Do you want a blowjob or not?"

It took him less than ten seconds to pull her off the counter and have her on her knees in front of him. She shifted uncomfortably on the rough, unforgiving floor. A second later, his wool jacket landed beside her, revealing another flannel shirt, this one blue. She knelt on the padding, undid his jeans, and wasn't surprised to find him flaccid.

"Poor baby," she said and pressed her cheek against it as she cooed.

"Jasmine," he said through clenched teeth.

For the first time since he tracked her down in the hospital, she was in charge. She looked up as she wrapped her hand around his dick and clucked her tongue.

"Maybe you got frostbite," she mused.

"Why don't you put your mouth on me, and we'll see if you're right?"

She chuckled as she massaged his balls. When he shivered, her playful mood died.

"Seriously, Roth, you should go by the fire—"

She didn't finish her sentence because he grabbed his dick and shoved it in her mouth. When she tried to draw back, he held her in place. She glared up at him and found him watching her with predatory focus.

"Suck me," he ordered.

Fine. If he wanted to catch pneumonia because he wanted a blowjob instead of warming up in front of the fire, that was his issue. She cupped his balls, which felt like cold iron, and used her mouth to coax his dick to come out of hiding. Icy hands sank into her hair, and as he began to lengthen, she pulled down his jeans and ran her hands over more of his chilled skin.

He undid her robe and pushed it off her shoulders. She took her mouth off him to hold on to it.

"Stop, Roth!"

"I don't want you to smell like her," he growled.

She gave it up since he made it clear he was going to rip it off if she didn't comply. "You're such a bully!"

He cupped her face with one hand and redirected her mouth back to his cock. "You like bullies."

"I don't," she muttered and frowned when she saw his skin covered in goose bumps. Maybe a little dirty talk would warm him up.

"I've always loved your cock," she breathed, letting her hot breath feather over it. Veins pulsed beneath her hand as she kissed the head of it and sat up to lick his lower stomach. She pressed her nude body against his legs and shivered as she absorbed the cold.

"You jacked off on me while I was asleep, didn't you?"

"Twice," he said in a guttural voice that made her breasts tingle.

"Do you know how long it took to wash the cum out of my hair?"

He planted his boots on either side of her while she worked him. Her hands stroked his muscled thighs, which no longer felt like frozen tree trunks. She licked around his groin, nipping here and there, while his hand flexed in her hair.

She glanced up and saw his chest moving double time beneath his shirt. Her hand drifted down her body and between her spread legs. "You're right, Roth. I can still feel you."

He yanked her off her knees and plopped her on the counter. He slid inside her with a groan filled with pain and relief. Her arms came around him as he shuddered.

"Why do you feel so good?" she whispered against his neck and raked her nails down his back, wanting to unleash his beast. "I hate that only you can give me what I crave."

He began to move. Deep, powerful strokes that made her inner walls flutter around him. She tucked her face against him and breathed in his musk, which smelled like her body wash and a hint of evergreen.

"I have wet dreams about you," she confessed, making his rhythm falter. "You're my favorite nightmare."

She rocked against him to get him moving again and smiled when he groaned. She clasped the back of his neck and tugged on his earlobe with her teeth before she gave it a little nip.

"I hate that you're from my father's world, that you care about the stock market, hedge funds, and investors. I wish you were normal, a cowboy who clocked out and came home to fuck my brains out."

He gripped her hair and yanked her face away from his neck so he could pierce her with a forbidding gaze that held the promise of violence.

"Cowboy?"

She gave him a cocky smile. "I want a good rider."

He tightened his hold, making her eyes water. "Don't talk to me about other men."

"You know there have been others. You read the books," she said hoarsely and ignored his stinging grip. "How else was I supposed to cope? You showed me who I really am, and then you left me."

"*You* left *me*," he hissed.

"I did what was best for both of us."

"You don't know what's best for me."

A tear slid down her cheek as his brutal grip made her scalp prickle. He looked homicidal, but she didn't care.

"You unlocked something dark in me I didn't know I had," she purred as she stroked his sides. "I tell them what I want, but they don't give it to me raw the way I need it. You give it to me without asking. It isn't fair."

She caused herself considerable pain to get close enough to press her lips against his.

"Why couldn't you just love me?" she whispered.

He yanked her backward until she lay flat on the counter. He drew her legs together and clasped them to his chest as he began to power into her with hard thrusts that made her body arch in an effort to ease the pain. He battered into her with such force that she screamed.

"Come, Roth!" she pleaded.

"I'll come when I'm damn good and ready," he growled. "Your job is to take what I give you."

Her hands scrabbled over the counter as he sped up his thrusts. The sharp sound of his balls slapping against her ass accompanied her moaning and his harsh breathing as he planted himself deep.

Her head tossed from side to side. "Roth, I don't—I can't—"

Her body bowed as she rode the crest of pain and pleasure and then exploded off the end of it. He rode her through her orgasm and didn't let up on his pace as he chased his climax. She writhed on the counter. Her body was an aching, throbbing mess, and she wasn't sure how much more she could take. With the last of her strength, she sat up, cupped both sides of his face, and kissed him. She kissed him the way she used to, before he shattered her world and made her feel like nothing.

He rammed home. When she winced and tried to draw away, he gripped her nape, keeping their lips sealed as he came. She felt the warm gush of his seed, and when he released her, she pressed kisses over his cheek and neck as he panted. She ran her hands down his damp flannel and smiled. Apparently, fucking could save someone even if they were half frozen.

"We haven't used anything," she said quietly. "I'm on the shot, but we haven't been using condoms."

"I'm clean."

So was she, but... "You don't care if I'm on anything?"

"It doesn't matter."

He stepped back, leaving her on the counter, legs splayed, completely exposed.

"What do you mean, it doesn't matter? How could it not matter? You're not worried that I'd throw a paternity suit at you?"

He zipped his pants. "No."

She reached for paper towels to clean herself before she hopped down. She couldn't believe his cavalier attitude. For someone obsessed with building an empire, she would have thought he would be more paranoid about hookups.

"I don't understand," she said as he picked up one of the sandwiches and took a bite.

"Don't worry about it."

She crossed her arms. "Why are you so casual about this?"

"I'm not."

"You are!"

He gave a one shoulder shrug. "You were always on something."

"It isn't like you to assume with something this important."

She watched him finish the sandwich and go for the soup.

"Roth!"

"What?"

"What aren't you telling me?"

He eyed her over his bowl. "It would be impossible for you to get pregnant."

"Why?"

"I got a vasectomy."

There was a short silence in the kitchen as she tried to digest that. "You had a vasectomy? Why?"

"I would think that's obvious."

So, he wouldn't get all the women he fucked pregnant? Did he really fuck around that much that he had to get snipped? As she tried to process this information, a thought crossed her mind that made her go very still. "When?"

"When, what?"

"*When* did you get the vasectomy?"

If she wasn't watching him so closely, she would have missed the way he tensed. Something icy and sharp sliced through her middle as her intuition pinged.

"You got a vasectomy when we were married?"

"Yes."

She felt as if she had been punched. Her ears started ringing, and the breath whooshed out of her lungs.

"I don't want children," he said.

For several seconds, she didn't react. She couldn't. He had just dropped a nuclear bomb on a world she was trying to rebuild and decimated the foundation to rubble. She thought she had gained some perspective and peace with the decisions she had made with her father and now closure with Roth, but with a few words, he shoved her back under the arctic waters of their past.

When she could breathe past the ice forming around her heart, she started toward the exit. She had to get away from him. Years of neglect, humiliation, and fury geysered up inside her. Her eyes burned with tears. Fuck him. Fuck him *hard*. They had been divorced for years, and he still found new ways to hurt her.

When his hand closed around her arm, she wrenched away

violently.

"Don't you fucking touch me," she said in a lethal voice that trembled with rage.

"We never talked about having children."

She held up a hand. "Don't."

He grabbed for her again, and she lost it. She lashed out with every ounce of fury pumping through her veins. Roth's head snapped to the side as her palm cracked his cheek. He glared at her as his fingers dug into her arm, but she didn't flinch. Physical discomfort couldn't compete with the pain radiating from her chest.

"I took care of it."

"Took care of it for who?" she hissed. "You? You're so busy trying to protect yourself from me, you never realized I'd never use a baby against you! I have more self-respect than to trap a man who doesn't want to be with me. Let me go, Roth, or I swear to God—"

"It had nothing to do with you."

She swung again, but this time, he caught her hand and yanked it down. That didn't deter her. She stomped on his foot, but he was still wearing those hulking work boots, so it made no impact. When she tried to knee him in the balls, he thrust her against the wall and pinned her there with a hand around her throat. Still, she fought. She was totally out of control and didn't care.

"I hate you!" she screamed.

"Stop, Jasmine!"

She didn't stop until she was exhausted. When anger faded, leaving only sorrow in its wake, she slumped against the wall with tears pouring down her cheeks. She sacrificed everything for him while he held her at arm's length.

"I never intended to have children."

"Fine," she said. "Get your hands off me."

His hand tightened around her throat. He was adding new marks to the ones he had already left, but she didn't care. Nothing mattered anymore.

"Look at me."

"Let me go."

"Not until you look at me."

She lifted her face and stared at him with all the fury pulsing through her. He looked as impassive and untouched as he always did. How had she ever convinced herself that he gave a shit about her?

"Now, let me go," she said raggedly.

"Talk to me."

It was so absurd to hear that line from him that she let out a humorless laugh. The knife he had plunged in her heart sank even deeper. "Now you want to talk? After you made decisions about our future without talking to me? Fuck you, Roth." The laughter vanished as quickly as it had appeared. "You hated my father so much that you got a vasectomy so we wouldn't have kids?"

"It had nothing to do with your father. I just don't want children."

"I suppose it had nothing to do with me either? You just keep showing me that we never had a real marriage. I was just a prop to get you where you wanted, and when I didn't get you there, you ditched me."

"You left—"

"I wasn't even a factor in your decision-making! You built a life you didn't want me to be a part of. You didn't want children with me; you didn't want to share a home with me." She sucked in a shaky breath. "I can't believe you're still hurting me." She closed her eyes and pushed at his arm with cold, trembling hands. "Let me go."

When he dropped his hand, she sagged before she caught herself. She panted against the wall and gathered what strength and dignity she had left before she met his gaze.

"How would you feel if I told you I tied my tubes because I didn't want your blood tainting the Hennessy line?" she asked hoarsely.

His expression didn't change, but the energy in the room did.

She lifted her chin. "Exactly. Now you feel a tiny fraction of what I do."

She walked out of the kitchen and locked herself in the bathroom. She turned on the shower, climbed in, and fell to her hands and knees. The steaming water hit her cold flesh, but she welcomed the sting. It was over. They were finally ash.

CHAPTER 6

$\mathcal{A}$fter she showered away her latest monumental lapse in judgment, she tamed her knotted hair, which bounced around her bruised shoulders. She braved the cold loft to change into a turtleneck sweater that would cover up all signs of depravity and cake makeup on her face, so she didn't look as haggard as she felt. Her cranberry-colored leather jacket, scarf, beanie, and ankle boots were no defense against the frigid Colorado day, but it would have to do.

When she descended the staircase with her luggage, she found Roth standing in front of the large picture window. When he started toward her, she prepared to knock him in the face, but all he did was reach for her bag, which she relinquished. When he stalked out to the truck, she tidied up the best she could and threw the soiled linens in the washer and started a load. If she was talking to Douche, she would have reminded him to toss it in the dryer once he brought Kaia home. As it was, she averted her face and slipped past him, turning sideways, so she didn't touch him since he was standing in the doorway like an Indian chief. She wanted to admire the diamond dust, but the cold penetrated her clothing and took her breath away, so she hurried to the truck instead.

The trip down the mountain was nothing like last night. It was remarkable the difference a few hours could make. The world around her shimmered with a pure innocence she wished she could go back to. Under other circumstances, she would have enjoyed the beautiful scenery, but the suffocating proximity to this asshole made the hour-long trip hell. She needed to get away from him so badly, her skin itched. He lied and betrayed her in so many ways, it made her head spin. The worst part was that she had wanted children with him. She had fantasized about having a son who looked like him, or a girl with his eyes. The fact that he had stolen even that dream from her made her want to rip his face off. If possible, this hurt more than anything he said to her in London because it showed, in no uncertain terms, he had never pictured a future with her. Their relationship had been a sham.

When he parked at the hospital, she had her door open before he came to a full stop. She charged toward the doors, determined to say her goodbyes to Kaia and get out of here, but Roth's long strides quickly caught up to her. They walked into the hospital with enough space between them for a gurney to pass through. In the elevator, she stood in the corner with her arms wrapped around herself. Like the car ride, neither of them spoke. When they reached the ICU, the nurse escorted them to Kaia's room. She listened with half an ear as the nurse discussed the care Kaia would need.

When she entered, Kaia's face lit up, but when her eyes went past her to Roth, her face went dead white.

"James?" Kaia whispered.

Jasmine rounded the bed and watched as mother and son stared at one another. As the silence stretched, the nurse's gaze went from Kaia and Roth to her. Jasmine shrugged to show she didn't know what was going on. She married into the Roth clan, but knew very little about their dynamics. Neither Kaia nor Roth had ever explained their very distant relationship, and she had never pried.

Roth didn't react to the changes time had wrought in his mother. His expression was as impassive as ever.

"I-I didn't think you'd come," Kaia said in a shaky voice.

"If I couldn't, I would have sent someone," Roth replied coolly.

Jasmine couldn't help herself. "Sent someone?"

When Roth looked at her, she dropped her gaze to his beard.

"Some business can't wait," he said.

He could be her father's twin. Divorcing Roth was the best thing she ever did. She saved herself from a lifetime of being ignored and begging for scraps of affection.

Kaia's eyes filled with tears as she took in Roth's outfit. "You're wearing his clothes?" she asked in a quavering voice.

Roth eyed his mother like she was a stock that wasn't behaving the way he wanted it to. "I had no choice."

Kaia's stunned gaze shifted to her. "You two talked?"

"No," she said shortly and leaned forward to kiss Kaia's cheek. "I'm glad you're all right. Now that he's here, I'm going back to New York."

Kaia gave Roth a wary glance and gripped her hand. "Are you sure you can't stay?"

A doctor entered and shook Roth's hand. This was her moment to get out of here.

"No, I'm so sorry, but you can visit me once you're recovered," she said hastily. "You take care, okay?"

"I don't know how to repay you," Kaia said, hanging onto her arm.

"No need," she said and patted Kaia's hand. "Get well soon, okay?"

"I will."

Jasmine eased around the medical staff and slipped out the door. She focused on the exit and didn't take a breath until the double doors of the ICU closed behind her. As she power walked down the hall and pulled out her cell phone, she ducked into an empty waiting room and dialed Sunny.

"Girl," Sunny began.

"Get me a plane," she ordered.

Sunny's tone instantly became formal and no-nonsense. "Absolutely, Ms. Hennessy. Where are you?"

"I'm—"

The phone was yanked from her grasp. She whirled as Roth glanced at the screen and then put it to his ear.

"That won't be necessary," he said and hung up.

"What the hell are you doing? Give it back!"

He tapped the screen, and his brows came together. "You spoke to Lyle Caruso this morning?"

"That's none of your business! Stop going through my phone!"

"Did you tell him about us?"

She was lightheaded with rage. "There is no *us*. Now, give me my phone."

He stared at her for a full thirty seconds before he started tapping the screen. She lost it and launched herself at him. He grabbed her hand and twisted it behind her back, forcing her to bend over to avoid having him snap it.

He pressed his mouth against her ear. "Don't push me, Jasmine."

"I'm not pushing you! I just want to get away from you."

He released her. She rubbed her throbbing shoulder and bared her teeth when she saw him still messing with her phone.

"I swear to God, if you don't—"

He pocketed it, and said, "We'll leave in thirty minutes."

"I don't need a ride to the airport. I'll call a cab."

"I already have a plane."

She stared at him. "You're going to leave Kaia?"

"She's coming with us. I hired a nurse to care for her while she recovers."

She shook her head to clear it. "Okay, good, but I'm going to New York."

"So am I."

Alarm bells went off in her mind. "You live in London."

"I moved my headquarters back to New York."

She had the sensation of falling. "I thought you were doing well in the UK."

"I am, but I always intended to move back, and now I have."

What the fuck? The city wasn't big enough for the two of them. Did her sisters know? Of course, they did. Why hadn't they told her?

"I'm surprised you'd want to return to New York," she said faintly

"Why? Because your father and his business partners ran me out of the city?"

There was no use beating around the bush. "Yes."

"They can't touch me now."

Her stomach churned. "Thanks for the offer, but I can get back to New York on my own."

"We'll leave in thirty minutes," he said again.

His gaze went beyond her, and a moment later, the door opened. She turned, hoping it was a doctor or some form of law enforcement. The two men in the doorway definitely had some kind of military training, but they weren't cops. Dressed in matching suits, overcoats, and even sunglasses, they couldn't look more different. One of the men had alabaster skin, a bald head, and blond brows. The other had slicked back hair, a full beard, and dark skin that made her think he was from the Middle East. The dark one held out a leather bag to Roth.

"Change of clothes, sir," the guard said with a hint of an accent she couldn't place.

Roth took the bag, and said, "Don't let her leave."

She watched his progress through the window as he walked down the hallway and disappeared. She stared at the guards who had their hands folded over their middle. Their expressions were impossible to read with the sunglasses concealing their eyes.

"Get out of my way," she said.

They glanced at one another and then back at her.

She stepped up to them and put her hands on hips. "Do you know who I am?"

"Jasmine Hennessy-Roth," the fair one said, also with an accent she didn't recognize.

Her hands balled in fists. "Just Hennessy."

The guards shrugged, as if it was all the same to them.

"I'll pay you one thousand dollars if you let me borrow your phone," she said.

No reaction.

"Two thousand."

No reaction.

"Ten."

"Roth said to keep you here. You aren't going anywhere, ma'am."

"I could have you arrested for kidnapping."

They shrugged, unfazed by the threat of legal trouble, and why would they be? Roth would bail them out. Fuck. She sank into a chair as a tension headache threatened. She was physically battered, tired, and trapped. She just wanted out. She buried her face in her hands and took a deep breath.

"Can I get you something, ma'am?"

She didn't need to look up to know it was the Middle Eastern one.

"Aspirin and water," she murmured.

She heard the door open and close and fought the urge to scream. She was going back to New York. That was all that mattered, right? A few more hours with Roth and she wouldn't be alone with him. These guards would be there, and Kaia as well. She could do this.

"Here."

She looked up and took the chilled water and aspirin from the guard. "Thank you."

"You're welcome."

She swallowed the pills and half the bottle before she set it on the empty seat beside her. "What's your name?"

"You can call me Mo."

"And where are you from?"

"Turkey."

She nodded and looked at the pale one by the door. "And you?"

"Johan."

"And you're from?"

"Denmark."

Interesting. "How long have you been with Roth?"

"Going on four years."

She nodded and watched people walk past the waiting room. Their faces were pinched with stress and worry. After spending a week in a hospital watching over her father, she wasn't happy to be back. The dour mood was the same in every hospital.

"I'm sorry about your father."

73

Her gaze went back to the guards who were watching her closely. She inclined her head. "Thank you."

She didn't remain sitting long. Not when her ass, thighs, and pussy were swollen and aching. She paced, fingers itching for a pen. Writing was her yoga. It kept her sane, organized her thoughts, and helped her escape reality when it was too much for her to handle. She wanted to get lost in a story where the character's world made sense, and she was in control. After spending most of her life following everyone's rules, writing was the one place she was free.

A woman wearing a white parka with a fur-lined hood caught her eye. She was sure the woman wasn't a local, and it had more to do with her exotic looks than the designer bag on her shoulder. She had beautiful dark skin with a scarlet lip and dark hair pulled back into a ponytail. The woman looked through the glass, stopped in her tracks, and waved. Jasmine looked behind herself to make sure the woman was looking at her. The woman opened the door, pushed the guards aside, and strode up to her with her hand outstretched, wearing a megawatt smile. Good manners forced her to shake the woman's hand without knowing who the hell she was.

"I'm Sarai, a huge fan," the woman said, dark brown eyes sparkling. She glanced at the guards and then back at Sarai. "Uh, okay."

Sarai leaned forward and winked. "Thalia."

Her heart skipped a beat. "You're his assistant?" she guessed.

"Yes."

She didn't know how to react. This woman was a fan of her work and had given her books to Roth, so he could discover that his ex-wife wrote an erotic series based on their relationship. This woman knew more about her than her own family. She withdrew her hand and nodded.

"Can I borrow your phone?" she asked.

Sarai reached into her pocket. "Of course. Is there anything else I can do for you? We should be leaving in about fifteen minutes."

She gave her a tight smile. "See, that's the problem. I don't want to leave in fifteen minutes. I want to get back to New York on my own."

Sarai paused in the middle of handing the phone over and hid it behind her back. "Roth gave explicit instructions."

"His instructions don't affect me." She held out her hand. "I want to make my own arrangements."

Sarai gave her a professional smile. "He should be available shortly to speak to you about your concerns."

She narrowed her eyes. "I don't want to disturb him."

"I'm sure he won't mind," Sarai said smoothly.

Sarai's phone rang. She held up a finger and gave Jasmine an apologetic smile as she turned away and answered in a foreign language. Johan muttered something under his breath, and Mo shook his head.

This was absolute bullshit. She walked up to the guards who looked down their noses at her. When she pressed against them experimentally, they tensed.

"I don't think you should be—" Mo began in an offended tone.

Still talking on the phone, Sarai hooked an arm through Jasmine's and led her away from the exit. She finished the call and smiled at her.

"So, how far along are you on the fifth book? Everyone's talking about it."

She opened and then closed her mouth. She had never spoken to a reader face to face, and it was disconcerting on multiple levels. Her work was private and sacred to her. It was the one thing that was hers alone, yet this woman was talking about it so casually, as if they were discussing the weather and not something that came from her soul. She didn't know how to feel about this woman.

"I love your young adult fantasy novels as Minnie Hess, too. Do you think you'll complete that series as well?" Sarai asked.

"I... don't know."

"It was the hardest thing I've ever done to give Roth those books and wait for him to figure it out for himself. Gah! I waited over six months. I never thought he'd read them, and then he did, thank God."

"Why did you do that?" she asked bluntly.

Sarai blinked. "They're about him. He should know, right?"

"If I had wanted him to know, I would have told him myself."

Sarai searched her eyes for a moment, and then hers widened. "You didn't want him to know?"

"No!"

Sarai covered her mouth with her hand. "But... hasn't anyone figured it out?"

"No!"

Sarai looked horrified, but that didn't mollify her. She untangled her arm from his assistant's and paced away.

"I thought... I thought the series was a love note to him," Sarai said faintly. "I thought it was romantic."

She whirled. "It wasn't for him; it was for me. And how could it be for him when I divorced him?"

"But Roth's still in the series, a supporting character. I thought..."

She wanted to throw something. "That's just fiction!"

"But... but the books follow your life so closely. The fourth book ended with you and your father repairing your relationship after all these years..." Sarai pressed a hand against her chest as her eyes filled with tears. "I'm so sorry to hear he passed. That's so tragic. You two have become so close, traveling and even living together. I can't imagine how you must feel about losing him so suddenly."

Jasmine stared at her. "Are you stalking me?"

Sarai gave her a guilty smile. "Is that bad?"

"Yes! What the hell?"

"I can't help it. Romance is my guilty pleasure, and you wrote one of my favorites. I re-read your series at least once a month, and I see you post on social media every now and then. If I follow your personal life, it enhances the reading experience because I know where you're getting your inspiration from."

She had never been struck speechless until this moment. She was still trying to cope with the shock of meeting a super fan who knew her real identity and the details of her personal life when Roth walked into the room. He was dressed in a fancy overcoat with a high collar and black scarf. He was back to looking like a rich, heartless business-man. When he looked at her, she averted her gaze.

"We're ready. Let's go," he said.

Everyone waited for her to move first. Once she passed Roth, he took the lead, his longer strides easily outstripping her, so he reached the elevator a good ten seconds ahead of anyone else. Sarai's eyes flicked between her and Roth as if she were watching a tennis match. When she noticed Jasmine's glare, she looked up at the ceiling.

When they exited the hospital, two SUVs were waiting for them. She waited for Roth to climb into the back of one before she got into the other. She was pleased to find Kaia with a nurse at her side.

"I'm glad you're coming with us," Kaia said.

She tried to give Kaia a reassuring smile, but was sure it was more of a grimace as she climbed into the back seat and prayed this was the longest nightmare ever and that she would wake up soon. Johan climbed into the driver's seat and adjusted the mirror so he could see her. Did he think she was going to make a run for it?

Kaia and the nurse chatted all the way to the airport while she closed her eyes and tried to relax before she was locked in a confined space with Roth for several hours. Lack of sleep, the unrelenting cold, and her achy body intensified her tension headache. She was beginning to feel ill. All she wanted was a bed and to get away from all these people.

They pulled up to a private airstrip. She wasn't pleased it was starting to snow again. There was no way she was getting stuck here. She boarded the plane and immediately begged the flight attendant for more aspirin, which she procured before she found an empty seat. She chugged the ginger ale and pain pills and gave the jet a cursory glance. It was plush and warm and done in soothing neutral shades. She didn't care. She had been on dozens of jets. All she cared about was snatching the farthest seat from Roth. Unfortunately, there were only eight seats available, divided into four sets of two that faced one another. The guards, Kaia, and the nurse claimed the back seats, which only left the front four, two on each side of the plane with tables between. Roth and Sarai were sitting across from one another with their laptops out. Sarai had an iPad in hand and was going over his schedule. She had no choice but to take the chair across the aisle from them. She accepted the blanket the flight attendant offered with a shaky smile and huddled against the window. She pulled down the shade, draped the blanket over her head, and tried to block out the world.

"What's wrong?"

She didn't have to open her eyes to know who was bothering her. He was the bane of her existence, the dude who made a career out of torturing her. She gave him the middle finger from beneath the blanket and silently told him to go to hell. When the blanket disappeared, she moaned and covered her head.

"Go away!"

"What's wrong with you?"

"You. You're what's wrong with me. Leave me alone," she muttered.

Two weeks ago, she buried her father. Yesterday, she rushed his mother to the hospital during a heart attack, and then spent the night doing the dirty with an ex she hadn't laid eyes on in five years. Two hours ago, he roused a past she thought she had come to terms with and then forced her on a plane with him and his entourage. The more apt question was, what was *right* with her? Absolutely nothing.

"Are you sick?" he persisted.

"Yeah, I'm sick of your bullshit."

She heard a choking sound and realized her chair was back to back with Kaia's. She swallowed the filth she wanted to spew at him and kept her face averted.

"She asked for aspirin earlier," Johan piped up.

"You have a headache?" Roth asked.

Why was he acting like he cared? "Yes, I have the migraine from hell. Leave me alone."

The blanket came back over her. She huddled beneath it like a kid in a tent. She didn't care what she looked like, not when her head was threatening to split open. As the engines revved, she covered her ears with her hands. Once they were in the air, she propped up the leg rest and stretched out, turning her body away from Sarai and Roth. Thankfully, she couldn't hear them over the deafening hum of the plane. Good.

A HAND SHOOK HER AWAKE. She groaned and slapped it away. She was warm and comfy and didn't want to be disturbed.

"Jasmine."

That voice jerked her out of a dreamless sleep and back to nasty reality. She opened one eye and saw Roth's angry mug hovering over her.

"We land in fifteen minutes."

Damn, it wasn't a bad dream. She sat up and touched her messy hair. The migraine was gone, but she was so tired, she felt hung over. Weeks of little sleep had finally caught up to her, and she needed her bed, STAT. She rubbed her eyes before she remembered she was wearing makeup. Damn. She staggered to the bathroom. The too bright mirror showed that her mascara was smudged, and she had definitely tossed and turned during her nap. After doing the best she could to make herself presentable and using one of the tiny bottles of mouthwash to freshen up, she felt a little better when she emerged. On her way back to her seat, she saw Kaia peering out the window. Seeing Kaia alert and active gave her gloomy mood a boost.

She paused beside Roth and held out her hand. "My phone."

She felt Sarai's curious gaze as Roth pulled the phone out of his breast pocket and handed it over. She turned it on as the plane began to descend. She ignored all the chirping noises as she texted Lyle to let him know she was back in New York. As the plane taxied, she dialed Sunny.

"You're killing me," Sunny said.

"I know. I just landed. Can you pick me up from—"

The phone was snatched from her hand. Before she could unbuckle her seat belt, Roth told Sunny her services wouldn't be needed again and hung up.

"What the hell is your problem?" she snapped.

"We have transportation waiting."

"Fine. Go on your way. Don't let me hold you back."

"We're going to drop you off."

"No, you're not."

He placed her phone back in his breast pocket. She shot up from her seat, ready to pummel him with a pillow, when the flight attendant came up to her.

"You feel better, miss?"

She swallowed her rage. "Uh, yes, thank you," she said hoarsely.

She stepped aside to make way for Kaia who needed to deplane first. As she gathered her things and made sure nothing had fallen out of her purse, Roth walked out with Johan and Mo on his heels, leaving her with Sarai who hefted a large workbag over her shoulder.

The smirk on the other woman's face caught her eye. "What's so funny?"

"Nothing."

"Jasmine!"

Roth's shout set her teeth on edge. Sarai's smirk turned into a full-blown smile. She shot Sarai a scathing look before she walked off the plane to find two Bentleys waiting for them. She ignored the car Roth stood next to and tried to board the one with Kaia, Johan, and her nurse, but Sarai took the last seat.

"Jasmine, let's go," Roth said impatiently.

She stalked up to him as the other car pulled away. "Give me my phone."

"Get in."

"Ms. Hennessy?"

Mo held the back door open for her. Fine. The faster she got in, the quicker she would get home and away from him once and for all. She sank into the buttery leather seat as Mo got behind the wheel. She was about to relax when Roth got into the back seat with her.

"Sit in the front," she ordered.

He ignored her and answered his phone. At least there was a massive console between them. She was tempted to turn on the TV on the back of Mo's seat, but she was too tired to fiddle with the buttons.

This was the longest one-night stand in history. She closed her eyes and tried to block him out. Not much longer... They hit traffic (no surprise), and when Mo asked for her address, she glanced at

Roth, who was on his third call. She gave it reluctantly. Her leg began to bounce as they neared her Chelsea apartment. If they went a little farther, she could hop out of the car and walk the last few blocks...

Her phone landed in her lap. She glared at Roth, who seemed absorbed in his call. She unlocked her phone and saw that she had forty-two voicemails, over one hundred missed calls, and two hundred unread texts. *Fuck.* She checked Lyle's message first. They were expecting her in two hours. She glanced at the barely moving traffic and shrugged. She'd arrive when she arrived. She texted Sunny to let her know she'd be at her apartment in thirty minutes and would need transportation to Midtown, where both of her sisters lived.

The bulk of her messages were from college friends or former acquaintances who were offering their condolences on her father's passing and asking how she was doing. She didn't answer because their act of sympathy was a ploy to get inside information on her father's trust, which she and her sisters had been mum about. The rampant speculation on how Maximus divided his billion-dollar fortune between his three daughters made her sick. She hadn't read a paper or been on social media since her father went into the hospital. Vigilant security kept most of the invasive paparazzi at bay, but that didn't stop them from shouting offensive questions at her when they could. She had been dubbed the scandalous, wild Hennessy. She didn't have a sex tape, but breaking off her engagement with Ford Baldwin for a virtual unknown had amounted to the same thing. Despite her master's degree in business, everyone assumed she was an airhead. No one wanted to see her at the helm of Hennessy & Co with her sisters. Not that she cared. She gave up her rights to Hennessy & Co seven years ago and was content with the path she had chosen. Everyone assumed she lived off her father because no one knew she had a writing career or that she was quite successful in her chosen field.

Roth's low rumble was getting on her nerves. She cracked the window, letting in the sound of honking, people shouting at one another on the sidewalks, and noisy construction. She relaxed a little. They weren't in a remote cabin in the mountains any longer. She wasn't dependent on him because Mother Nature decided to blow her icy rage across the state or because he had knowledge of generators when she didn't. No. They were back in the city where there were cabs, stores, and witnesses if he tried anything. Not that he would. He went back to work the moment they landed. He was in his element—wheeling and dealing—just like her father.

When Mo pulled up to the sidewalk in front of her apartment building, she sprang out of the Bentley. She was so relieved, she wanted to grab one of the stranger's speed walking past and give them a hug. Mo pulled her suitcases from the trunk and set it on the sidewalk. She wasn't pleased when Roth emerged from the back seat.

"I got it!" she said as she reached for her things.

Roth slung the duffel over one shoulder and grasped the handle of her blush-colored suitcase.

"I don't need your help," she said and tried to pull the duffel from his shoulder.

He pried her hand from the strap and towed her toward the building.

"I swear to God, Roth, I'm going to—"

She broke off as three men lounging against the wall ran forward with cameras. Oh, fuck. She turned her face away and heard car horns blast. Two men ran into traffic with their cameras in the air, desperate to get a shot.

"Ms. Hennessy, Ms. Hennessy! Did you vacation with some of the money you inherited?" someone shouted.

"Is there anything you can tell us about your father's will? Did he leave everything to your sisters? How does that make you feel?" a man asked as he leaped in front of them.

"Is that...?"

"It is! Mr. Roth, did you come back to the States now that Maximus Hennessy is dead? Did you come back to pick up where you two left off?"

Roth pulled her beneath the shelter of his arm as Mo cleared a path to the door. The camera flashes and offensive questions were meant to rile them, so the paparazzi could get a juicy shot. The photographers jockeyed for position and even followed them into the building. She kept her back to them until the elevator arrived, and Roth pushed her in. Mo kept the paparazzi in the lobby as the doors closed.

"You live in a building without security? What the hell are you thinking?" Roth snapped.

"I thought they would have lost interest by now," she said as she slumped against the wall.

"Where's your security team?"

"They're on their way." She gave him a hot glare. "They would have been here sooner if I had my phone."

The elevator stopped on her floor. She stepped out and turned to him.

"You don't have to come with me."

His hostile expression told her he wasn't handing over the bags. She ground her teeth as she strode to her apartment and unlocked the door. She turned to him and held out her hands.

"Thanks for all the fucks," she said with a plastic smile. "I hope I don't see you for another five years."

He bumped her aside and strode in.

"You can't come in here!" she bellowed.

He slammed the door, and with a flick of his finger, locked the door. He dropped her duffel with a loud thump. The hungry gleam in his eyes made her heart leap into her throat.

"Don't you—"

He clasped her face with both hands and yanked her forward. When their mouths collided, she slammed her hands against his chest and pushed, but she was no match for him. He backed her against a wall of exposed brick. He was kissing her with an intensity different from anything they shared in Colorado. He unzipped her jacket and grasped her tender breasts. She gripped his wrists and tugged desperately. She couldn't let him take her over again. He allowed her to pull his hands down. She felt a moment of relief before his fingers undid her jeans.

She ripped her mouth from his. "No, Roth."

He kissed her jaw and tugged down her turtleneck so he could get at her throat.

"I'm not playing your game," she said through clenched teeth.

He bit her neck as he pulled her jeans down.

"Fuck, Roth, *stop!*"

She let out an outraged shriek as his hand dipped between her legs. "You can't do this!"

He pinned her to the wall with his shoulder, face less than an inch away. Her eyes watered with rage and need.

"I'm doing it," he said in a guttural voice.

"Why?"

"Because I need it."

He knelt and forced her legs to part as much as she could with her jeans around her knees. She tried to turn sideways to protect herself from him, but the steely grip on her thighs widened her stance to make room for him.

"Please..."

Her voice died as lust took over. The sight of him on his knees before her was a fantasy she never thought she'd see again. He closed his eyes as he feasted. He wasn't going down on her so she could take him. He did it because he loved her taste. The ecstasy on his face made her hot and weak and stupid. When her thighs were quaking, he straightened. She closed her eyes against the sight of him. Even as self-loathing cascaded through her, she didn't move as she heard the sound of his belt coming out of its loops or the rasp of his zipper. He cupped her ass and raised her to her tiptoes. As he slipped inside her, she bit back a moan. She wanted to spread her legs, but she couldn't, not with her jeans around her ankle boots.

"You fucked up, letting me get a taste of you again," he breathed against her temple.

She bared her teeth. "This is the last time."

His dark chuckle made her body erupt in goose bumps.

"It is!"

He slid in to the hilt and stayed there, forcing her to adjust to his size. Her pussy fluttered around him.

"You feel that, princess? That's you giving yourself to me."

Her neighbor across the hall opened his door. She stiffened, but Roth didn't stop. He fucked her nice and slow as two men began to talk. It sounded like they were right outside her door, less than six feet from where Roth was fucking her.

He gauged every emotion that flitted across her face. She glared at him, hating him yet desperate for one last taste. His hands left her ass, allowing her skin to scrape against the bricks with each thrust, adding more sensation to her overloaded senses.

"Yes, my cat gave birth. Eight kittens. You want one?" a man asked just outside her door.

"What colors do you have?" someone asked.

"All kinds. You want to see?"

"Want a kitty?" Roth whispered as she shifted restlessly against him.

She reached up and dug her nails into the back of his neck. "No, I want you to finish me."

His eyes dropped to her lips. "Ask me nicely."

"Fuck you."

He linked their hands together and pinned them over her head. He crowded her, limiting her movements, as he sped up. The fact he was fucking her standing up with her legs clamped together made him feel bigger than ever. It was just too fucking good. He adjusted and hit her just right. She let out a strangled gasp. The voices in the hallway faltered.

"You want them to hear you?" Roth murmured.

"I don't care!" she said loudly, past caring about anything but her climax.

She bucked against him and tipped her head back as she reached for bliss. She let out a desperate moan that no one would mistake for anything but a woman in the throes.

"Roth!"

Sensing she was close, he gave her what she needed, grinding her ass against the bricks to coax her overused body into another orgasm. She muffled her scream against his chest as he sped up, fucking her mercilessly until he spilled. She lost her breath as he sagged against her with his face buried in her hair. When he released her hands, they dropped to her sides, and for a moment, they stayed like that. There were no voices in the hallway. Either they had left, or they were in their apartments jacking off.

When her brain lurched into gear, she shoved him. "Now, leave."

Roth pulled out of her, causing his cum to slide down her leg and drip on her jeans, another reminder that he had no need for a condom because he was shooting blanks. Self-loathing and rage ripped through her.

"Step back," she ordered.

His phone began to ring.

"See, that's the real-world calling you. Bye."

As he stepped back, she yanked up her jeans with a grimace. Roth glanced at his phone before he pocketed it without answering. He zipped his pants and slid a hand through his tousled hair.

His eyes met hers. "I put my number in your phone. Use it."

She crossed her arms and jerked her chin at the door.

He gave her a long, considering look. "You won't be able to avoid me."

"Please leave," she said.

She didn't think he was going to, but he finally did. When the door closed behind him, she turned the deadbolt. She looked through the peephole to make sure he really was gone before she rested her face against the door and screamed.

CHAPTER 7

$\mathcal{T}$he cavalry arrived by the time she stepped out of the shower. She put on a robe and looked through the peephole before she let in four guards and Sunny. When the guards caught sight of her, they immediately averted their eyes, while Sunny shook her head and pointed her back into the bedroom.

"Your father would have a heart attack if he could see you right now," Sunny said.

Jasmine grunted as she snagged a Yoo-hoo from the fridge and went into her bedroom. She wasn't entirely surprised when Sunny followed. She dried and styled her hair, then perched on a stool in front of the vanity.

Sunny lounged in the open doorway. She was a black woman in her late sixties, a former Marine who had created her own security firm before she sold it. She spent a year on a cruise before she came out of retirement and became her father's security coordinator. Dressed like a butler in a black pantsuit, she wore braids swirled into a fancy bun on her head over six inches high.

"You can't stay here. It isn't safe," Sunny said.

"I know."

"What's that on your neck?"

She yanked up the collar of her robe. "Nothing." When Sunny started toward her, she held up both hands. "It's nothing, I swear."

"Someone put their hands on you."

"Not without my permission."

Sunny cocked her head to the side. "You went to some BDSM resort or something?"

She shrugged and tried to look casual. "Something like that."

Nearly freezing to death in the mountains was far from a resort, but the BDSM story was better than admitting she'd hooked up with her ex multiple times. She glared at herself in the mirror as she began to apply her makeup. Her ego was bruised. The fact she had given in to him so easily sickened her. Had the past five years taught her nothing? She was a successful businesswoman in her own right, so why had she allowed him to—

"Next time you want privacy to get your kink out, maybe I can hire some female guards, so you won't feel self-conscious," Sunny said.

"No need."

"Why?"

"I'm done."

Sunny snorted. "Sure. I know what you write."

Sunny was privy to her Thalia secret even though she had never read any of the books. Sunny got the gist, though, and kept her opinions about it to herself. Sunny was locked up so tight, Jasmine couldn't determine if she was gay, straight, or asexual. The woman never mentioned partners or expressed any interest in either sex.

"I mean, I won't be taking off. I learned my lesson," she amended.

Sunny's brows rose. "Is that right?"

"Yes, that's right," she said as she finished applying her foundation. "After this, I'm going back to Tuxedo Park, so you don't need to worry."

"It'll be months before interest in you dies down," Sunny said, and then shrugged. "And maybe not even then."

Her rigid hand motions made her bronze eyeshadow a little heavier than she wanted, but she was going to go with it.

"Who was the man who answered your phone?" Sunny asked.

She made a face as she got caught in her lie. She debated whether to tell the truth and then remembered the paparazzi downstairs. They ruined everything. Now she was going to have to tell her family about Roth, which wasn't going to go over well. She flicked her makeup brush irritably.

"That was James," she said casually, hoping Sunny wouldn't recognize his first name.

Less than two seconds later, she heard, "James *Roth?*"

Sunny had been around her father long enough to know that name very well. She sighed as she applied mascara. "Yeah."

Sunny wasn't leaning on the wall anymore. She was standing straight and on high alert.

"I visited his mother in Colorado. She had a heart attack while I was there. Roth brought her back to New York to care for her while she recovers," she said as she chose a deep red matte lipstick.

"And he answered your phone?" Sunny asked carefully.

"He insisted I ride back with them." She rose and avoided Sunny's dissecting gaze as she went to the closet. "I'll be ready in fifteen."

After Sunny left, she blew out a long breath. Sunny could put two and two together. The injuries weren't from a BDSM resort, but Roth, which made her a textbook cliché to hook up with her ex. Hell. She went to her closet and dug out a black dress with a high collar and pulled on thigh high boots and added some accessories. The paparazzi were here for a shot, so she'd give them one that hopefully overshadowed the one with Roth. She grabbed one of the few designer bags she still owned and a coat before she walked into the living room.

The guards immediately got to their feet. She didn't say a word as she walked to the door. They congregated around her, and this time when she faced the paparazzi, she kept her head high and hoped they got a much better photo. The sun was setting as she ducked into an SUV and settled beside Sunny, who talked into her earpiece. She texted Lyle that she was on her way and prepared to face her sisters, who she hadn't seen since the funeral.

What should have taken ten minutes with no traffic took close to forty. She climbed out of the SUV and looked up at Hennessy Tower, a glass building that spiraled toward the sky. Sunny and two guards accompanied her, but there was no need, since the staff didn't allow the paparazzi within fifteen feet of anyone entering the building. There were a few flashes from the dejected paparazzi, but nothing compared to the circus at her apartment. The workers of Hennessy Tower inclined their heads as she passed through the revolving door and crossed the massive lobby. The elevator operator acknowledged her with a smile before he selected the top floor.

The elevator opened into an entryway that rivaled the Sistine Chapel. Security stepped aside to let her pass. She passed a mini waterfall and koi pond before she rounded the corner and faced the grand living room. It was everything one would expect from a home worth upward of fifty million. A white piano sat in the corner of the room, while the walls were decorated with expensive art. The cream furniture trimmed in gold was custom, as was everything in the two-story penthouse inhabited by Colette, Lyle, and their housekeeper and cook. Everyone lounging in front of the golden hearth turned their heads as she paused on the threshold.

"Aunty Minnie!"

Two children ran toward her. She knelt and fell back on her butt as Bailey and Kye hurtled themselves at her.

"Uncle Lyle says you're in trouble," Bailey whispered in her ear.

"What's new?" she whispered back.

Bailey bugged out her eyes, which were the same icy blue as her mother's. "Are you going to get a time-out?"

"Maybe," she said gravely, and then patted the butt of the little boy who was clinging to her. "How's my boy?"

"Miss you," he said against her neck.

Her heart melted. She rose with Kye in her arms and faced a formidable jury eyeing her with varying degrees of disapproval. Her sisters, Colette and Ariana, stood side by side. She was taller than average at five foot seven, but small in comparison to her sisters, who towered over her at six feet. They were blonde bombshells with glacial blue eyes. The resemblance between them was uncanny, considering they had different mothers.

Colette was ten years her senior and detached, rigid, and unbending—the female version of their father. She was the CEO of Hennessy & Co, a role she had been groomed for since birth. Maximus paired Colette with Lyle Caruso, a brilliant hedge fund manager and passionate Italian. Colette and Lyle were a New York power couple frequently featured on magazine covers. They had been married over a decade, so she figured Colette wasn't as frigid between the sheets as she appeared in her everyday life. They nearly divorced last year when Colette refused to have kids, but she had given in once she was reminded of the marriage contract. It was about legacies, after all, not love.

Colette wore a white coat dress with gold buttons along the front of it and a black belt high around her swollen belly. Despite being six months pregnant and in her own home, she was still wearing heels after a long day. Colette was a stickler for formality, just like their father. It was one of the reasons Jasmine had taken the time to make herself presentable. Lyle, conversely, wore black slacks and a shirt with no tie. His head was shaved on the sides, while he left the top long and slicked back.

Her other sister, Ariana, was eight years older than her and the COO of Hennessy & Co. Ariana was just as intimidating as Colette but had softened after having Bailey and Kye. Their father, Rami Khan, was a brilliant software mogul. He was a quiet man, but no less powerful than the others in the room. He wore a sweater vest and had gold Harry Potter glasses perched on his nose.

"Sorry I'm late," she announced.

"I'm glad you could make it," Colette said.

She doubted it, but kept that thought to herself.

"What the hell, Minnie?" Lyle snapped.

"What?" she asked as Ariana shot him a severe look for his language.

"What are you doing with Roth?" Lyle demanded.

The smile fell from her lips. "What are you talking about?"

"There's a picture of you and him on a gossip site. Colette got tagged in it. Is it true?"

Her stomach curdled. She had known she would have to mention it tonight, but she'd been hoping to ease them into it and not have to discuss Roth as soon as she walked in. They were all staring at her, waiting for an explanation. Even Kye and Bailey watched her, realizing something significant was going on, though they didn't understand it.

"I went to Colorado to see Kaia. She had a heart attack while I was there, so Roth flew in," she said.

Lyle spread his arms. "And? How did he end up with his arm around you at your building?"

"We flew back together, and he was shielding me from the paparazzi."

"That's it?" Lyle pushed.

"Yes."

"You know he moved back to New York?" Colette asked.

She switched her gaze to her oldest sister. "He dropped that tidbit before we came back. Why didn't you tell me?"

"I didn't want to upset you."

"I would rather hear it from you than him."

"You're hardly in the city. I didn't think you'd run into him," Colette said with a delicate shrug.

Before Jasmine could snap, Ariana spoke up. "Are you all right?"

"Sure," she said dismissively as she kissed Kye's cheek. If they really cared, they wouldn't have walked away when she needed them.

"Let's eat," Lyle said as he came forward and gave her a hug. "It's going to be all right," he said quietly.

She gave him a long look. "Whatever you say."

Rami took Kye from her and herded his children ahead of them.

"You can't do anything without making headlines, can you?" he teased.

"I have to keep up my reputation," she said and gave him a hug. "How have you been, Rami?"

"Busy, of course," he said and slung an arm over her shoulder as he led her into the formal dining room.

She had a better rapport with her brothers-in-law than her sisters.

Maximus raised his daughters to be female generals in the male-dominated business world. They had been raised in the public eye and taught from a young age never to show emotion since it was a weakness that could be exploited. Lyle and Rami, on the other hand, were much more casual about showing affection and didn't feel the need to be super macho.

She took a seat at the table and reached for the glass of wine waiting for her. Servers came out with artfully arranged Asian cuisine. She wasn't surprised by the polite inquiries her sisters volleyed her way. They wanted to discuss business and mutual acquaintances she didn't give a damn about.

She turned her attention to her niece and nephew, who were much more interesting. Kye and Bailey wanted to tell her everything they had seen and learned in the weeks she had been gone. Bailey was learning French and German and switched between both languages as she spoke. Kye was partial to Spanish and spoke in broken sentences. The kids were the main reason she bothered to come when she was still raw from her encounter with Roth. They were warm and loving and eager to tell her about their lives full of travel, observations, and education. Ariana and Rami were definitely following the same curriculum she had been raised on, aside from boarding school. Bailey and Kye would be attending private school in New York, which meant she would be able to see them more often.

As the adults discussed market swings, capital gains, and investors, she focused on the kids who were a beacon of light in her otherwise dreary world.

"Mommy says you miss Papa a lot," Bailey said.

She blinked back the instant flood of tears. "She's right."

Bailey pressed a hand against her cheek, compassion radiating from her eyes. "It's going to be okay. Papa's in a better place."

She nodded as a tear slipped down her cheek. "Yes, he is."

"Miss Papa," Kye piped up.

She pulled him against her and kissed the top of his head. "Me too, baby."

"Are you going back to the castle?" Bailey asked as she got up on her knees on the chair.

Her mouth curved. "Yes."

Bailey glanced at her mom before she leaned forward. "Can I come?"

"I think she has you on a tight schedule."

"But if you tell her you're sad, she might let me come with you."

Bailey was learning the art of negotiation quickly. She was logical and persuasive and not even five years old.

"Come too!" Kye said loudly before his sister shushed him.

"I've been away for a while. I have some work to do, but if your mom lets you, I'll pick you up in a week or two," she said.

Bailey sighed and sank back on her seat, arms crossed. "I want to see the horses."

"You will."

"I want to see them *now*."

She tapped her niece's nose. "Be good and you will. No pouting."

After dinner, she played with Kye and Bailey before Ariana declared it was time for bed. She kissed the kids before Rami took them two floors down to their penthouse. Lyle locked himself in his office while she and her sisters, by mutual accord, settled in the grand living room.

When Jasmine glanced at the fire, memories of her and Roth fucking in front of a similar blaze swamped her before Colette cleared her throat.

"You haven't responded to my messages," she said.

Jasmine switched her attention to her sister as remnants of the flames danced in her eyes. "I don't know what we have to talk about."

Colette and Ariana glanced at each other. They were so in sync, talking wasn't necessary. Growing up in the shadow of two talented, gorgeous sisters hadn't been easy. She was always ten steps behind, and no matter what, she would never catch up. Roth freed her from the Hennessy mold. She stopped trying to be the perfect daughter and employee and decided to be herself. Her sisters played a high stakes game she wasn't built for. She was glad she had gotten out before she married Ford and got stuck in a world where money was king and image was everything. When she broke off her engagement, her sisters had been just as angry as their father. Neither of them reached out during the estrangement, and when she reconciled with their father, Colette and Ariana went along with it, but not without exchanging looks filled with silent condemnation. She had always been an outsider.

"This news with Roth is… unexpected," Ariana said, obviously trying to ease the tension in the room.

Her pussy pulsed. She crossed her ankles and fisted her hands in her lap.

"Do you think it's a coincidence that he came back to New York after Dad passed?" Colette asked.

She blinked. "What?"

"He moved back right after the funeral."

She frowned. "Of course, it's a coincidence. What else could it be?"

Colette and Ariana glanced at one another again.

Ariana sat forward. "We reacted badly when the will was read. We wanted to let you know we don't harbor any resentments about your inheritance."

"I don't believe that for a second," she said. After dealing with Roth, her patience was at an all-time low. She wasn't interested in their polite bullshit.

Her sister's visibly stiffened. It was clear they weren't expecting her to be so blunt.

"I didn't know he would name me as executor," she said, looking directly at Colette. "And I didn't know I would inherit his remaining assets. I never asked for anything."

Colette lowered her gaze, while Ariana shifted uncomfortably.

"You walked out after the will was read," Jasmine continued. "You forced me to make that decision about Dad alone. You weren't there when he passed." Her breath caught, and she looked back at the fire as she fought to keep her composure. "Be honest for once. You were pissed."

"You're right."

Colette sat on the edge of the couch, calves pressed together and angled to the side like a royal. If she hadn't seen Colette vomit before, she might suspect her sister wasn't human. Colette never showed weakness, but tonight, something was different about her.

"I wasn't expecting you to be the executor or sole heir," Colette said in a hesitant tone as she searched for words. "I reacted horribly." Colette inclined her head. "I'm sorry, Minnie."

"I didn't handle it any better," Ariana added. "I apologize."

Jasmine didn't react. She wasn't sure what was more shocking. Seeing Roth or receiving an apology from her sisters.

No one had been more astounded by her father's will than her. Before she could come to terms with the fact that her father's fate rested in her hands, the attorney announced that she had inherited his remaining assets, valued at over three hundred million dollars. While she was trying to comprehend all of this, Colette and Ariana had walked out of the room and left her to deal with the decision to take her father off life support. Standing beside her father's casket, she had never felt more alone. Her father's peers had pointed out that she didn't measure up to her sisters. No amount of time would bury the scandal she caused, and it resurfaced every time she did. Despite her reconciliation with Maximus, she didn't expect anything. Maximus was a hard man who never went back on his decrees. Her sisters kept Hennessy & Co going after he got sick, and they worked their butts off while she walked her own path. She didn't think she deserved anything, but at some point, Maximus had a change of heart and hadn't told any of them about it.

"We received letters," Colette said.

"Letters from who?" Jasmine asked as she tapped at the corner of her eye.

"Dad," Ariana said. "We both got one. They were delivered a couple of days ago. He explained his reasons for making you his sole heir."

Jasmine straightened. "What did he say?"

"I'm sure you have a letter waiting for you at the estate that explains that," Colette said as she rubbed her temples.

It was clear the pregnancy was taking its toll. Normally stoic, decisive, and straightforward, Colette looked uncharacteristically weary.

"Are you okay?" she asked.

"She's supposed to be on bedrest," Ariana explained as she rubbed Colette's lower back. "You need to lie down."

"I will in a little while." Colette tried to maintain her erect posture. "We left you with a heavy burden you didn't ask for, and I'm sorry. I don't know how we can make it up to you. I wasn't thinking clearly."

Jasmine looked down at her hands as her emotions stirred.

"You forgave him after he disowned you and were there for him when he really needed you," Colette said as she rubbed her tummy. "You gave him the best years of his life."

Jasmine's mouth trembled as grief rose again, so strong that she couldn't take a full breath.

"You did the right thing, Minnie," Ariana said. "You didn't let him suffer. You let him go."

She buried her face in her hands as the tears came. Soft, feminine voices murmured comfortingly as her sisters settled on either side of her. Colette tipped her sideways, onto her lap, which only made her cry harder. Hands moved through her hair as the tears she thought she got rid of in Colorado made another appearance. Grief made even the most hardened people offer her comfort. First Roth and now Colette. What was the world coming to?

"We got our inheritance years ago when he divided his remaining shares of Hennessy & Co between Colette and me. You never said a thing," Ariana said.

"Why would I?"

"You're a Hennessy."

She never felt like a real Hennessy. She didn't embody the traits that made their family so revered in society. The only thing she had done was cause problems with her father's partners and taint their name with scandal. And for what? A man who hadn't even loved her. She didn't deserve anything her father or sisters had worked so hard for.

"Ariana and I received lots of boons from Dad. You received the

97

least. Leaving you his estates was his way of honoring you," Colette said quietly.

"I have money," she whispered.

"He told us that as well," Ariana said.

The tears stopped coursing down her cheeks. "What?"

"I don't understand why you kept it a secret. You let us think you had no job. Where did the name Thalia Crane come from, anyway?" Colette asked.

She leaped to her feet and faced her sisters with her hands on her hips. "That wasn't his to tell!"

"He was proud of you."

"He promised!"

Colette and Ariana glanced at one another. Their somber expressions melted into grins.

"What?" Jasmine growled.

"Did you make him pinky swear?" Ariana asked.

She glared at her sister. "If you tell Rami, I'll kill you."

"He already knows."

Jasmine grit her teeth. Her anonymity was being blown out of the water. At this rate, the whole world would know her identity by the end of the year.

"So, you're a writer," Ariana said with a shrug. "What's the big deal?"

"The big deal," she stressed through clenched teeth, "is that I'm the new *Fifty Shades,* and I've already caused enough damage."

Ariana waved her hand. "You're an artist."

"I bought the boxed set," Colette added. "I'm going to read the series when I'm on maternity leave."

Jasmine covered her face with her hands and moaned.

"What? I'm trying to be supportive!" Colette said defensively.

"You'll gouge your eyes out once you read it," Jasmine predicted.

"You don't know that."

"Look at you!"

Colette looked down at herself. "What?"

"You're *you!*"

"What does that mean?"

"You're wearing pearls and Mrs. Straitlaced. You can't handle it."

Colette tipped her nose in the air. "We'll see about that."

Jasmine paced toward the view of the city lit up at night. "This is not okay."

"Don't be so dramatic, Minnie. Your dream of being a writer came true. What does it matter what we think?"

"It doesn't," she muttered, even though it was a damn lie.

She respected her sisters for who they were and what they accomplished. She would rather have them believe she did nothing than read the writings of her soul and sneer at it. It was one of the reasons she had concealed her identity. Writing was hers alone... or it had been before Sarai and her father decided to tell the whole planet.

She wandered toward a gold mirror hanging on the wall to see the damage her latest crying session had wrought on her face. She looked awful. Good thing she had sunglasses in her purse.

"Dad was really proud of you," Colette said.

She sighed. "I know."

Even while they were estranged, Maximus had kept an eye on her. He tracked her writing career, was aware of Thalia Crane's success, and was notified immediately when she left Roth and filed for divorce. When she came to him for help, he already knew everything.

"Is the series about...?" Ariana began before Colette shushed her.

"Yes, it's about Roth and me." It was a lost cause to act like it wasn't. It would be obvious to her sisters if they read the books. "And I just found out he knows, too."

Her sister's horror summed up how she felt when he'd dropped that bomb on her. She had never spent time with her sisters. They were usually too busy for that. They had obviously cleared their schedules for the evening, which showed how much this talk meant to them. Weeks of guilt and loneliness seeped away.

"He knows?" Ariana choked.

"Yep."

"How did he find out?"

"His assistant read me as Minnie Hess and then checked into

Thalia Crane since she's an avid romance reader, saw the similarities between the writing style and story, and put it together. *Then*," she said with relish, "she gives him the books as a gift, and he fucking reads them."

Ariana's hands went to her mouth while Colette twisted her pearl necklace.

"Why would she do that?" Colette asked.

"Exactly!" She threw up her hands. "She thinks I wrote the series as a love note to him or something. Ugh!" She crossed her arms and tapped her foot irritably.

"Did you?" Ariana asked.

"Of course not!"

"How did he take it?" Colette asked.

She shrugged. "He was more flattered than anything else, I think."

"Well, that's something, at least." Colette cocked her head to the side. "Is he…? Did he say anything about us?"

Jasmine frowned. "What do you mean?"

"About Dad or the company?"

"No. Why?"

Colette and Ariana glanced at one another before returning their attention back to her.

"We were wondering if he was going to cause any trouble now that he's back," Ariana said.

"Why would he? His fight was with Dad, not you."

Colette shifted uncomfortably and then winced.

"Why are you supposed to be on bed rest? Is something wrong?" she asked as she circled back to her sisters.

"She has high blood pressure," Ariana said as she kicked off Colette's heels and forced her sister back against the cushions. "If you don't relax, I'm going to tell Lyle."

"Why haven't you told him?" Jasmine asked.

"I'm in the middle of something at work. Once it's done, I'll relax and prepare for the baby," Colette said irritably.

Jasmine perched on a gold coffee table facing them.

Colette eyed her thoughtfully. "Dad was proud that you made it in your own arena."

Jasmine nodded. He had mentioned that to her before.

"He said you don't fear failure and that's why you've become a success."

"I'm not making millions," Jasmine said defensively.

"If your sales trajectory and book releases stay consistent, you should hit that figure within the next three years," Colette said.

"Will you stop digging into my shit?" she snapped and shook her head. "You're just like him."

"Less than ten percent of writers live off their earnings, so your income is impressive. You built something out of nothing, just like grandpa." Colette rubbed her tummy as she stared at the fire. "I like rules."

"I know you do," Jasmine said and shot a bewildered look at Ariana, who shrugged.

"I know how the game works. I also know the players and my place in the hierarchy. I'm at the top. Dad said I won't go forward if I'm too afraid to make mistakes."

Jasmine tilted her head to the side as she examined her sister. "Those pregnancy hormones are doing a number on you."

Colette's mouth set into a thin line. "Lyle thinks it's funny."

"I can see his point. You're not yourself."

"No, I'm not. I hate it. I can't think straight. I'm reacting without thinking. It's so unlike me."

"It'll pass," Ariana soothed, patting her thigh. "Soon, Polara will be here, and it'll all be worth it."

"Polara?" Jasmine echoed with raised brows.

"Your second niece."

"Polara?" she said again.

"What's wrong with Polara?" Colette asked sharply.

"Nothing. I've just never heard it before. Sounds like a heroine from a fantasy novel."

"Polara's a badass name," Colette said severely.

While she tried to bite back a smile, Ariana eyed her soberly.

"We apologize for the way we acted. You never took anything from him. He stopped paying your tuition and you managed. We should have expected him to do something like this for you."

She shifted uncomfortably. "I don't need the money, though, and I don't want to manage it."

"We have people who will monitor it for you. You don't need to worry about it," Colette said, sounding much more like herself now that they were talking about business. "If you want to sell one of his properties, let us know. We may want to buy it from you."

She let out a long breath. "Ooookay."

"You forgive us?" Colette asked.

"Yes."

She didn't have to think about it. She hadn't expected an apology or even an acknowledgment of what they'd done. Their family never discussed sensitive subjects, but it seemed their father's death had affected her sisters as well. The weight she had carried to Colorado and back lightened considerably.

"Are you going back to Tuxedo Park?" Ariana asked.

"Yes."

Colette sighed as she finally relaxed into the cushions. "Are you going to be okay there by yourself?"

"Yes. It was hard being there after he passed, but I think I'll be okay now." She pursed her lips. "I think I need to get rid of my apartment in Chelsea."

"You shouldn't have gotten it in the first place. I told you to stay at —" Colette began but stopped when Jasmine waved her hands.

"I don't want to stay on the Upper East Side."

"Why not?"

She glared at her sister. "I don't want to see all my classmates and have to answer questions about why I'm not married or have kids when I walk to a coffee shop."

"Do you want us to handle your apartment?" Ariana asked.

She sighed. "Yes. I don't think I want to go back with the paparazzi there. I'll probably head out of the city tonight. I have a lot of work to do anyway."

"Please let us know if you decide to travel," Colette said slowly, eyelids fluttering as she struggled to stay awake. "It's just us now. And we're gonna do the same with keeping you informed about our whereabouts, especially if you want to be there for the birth."

"Yes, I want to be there," she said immediately.

"So, it's settled," Colette said as she finally gave in and closed her eyes. "No going off without security. You have to take precautions now."

"I will. I'm going to head out now," she said and got to her feet. She went to Colette, who instantly tried to sit up. She pressed her back down and kissed her cheek. "Get some rest."

Colette clasped her face between both hands. "I'm truly sorry, Minnie."

She swallowed hard. "I know."

"I haven't been a good sister to you," she said quietly. "No wonder you went to Colorado. We've never been there for you, have we?"

"Stop."

Colette let out a shaky sigh. "This is why I never wanted to be pregnant. I'm starting to care about people."

Jasmine grinned. "The ice queen's melting."

"I am who I have to be," Colette said sternly as she kissed her cheek. "But I want to do better for Polara than what my mom did for me. You never had a mom, but you're better with kids than me. Why?"

"You think you have to do something. You don't. All you have to do is listen. They'll do the rest."

Colette searched her eyes. "I worked with Dad every day, but I didn't know anything about him. I didn't ask questions; I just followed orders. You had a different relationship with him. He changed once he got sick, and I didn't have time to see him once I took over the company. You got the best of him. I was envious of that."

She didn't know how to respond to her sister's blunt honesty.

"I would have done anything for him, but he entrusted his life to you. I didn't handle that well either, but I know why he did it," she whispered.

"Why?"

Colette's eyes watered. "Because I wouldn't have held his hand when he crossed over."

A tear slid down her cheek.

"I wouldn't have known what suit he wanted to wear in his casket."

As Colette's face crumpled, Jasmine hugged her. Colette didn't make a sound, but her body shuddered as she cried. Ariana blinked back tears as she rubbed Colette's back.

"Now I feel sick," Colette announced as she dabbed at her face with her sleeve. "How do people handle emotions all day long?"

"Practice," Jasmine said dryly as she helped her up. "Let's get you to bed."

It was a measure of how exhausted she was that Colette let them tuck her in like a child.

"I've never seen her like this," Ariana confessed as they walked back into the great living room.

"Me either. It's scary."

Ariana gave her a hug. "We'll send you some emails about business things, but we promise to leave you alone, so you can write."

"All right. Keep me posted about Colette."

"Will do."

As Ariana exited, she headed for Lyle's office and knocked on the door.

"Come in."

She walked in and found him sitting at a massive desk with the skyline behind him.

He raised a brow once he got a look at her face. "I assume you guys made up?"

She plopped in a seat in front of his desk. "Yup. Your wife's in bed."

He frowned and shrugged back the sleeve of his shirt. "It's nine o'clock."

She leaned forward, and whispered, "She broke down."

"What the hell does that mean?"

She mimed crying and smacked his desk. "Like, full on." When he grinned, Jasmine snapped, "What the hell is so funny?"

"The baby's changing her."

"Is that why you insisted she get pregnant?"

He settled back in his seat with a cocky grin and didn't respond.

"You're sick."

He shrugged. "So, you guys hashed it out? You're all good?"

"Better than we've ever been." She shook her head. "Feels like the world's turned upside down since Dad died."

"Death changes people's perspectives." His expression turned serious. "You guys talked business?"

"They'll handle the accounts. I have no interest in the money. All I wanted was the country estate. I have what I need."

"Good." He steepled his fingers. "You have anything else to tell me?"

She tensed. "What do you mean?"

"About Roth."

"What about him?"

"He's your ex-husband."

"I know that."

"And you divorced him."

"So?"

His eyes narrowed. "He's back in New York."

"That has nothing to do with me."

He tipped his head to the side. "Roth's done well for himself."

"Seeing his face on magazines told me that."

"He has his hands in everything. Real estate, hedge funds, stocks..."

"Good for him," she said coolly.

"Stay away from him," Lyle warned.

"That's my plan. I'm going to Tuxedo Park tonight."

"Smart girl."

When she rose and turned to leave, he clucked his tongue to get her attention. She made a big show of rolling her eyes as she went to him and gave him a peck on the cheek.

"I know we're fucked up and don't talk, but you know we care, right?" he murmured.

"Yeah," she said. "I'll be in touch." She was almost out of his office when she turned back. "You're letting her name your kid Polara?"

He shrugged. "She can do whatever she wants as long as she gives me an heir."

"You guys have a weird marriage."

"All marriages are weird."

She shook her head as she left his office. Sunny and her guards were in a room off the entry hall. They rose as she approached. She donned her sunglasses as they boarded the elevator.

"I want to go to Tuxedo Park," she told Sunny.

"Do you need anything from your apartment?"

"When you can, have someone deliver everything to the estate. I won't be going back."

Sunny nodded and spoke into her earpiece as the doors opened into the lobby. There were more paparazzi now than when she arrived. They were too far away for her to hear their questions clearly, but she heard Roth's name mentioned several times. That stupid picture of them was getting attention she didn't want or need. Shit.

She ducked into the SUV at the curb, closed her eyes, and tuned everything out as they drove away from Hennessy Tower. Her mind filled with white static, and she didn't try to change the channel or make sense of her feelings. She wanted to cry her heart out and let it all hang out, but she couldn't. Not until she was in her room at Tuxedo Park. She breathed deep and willed herself to sleep, but she was too wired.

In the past twenty-four hours, she had two monumental shifts in her life. The first being the bombshell Roth dropped about his vasectomy. And the second was this unexpected turnaround with her sisters.

Her time in Colorado with Roth was a fluke. Everything had been working against her—the snowstorm, the lack of electricity, and the fact she was emotionally fucked after her father's passing. She wasn't going to bemoan her choices because it was done. She had fucked the ever-living hell out of him, and he proved once and for all that they never had a real relationship. A husband who got a vasectomy was one who didn't want a permanent tie to his wife. She had beaten him to the punch by initiating the divorce. The only reason he fought was a need to prove her father wrong. Well, fuck him. He had humiliated her for the last time. They were over. They didn't move in the same circles, so there was no reason to have another incident like the one in Colorado. *I put my number in your phone. Use it.* She grabbed her phone and found him under Roth, no first name. Even if she deleted him, he could still message her, so she blocked him. He could call or message all he wanted, but she would never know, and that was how she wanted it. If he wanted a hot fuck, then he could get it from any woman he chose. She wasn't available.

They quickly left New York City behind. No traffic meant the hour-long trip to Tuxedo Park would take even less time. She knew the route well, as she had been chauffeured from the village to the city countless times. Tuxedo Park was forty miles from Midtown, but the two places couldn't be more different if they tried. Tuxedo Park was a gated community with a twenty-four-hour guard who only allowed access to residents and their guests. There were no stores, gas stations, or banks within the walls of Tuxedo Park. The village was locked in a time warp where crime was non-existent, residents left their doors unlocked, and most people rode bikes everywhere. It was a haven in the midst of a chaotic world.

Maximus had banished his personal assistant, Elena Rogan, to Tuxedo Park when she became pregnant. Jasmine didn't remember much about her mother, since she was killed in a car accident when she was three. According to Maximus, the autopsy revealed she was pregnant with another man's child. Maximus suspected it was one of the staff and had dismissed all of them immediately. Instead of bringing Jasmine to New York, he left her at Tuxedo Park where the household staff raised her, and she attended the local private school before she was shipped off to boarding school when she was ten years old.

Both of her sisters were the byproduct of Maximus's marriages to high-profile women. Colette's mother was the daughter of an oil tycoon, while Ariana's mother was a supermodel. Maximus insisted on being very hands-on with Colette and Ariana. They grew up in his offices, so he could teach them to take over when their time came.

Born eight years after Ariana, Jasmine had been an unwanted embarrassment from day one.

She grew up with her mother's sins on her shoulders. She tried to be the best at everything and fell short every time. Maximus had always looked at her differently. It didn't help that she was a replica of her mother—brunette and curvy, with light-brown eyes. She stood out like a sore thumb next to her tall, blond sisters. She was dubbed the black sheep before she spoke her first word, and had never been able to shirk the title. The one time she had come close to making her father proud was her engagement to Ford Baldwin... and that had ended in the scandal of the decade.

The fact that Maximus had acknowledged her in his will was nothing short of astounding. No one could have predicted that, least of all her. He had made her rich beyond her wildest dreams. She didn't have to work another day in her life if she didn't want to. Could she really blame her sisters for reacting the way they had? Maximus had known how this would go down and had the foresight to prepare letters to explain his decision. What had he said that would make her sisters not only accept his decision, but apologize? Colette's breakdown was shocking. Was it the pregnancy, letter, or something else that prompted her to show such vulnerability? Whatever it was, she was grateful. She missed Maximus terribly, but something beautiful and unexpected had come from his death. Her sisters were reaching out for the first time in her life. They wanted to be a real family. She wasn't sure how this was going to pan out, but she would nurture the seeds Maximus planted and hope for the best.

When the SUV stopped, she came out of her stupor. One of the guards opened her door, and she took his hand as she stepped down. Her housekeeper Thea stood in the open doorway of the house. Jasmine gave her a wan smile and a tight hug.

"Are you okay? Do you want to eat?" Thea asked.

"No, thank you. Just bed for me."

Thea put her arm around her waist as if she were injured and walked her up the massive staircase to her bedroom.

"How long are you staying, miss?" Thea asked.

"I'm never leaving again," she mumbled. She went into her ensuite bathroom and washed her face before she kicked off her boots and shrugged off her coat. The covers were folded back, so she slid right in. "Leave it, Thea," she mumbled as the housekeeper carried her boots and coat to the closet. "It's late. You didn't have to come here just for me."

"Of course, I did. Do you know what you want for breakfast?"

"Coffee."

"And?"

She eyed her balefully. "More coffee."

Thea kissed her on the brow. "Will do. Welcome home."

CHAPTER 8

FOUR YEARS AGO

*I*t had been three years since she saw her father. She was so nervous that she hadn't been able to eat for two days. She was surprised that out of all the real estate he owned, Maximus had taken up residence at Tuxedo Park. He had never been fond of the place, especially after her mother inhabited it.

Her shoes squeaked on the polished wood floor as she crossed the main hall and turned toward the library. One of the doors stood ajar. She stopped just shy of the entrance and tried to control her roiling stomach.

It had been almost a year since she left Roth. She wanted to move on, but he was making things difficult. She felt as if there was a noose around her neck. He demanded to see her, but she refused. She was desperate to break ties with him at any cost. Her father was the only man powerful enough to make that happen.

She took a deep breath, closed her eyes, and tapped lightly on the door.

"Come in."

She kept her gaze lowered as she stepped into the doorway. She was half-convinced the guard at the gate had given her father the wrong name, and that was the only reason she had been granted access.

Maximus didn't shout at the sight of her. There was only a buzzing silence, which was worse.

"Are you just going to stand there?"

She flinched. Just the sound of his voice made her feel ill. It took a few seconds for her legs to work. She stopped several feet from his desk. She was defeated, exhausted, humiliated, and desperate to get through this without hurling on his expensive rug.

"I filed for divorce," she whispered.

She hunched her shoulders, waiting for the barrage of insults, but Maximus said nothing.

"H-he won't sign," she continued.

"What do you want from me?"

She swallowed hard. "I-I was hoping you could convince him to agree."

"If you want something, look at me."

She gathered what little courage she had and looked up. The change in his appearance was shocking. He had his first stroke shortly after he disowned her. When she tried to visit him at the hospital, she was turned away. His health deteriorated, forcing him to step down from Hennessy & Co, but nothing prepared her for this transformation. He had lost a significant amount of weight, his hair was a blinding white, and his face had age spots all over it. His hair was thinning, and the muscles in his face weren't working right. He had aged a decade in less than three years. Nevertheless, his gaze was as piercing as ever.

"Now, Jasmine," he said, "ask me."

He might look old, but he still sounded like a drill sergeant.

"Can you help me with Roth?" she asked.

"Help you how?"

She shrugged and then grimaced, knowing how much he hated useless gestures like that. "Ask him?"

"You think he'll sign if I *ask* him to?"

He was toying with her, making her feel stupid. Her lower lip trembled, and she broke his rules by looking down at her trembling fingers twined together in front of her. She hoped he didn't notice the tear that slipped from her eye and disappeared into the thick carpet.

She opened her mouth, closed it, and then took a step back. She made a mistake. Another one. After all she had done, he wasn't going to help her out of her mess. He wanted to watch her drown.

"Never mind. I'm sorry I bothered you," she said and whirled away.

She rushed to the door as her face crumpled and tears began to stream down her face.

"Jasmine."

She didn't stop. She slipped through the library door and ran. She was tired of everyone's manipulative games. Roth was right. She wasn't built for this life, and she didn't belong here. But where did that leave her?

She was trying to unlock her car door when the keys were snatched out of her hand. She opened her mouth to blast his security, but froze when she saw her father standing there. Instantly, she averted her face and began to swipe at her cheeks, mortified all over again.

"What did he do to you?" he asked.

The question caught her off guard. So much so that she looked at him. "What?"

"Did he abuse you?"

She shook her head.

His eyes narrowed. "And you're done with him?"

"I wouldn't file for divorce if I wasn't." It was the sassiest thing she had ever said to him.

He wasn't fazed. "I'll take care of it."

She couldn't believe her ears. "Y-you will?"

"But there are conditions."

Of course, there were. Her stomach knotted. "What are they?"

"You don't see him again. Ever."

"I don't want to."

"You agree to visit me several times a month."

"Pardon?" She was sure she hadn't heard him correctly.

"We need time."

"Excuse me?"

He shuffled his feet, the first sign of discomfort she had ever seen from him.

"I guess what they say is true. Getting old, sick, and weak forces you to look at things differently." He cleared his throat and looked beyond her down the long gravel drive to the massive wrought iron gates. "I have many regrets where you're concerned. I should have known what I did would push you toward him."

Out of all the scenarios she had gone over in her mind, one where her father showed some remorse about how he treated her in the past never crossed her mind.

"If you like, you can live here."

She glanced at her childhood home, a castle made of stone with turrets and brick arches, and then back at him. "Live here?"

He clasped his hands behind his back and lifted his chin. "How long do you think you can stay in that dump in Boston?"

She went cold with shock. "How do you know?"

"I've always had someone watching you."

"Why?"

"You're my daughter."

"Oh, I'm your daughter now?" she asked scathingly.

"You always will be."

"That's not what you said."

"You destroyed my friendship with Parker and cost me millions. For what? A man who only wanted to trade off your name. How could you not see that he was using you?"

His words set off an avalanche of pain. She closed her eyes and brushed a hand over her face. "How many times are you going to throw that in my face?" she whispered.

"That's the last time you'll ever hear it."

She opened her eyes and glanced around the historic estate. Everything was green and peaceful. She had forgotten how much she loved this place. "You'd let me live here?"

"You need a quiet place to work now that your career is taking off."

She looked back at him. "Career?" No, he couldn't know...

He gave her a steady look out of knowing eyes. "You think you can get anything past me?"

"You know?" she choked.

"Know and read, Thalia."

She felt faint. He read in detail about her affair with Roth. He read the anal scene, her fucking in an alley...? She was sick with embarrassment. "Y-you had no right!"

"You published it, didn't you?"

"Yes, but..." She couldn't wrap her mind around this catastrophe.

"I'm having lunch in ten minutes. You'll stay, and we'll discuss the next step."

"Next step?"

"I know someone who works at a publishing company—"

"No!"

"No, what?" he snapped.

"I don't want you involved in my career."

"Why?"

"Because..." Her hands tumbled through the air as she tried to find a reason why he should stay out of her business. "I need to do this on my own. I *am* doing it on my own. I need to know I'm good enough! I need something that's just mine."

"You're being childish."

"So be it."

He shrugged. "Fine. Let's go inside."

She didn't move. "I don't know if..."

His expression hardened. "You don't have a choice. If you want a divorce, I can make it happen, but you give me what I want."

"For me to visit you?" She shook her head, unable to believe that was his condition. She and her father didn't have a relationship, and she was wary of getting close to him. "Why?"

"I'm a sick and miserable old man… and a terrible father. You went easy on me in your book."

She swallowed hard.

"I still have time," he said gruffly. "I can change our story, and it would be nice to have company."

"You want me around?"

He scowled. "Didn't I just say so?"

"Um, I guess…"

"You guess what?" he asked impatiently.

She gave him a tremulous smile. "I-I guess we can start with visits?"

He gave a curt nod and started back to the house. She walked behind him and noticed his awkward gait. She paced at his side, watching him closely, ready to reach out if he needed help.

"A lot has changed," she said.

"Karma caught up to me," he groused. "My doctor said I shouldn't have survived my second stroke. I was forced to retire. Now I have too much time on my hands, which has forced me to reflect on other aspects of my life I failed in. I hate it."

She bit her bottom lip. "You… you actually read the book?"

"Yes."

She waited for him to continue, but when he didn't, she prompted, "And?"

One side of his lips curved into a smile. "You have more of me in you than I thought."

CHAPTER 9

$\mathcal{J}$asmine stared out of the twenty-five-foot lead-glass windows at Tuxedo Lake. It was a beautiful morning without a cloud in the sky. The glassy surface of the water reflected the orange leaves on the trees. Even though her surroundings were serene, she was anything but. She sat in the corner of the massive couch, chin on her knee, as she contemplated her dilemma.

The book wasn't going well. Was it even a book if the damn thing consisted of a few scenes and no storyline? The highly anticipated fifth book had a tentative release date several months from now. She had written the first chapters when Maximus had his stroke. After the funeral, she tried to pick up where she left off, but the idea she wanted to pursue no longer held any appeal. She tried sketching out new ideas, but nothing worked, so she gave up and took Kaia up on her offer to visit.

Her lip curled as she reached for her coffee and sipped. Going to Colorado had fucked with her head even more. Despite her best efforts, that fucker had crept into her mind. It didn't help that his character was in the fucking story and needed some kind of resolution. The only sendoff she wanted to give him was a bloody one. She wrote a scene where he was "accidentally" killed off. It made her feel marginally better, but if she tried to nix him, her fan base would freak out. Maybe it would help if she revealed his vasectomy. Then her fans would understand the heroine's mindset when she shoved him off a cliff. She set the cup down, picked up her pencil, and tipped it back and forth on the empty pages of her notebook. Why hadn't she written Roth out of the series after she and the character divorced him? Because the damn readers loved his ass, that's why. They thought he was redeemable. He wasn't, and she wouldn't let them talk her into giving him a good ending. If she couldn't kill him, he had to exit stage left as soon as possible... Possibly, a crazed hooker would take him off her hands.

The fact that her life heavily influenced the series had fucked her up royally. In book four, she reconciled with her father and peppered that with some fictional sexcapades. And now what? The heroine reunites with her father, who then dies? That was a downer. No one wanted to read that shit.

She had been back at Tuxedo Park for three weeks and hadn't gotten past chapter one. Logic told her to give the heroine a happy conclusion that was complete and utter fiction, but she couldn't do it. She was unable to write happy shit when her soul was black, tattered, and dripping blood. Everyone expected the series to have a happy ending, but not everyone got HEAs. *She* didn't. Yes, she got her child-hood home and was now rich enough to buy a country, but was she happy? Fuck no. But she also couldn't ruin the whole series by writing a realistic ending, either. She rubbed her temples. Reading was about escapism. It was why she had fallen in love with books as a child. She couldn't do that to her readers. No one wanted to see a character they had been rooting for give up at the end. So, what the fuck was she going to do? She had already sent out a newsletter explaining there would be a delay in the release due to some personal issues and a family death. There was an outpouring of support, but also some snarky and irritated emails from fans who had been waiting *forever*. Everyone wanted closure. So did she. She just didn't know what that meant.

She got to her feet. Another day with no journal entry or sketch. Oh, well. She turned to face her sanctuary and paused to savor the way the morning light lit up her favorite room in the house. The library was straight out of *Beauty and the Beast* with two fireplaces, its own stone terrace, and a second-level reading nook with ladders that went up to the ceiling. Left to her own devices in a world where she had no one, it was no wonder she had become a book lover. She lost herself in stories to escape the real world, which was frequently unkind. She started writing at eight years old and secretly submitted her work to publications and magazines. Everyone turned her down, and rightly so. She was a novice and still learning. She wrote throughout school and self-published her first book at twenty under the pen name, Minnie Hess. Back then, she had been proud of her accomplishment and told her family, who had been less than impressed. Despite lackluster sales, she continued to write and gathered a small fan base as she wrote romance and fantasy. It wasn't until she blew up her life and married Roth that she really had something to write about... and write it she did. It was ironic that writing their story as Thalia Crane gave her the money she needed to leave him.

She walked out of the library with her coffee cup in hand and entered the massive kitchen that had its fireplace. She refilled her cup and grabbed a protein bar. Once she was back in the library, she climbed the stairs to the second story, which she had claimed as her office. She told Thea to take some time off in the hopes that being alone would prod her muse.

She tapped her pencil on the empty page again. She was following the same routine she developed for the last book, which had been a breeze to write. Coffee, write in her journal to cleanse her mental palate, sketch out some ideas, then write. But nothing happened. Her fingers didn't type. They hovered over the white keys, immobile. For the first time in her life, there were no words. Words were the only thing she had been able to count on, and now even they had deserted her.

She forced herself to type. She wrote even though she knew the words on the screen would be deleted. The words didn't convey her thoughts correctly. They weren't right. Nothing was, and she didn't understand why. There was nothing to worry about. She had a home, no financial worries, and things were better than they had ever been with her sisters. Last week, Ariana, Rami, and the kids came out for the weekend, and they had a great time. Colette had texted her a couple of times and even called her once to see how she was doing. There was no word from Roth. He couldn't contact her, but still… Neither Colette nor Ariana brought him up, and that was good. If only she didn't have to deal with him in her story, everything would be peachy.

When her eyes crossed from staring at the unmoving cursor, she sat back. She was having the worst case of writer's block ever, and she didn't know how to snap out of it. The pressure of producing something that would please fans without selling her soul in the process made her temples pound. The character was her, but it wasn't. She should be able to separate the two, but they were intrinsically linked.

Her gaze strayed to her father's massive desk on the lower level. God, she missed him. Colette was right. She got the best of him. She had kept her word and visited him frequently. It took years to build a relationship and learn to trust him, but it was one of the best things she had ever done. Repairing her relationship with her father healed wounds she didn't even know she had and made a huge difference in her work. Last year, as his health declined, she moved in. Surprisingly, they had developed a routine she had come to love. In the mornings, they met in the library. He worked at his desk while she went to hers on the second level. He'd bark at her if he didn't hear typing. Her father might not understand or approve of her work, but he saw the effect it had on others. In the end, he supported her, and that was all that mattered.

She visited the kitchen once more, this time for a bottle of water and a granola bar. She snagged her jacket and beanie and pulled both on before she walked outside. The chill invigorated her as she walked along the lake. The historic estate was a turn-of-the-century master-piece set on a peninsula of three acres overlooking Tuxedo Lake. The house was built in the early 1900s and had been given modern updates while keeping the original design intact, which made it look like a castle. As a child, she imagined herself as the princess and wondered when her Prince Charming would save her. Ford wasn't a bad choice, but he hadn't asked her to marry him. In fact, he hadn't even proposed. Her father told her she would marry him and that was that. She liked Ford well enough. She had grown up around him and considered him a friend. She had been pleased to find out he would be her husband. Arranged marriages weren't out of the ordinary in her world, and she was eager to start another life. She had hoped she would fit in better with the Baldwins than her own family, but then Roth came along. He was the first person to express interest in her. Not Jasmine Hennessy, but Jasmine... Or so she thought. He pursued her, and she fell like a ton of bricks for him. Foolish girl.

One-hundred-year-old trees towered above her. Leaves drifted around her as she trudged over the crunchy piles. She passed the two-bedroom guesthouse and continued along the empty, narrow, winding road. Every time she walked, she considered getting a dog, but she knew herself too well. She traveled whenever the urge took her, and it wouldn't be fair to the dog if she was constantly taking off. Maximus had accompanied her on her last trip. His mobility hadn't been as good, and she could see daily tasks were becoming a struggle. She was planning to cut back on travel and be at home more in case he needed her. The morning she found him face down in the kitchen still haunted her. She sucked in a breath and walked faster.

She had lived in Tuxedo Park for most of her life and loved watching the seasons change. The village had never lost its magic for her. The estate was valued at eight million, a paltry sum for her sisters or father. She would have tried to negotiate with her sisters to keep the estate, but there was no need. She now owned it.

When a truck passed, she waved and got a honk in return. She sipped water as she walked, attempting to find inspiration in the smell of the leaves, the colors of fall, or the sound of the birds chirping in the trees. Nothing worked. How could it be that she had everything and nothing at the same time?

Maximus hadn't left her a letter. He probably thought giving her an inheritance was enough, but she would have valued a personal goodbye more. Why hadn't he?

Wasting time was a sin in her father's book, and in this, they agreed. She was a fucking writer, and she just had to push through. Whatever came out would have to do.

She jogged back to the house and plopped in her chair. She put her hands on the keys and forced her fingers to move. Words appeared on the screen. She paused, erased, and replaced those words with others. When those words didn't do the trick, she opened the thesaurus for inspiration and typed more. She stared at the screen, listed some ideas, threw her pencil, spun in her chair, and swore.

It was close to eight o'clock when she heard the front door slam. Only a handful of people had the gate code, so she looked toward the open library doors and waited. Thea appeared in a dressing gown with a coat over it.

She got to her feet. "What's going on?"

"Where's your phone?"

"I have no idea. Why?"

"Colette and Ariana have been trying to reach you."

"Is something wrong?"

"They need you in New York. Sunny's sending a car for you."

Her heartbeat sped up as she picked up on Thea's worry. "Did they say anything else?"

"No, miss."

By the time her ride arrived, she had looked under every paper, taken off every couch cushion, and looked in every drawer, but still couldn't find her phone.

She gave up and walked into the kitchen for aspirin and tea for the road. She opened the microwave to nuke her water and paused when she saw her phone on the glass plate. It was completely dead, no surprise. During the first two weeks at Tuxedo Park there was a frenzy of calls from attorneys, accountants, and other staff who now answered to her. There were legal documents to sign and many, many figures to discuss because of her inheritance. With her sisters' help, the process wasn't as painful as it could have been. They took care of her apartment in Chelsea and had her things delivered to the estate. Once the calls and appointments began to dwindle, she went back to ignoring her phone and trying to finish her book.

She didn't bother to change out of her tracksuit. It was late, she was tired, and it sounded urgent. Maybe it was baby related. She ducked into the SUV and plugged in her phone to charge it.

After she returned to Tuxedo Park, she convinced Lyle that she didn't need security on the estate. No one was admitted into the village without permission from a resident. With less than one thousand people in the community, nothing went unnoticed. Lyle didn't like it, but had finally agreed. Sunny had withdrawn her men and told her to call her whenever she left Tuxedo Park.

Once her phone had enough juice to turn on, she called Ariana, but her sister didn't answer. Neither did Colette. She frowned and messaged them in the group text: *What's wrong?*

While she waited for a response, she logged onto Thalia Crane's social media. She waded through the messages and notifications. Everyone was excited about the upcoming book, sending well wishes, waiting... She reassured them that she was on it, even though she had no idea what the damn book was about.

Ariana: *Are you on your way?*

Jasmine: *Yes. What's happening?*

Ariana: *We'll talk when you get here. We're at Colette's.*

The cryptic message was odd, but she wasn't too worried. If it were a real emergency, they would ask her to come to the hospital. She synced her manuscript to her phone and spent the rest of the ride butchering everything she wrote that day. By the time they pulled up to Hennessy Tower, she was beyond aggravated. She had no idea what she was going to do. Her deadline was looming, everyone was expecting a great ending, and she had nothing but a blank screen. This time, she wasn't in the mood to act cool, calm, and collected, so it was a good thing no paparazzi were around.

During the elevator ride, her fingers restlessly tapped her thigh as she counted the words in a sentence she couldn't get out of her head. She repeated the sentence three times before Colette's entry hall appeared before her. Eager for a distraction from work, she strode into the penthouse and rounded the corner into the grand living room.

Her sisters stood in front of the fireplace. Ariana had a hold of Colette's hands and was speaking to her urgently. When Ariana spotted her, she stopped talking. As Colette turned, a bolt of fear rocketed through her. Colette's tear-streaked face was ghost white.

"What's going on? Is it Polara?" Jasmine demanded as she rushed forward and pressed her hands over Colette's tummy. "Is she okay? What happened?"

"It's not the baby," Ariana said.

Jasmine eyed her sister's somber expression with growing anger and bewilderment. "Did someone die? What the hell's going on? You're freaking me out!"

"I made a horrible mistake," Colette whispered.

"Mistake? You?"

Colette gulped back tears. "An awful mistake. I don't know what to do. I didn't want you involved, but I don't think there's any other way, and I..."

"You what?" she snapped impatiently. "Spit it out!"

"He's going to destroy us," Colette whispered and swayed.

Jasmine wrapped her arms around Colette before she fell. With Ariana's help, they settled her on the couch. Before she could straighten, Colette grabbed her arm in a death grip.

"I have no right to ask, Minnie, but I don't know what to do."

Colette's voice was raspy, as if she was suppressing a scream.

"I don't know what you're talking about!"

"It's Roth," Ariana said.

Her heart skipped a beat. "What about him?"

She followed Ariana's gaze to Colette, who stared straight ahead as tears slipped down her face. She knelt before her sister and squeezed Colette's knee to get her attention.

"Tell me what happened."

Colette turned her face away, as if she couldn't bear to meet her eyes. "Two years ago, I decided to go through with some investments

Dad didn't approve of. They fell through, so I invested more to make up the difference, but we didn't profit from those either."

Jasmine glanced at Ariana who stood before the fire, arms crossed, lost in thought.

"I lost so much money that I sold some shares. A year after, more investments fell through, so I sold more... I thought I could buy them back later." Colette shook her head. "I was such a fool."

"I don't understand."

"He bought the shares," Colette rasped.

"Who...?" Her blood turned to icy slush in her veins. "No, he didn't."

"Roth owns a controlling share of Hennessy & Co." Colette put a shaking hand over her mouth as if she were going to be sick. "No one said a thing. They just sold it to him without giving me a chance to..." Colette focused on Jasmine. "The board of directors has been unhappy with me for some time. He could easily convince them to replace us. That's what this is about, right? He hates us because of what Dad did to him."

Colette sounded more like a lost and frightened child than a badass CEO. Jasmine didn't know what to say. Roth had a controlling share of Hennessy & Co? *Why?*

She looked toward her brother-in-law's office. "Where's Lyle?"

"No!" Colette surged to her feet. "He thinks I can't handle it, but I can! I just need more time."

Jasmine watched Colette march back and forth, dress billowing out behind her as she gnawed on her thumb, a nervous habit she hadn't seen her sister do in over a decade.

"Colette, calm down. This can't be good for the baby."

"Lyle would tell us to bow out, but I can't do that," Colette said under her breath before she circled back to Jasmine. "Roth won't speak to either of us. We've called his office, tried to make appointments... Today, I sat in his waiting room. I said I would take any time he had, but he refused to see me."

"She came home two hours ago," Ariana said.

The thought of Colette, pregnant and desperate, sitting in the waiting room all day heated her blood. That fucker. What game was he playing?

"I don't know what to do, Minnie. I wanted to keep you out of it, but I don't have a choice. Could you talk to him?" Colette asked.

She opened her mouth, closed it, and then said, "I have no sway over him. I don't even know if he'll talk to me." And she had blocked his number.

"You were married to him," Ariana said as she put an arm around Colette and led her back to the couch. "You saw him in Colorado. That counts for something."

Not to him.

"Did he say anything about this the last time you saw him?" Colette asked as she splayed her hands over her stomach.

"No." He hadn't said a damn thing. All of this had been set in motion before they met in Colorado, she was sure of it. Even as he was fucking her, he was planning to go after her family. Her stomach rocked with shame and fury. She thought she was the one using him when it was the other way around. Again. He managed to get another pound of flesh from her, and she allowed it. Her throat itched with the need to roar in frustration. He was always one step ahead of her, always pulling the strings…

"I don't know what he plans for Hennessy & Co, but we can't lose our company." Colette scooted the edge of her seat with an imploring look on her face. "Dad entrusted me with it. He believed I could handle it, and I…"

Colette's face crumpled into one of abject helplessness before she reined in her emotions through sheer force of will. Roth shattered her sister's confidence and was in the process of breaking her spirit.

"I can do this," Colette said fiercely. "I know I was an idiot. My pride got in the way. This company is everything to me. It's my life, our children's birthright. I can't… I can't lose this."

She stroked Colette's damp hair back as her throat closed up. "I'm sorry."

"What are you sorry for? This is my fault."

No, the blame lay on her shoulders. She brought Roth into their lives, and they were all paying the price.

The way her sisters were staring at her made her heart gallop in her chest. They were looking to her for help. They thought she could fix this, that she could somehow alter his course. Roth might desire her, but nothing came before business. She had learned that lesson the hard way.

"Just get him to meet with us, Minnie," Ariana urged. "We want to offer him a deal."

If he wanted to make a deal with her sisters, he would have done so. This wasn't about business or profit, it was about payback. No wonder Colette reacted the way she had when the will was read. Colette could have used that inheritance money to secure the company instead of letting someone like Roth take over. It took her less than thirty seconds to make up her mind.

"I'll buy back the shares," she said.

What little color Colette had left drained away. "That's not why we asked you here, Minnie."

"I know." She might not be a part of Hennessy & Co, but it was her family's legacy. Knowing how much it was recognized and respected worldwide, she would sacrifice just as much as her sisters to protect and maintain it, even if that meant giving up the millions she inherited mere weeks ago.

Colette dropped her face in her hands. "This is all my fault."

The pressure Colette was under to yield outstanding results would drive anyone insane. The fact that she was a woman in a male-dominated field and also the daughter of a legend didn't help. She had no doubt Colette would recover and do remarkable things if Roth didn't destroy her first.

She looked around the empty penthouse. "Where is everybody?"

"Rami and Lyle are traveling. I have a nanny with the kids," Ariana said.

"Does Lyle know about your money troubles?" she asked as delicately as possible.

Colette went rigid and unconsciously raised her chin as she

produced a handkerchief and began to mop up her face. "No, he doesn't. He has his businesses to worry about. This is mine."

"If he ever finds out that you didn't tell him, he's going to be pissed."

"Right," Ariana muttered.

"He won't find out because we aren't going to tell him," Colette said severely, sounding much more like herself.

As Ariana began to lecture Colette on how husbands and wives shouldn't keep secrets from each other, Jasmine stared out the window. What was Roth's end game? To destroy the Hennessy name? Humiliate her sisters? Seize everything that had once been her father's to show his power and influence? Maybe it was meant to be that Maximus left her that inheritance. Now, she could use that money to pay off her ex and be free of him once and for all.

"Minnie."

She turned to her sisters, who sat side by side on the couch.

"If you can't do this," Colette said quietly, "we'll find another way."

She took a deep breath. "No, I can do it. I'll give him a call."

"You have his number?"

She nodded. "Get some rest. I'll let you know if I get in touch with him."

Before they could say anything else, she walked out of the penthouse on legs that felt like jelly.

CHAPTER 10

"**W**here to?" the driver asked.

She stared out the window as they pulled away from Hennessy Tower. "Not sure yet. Just drive."

After two blocks, she pulled out her phone. She unblocked Roth's number and waited for a deluge of notifications or voicemails to pop up. Nothing happened.

Her gaze returned to the window. She wanted to beat her fist against the glass until it splintered. She thought she was done with corporate games, but Roth was drawing her back into the thick of it. He thought she wasn't suited for the business world because she didn't have the same ruthless streak he did, but he was wrong. She would do whatever it took to keep Hennessy & Co, even if it meant sacrificing every penny she had to fight him. Once upon a time, he broke her heart. That wasn't enough for him. He kept dicing it into smaller pieces. Did he want her to hate him? Mission accomplished.

She found his name in her contacts. Her finger hovered over the screen. She buried her feelings, tapped his name, and put the phone to her ear. It rang once, twice, three times. Maybe he wouldn't answer her call, just like her sisters. She was just a piece of ass to him anyway—

"Jasmine."

Her hand balled into a fist. "Where are you?"

"My office."

"I need to talk to you."

No response. She waited and then pulled the phone away to check that he was still on the line.

"Roth?"

"I'll be here."

"Where's your office?"

He rattled off an address she was very familiar with. His office was across from Hennessy headquarters. Motherfucker.

"See you in ten," she said and hung up.

She gave the address to the driver, who seemed relieved to have a destination. Emotions frothed inside her. *Business isn't personal.* She ground her teeth as her father's words drifted through her mind. The fuck it wasn't.

When the car stopped, she sat back. "Give me a moment," she said when the driver prepared to get out of the car.

"Ms. Hennessy?"

"A minute," she repeated and took a deep breath. She snuffed out her emotions. If she showed weakness, he would have the upper hand. He wasn't her ex-husband, friend, or enemy. He was a nobody, a faceless fuck who was messing with her family. She had several hundred million at her disposal. He wouldn't be expecting that. She would give him what he wanted, ensure Hennessy & Co was back in her sister's hands, and then peace the fuck out of here.

Someone knocked on the glass. She opened her eyes and saw an unfamiliar security guard standing outside her door. She cracked the window.

"Mr. Roth's expecting you," he said.

When she unlocked the door, he held out a hand to help her from the vehicle.

"I'll escort you," he said.

She looked down the empty sidewalks of the business district. It had to be close to eleven o'clock. She glanced across the street at her father's building and felt her swinging equilibrium stabilize. She would never be a CEO, but she was still a Hennessy. Maximus Carlsbad Hennessy didn't raise weak women. He had built a legacy that should live on for generations. It was up to her to make sure that happened.

She lifted her chin as she walked into the building. Their footsteps echoed eerily in the empty lobby. The guard didn't say a word as he pressed the button for the forty-fifth floor. The elevator was so smooth, she didn't feel it stop. They strode past a beautiful reception area filled with fresh flowers, then walked down a long hallway lined with offices with frosted glass sliding walls. The guard led her to the executive suite and knocked on the double doors.

"Come in."

She steeled herself as the guard opened the door. Roth sat at his desk with the stunning backdrop of New York City behind him. The view paired with his palatial office let everyone know immediately who was in control here. The white floor, espresso desk and neutral walls highlighted the strategically placed plants, statues, and artwork. She didn't have to ask him to know that everything in this room was top of the line.

The door closed as she walked toward him. His jacket was draped over the back of his chair, leaving him in a white dress shirt with the top buttons undone. His navy silk tie was loose around his neck. He looked stylish and expensive and every inch a tycoon.

"You finally used my number," he said and shrugged back the sleeve of his shirt to look at his watch. "We can fuck here or at my penthouse."

She stopped dead in her tracks a few feet from his desk. "I'm not here to fuck."

He gave a one-shoulder shrug. "I thought you needed more material for your books."

"Don't talk about my work!" She wanted to knock his computer off his desk and spit in his face. Instead, she smothered her emotions and focused on her mission. "I'm here because you bought a controlling share of Hennessy & Co."

He surveyed her coolly. "What about it?"

"I'm here to negotiate."

His eyes flicked over her. "Is that right?"

Her temper threatened to erupt. "You let my pregnant sister wait in the lobby all day?"

"I'm a busy man."

"Yet, here I am."

"I thought you wanted to fuck."

He was trying to make her feel cheap, and it was working. Whatever unspoken truce they had in Colorado was officially gone. He was showing her how little she mattered to him. Her stomach rocked. The urge to turn around and walk away was overwhelming, but she held her ground. She was her sister's only hope. At least she had gotten further than her sisters and was actually speaking to him face to face.

"I want to buy back the shares," she said.

"They aren't for sale."

"Everything has a price."

"Some things are priceless," he said as he steepled his fingers. "Like having Colette Hennessy-Caruso sitting in my lobby all day."

"You fucker," she said and took a step forward before she stopped herself. He was deliberately antagonizing her. To make her walk? She forced herself to think through the red haze.

"Colette got cocky. She took risks, which is good, but she took too many at once and didn't pull back when the first handful didn't pay off. We never borrow. You don't want to be indebted to anyone. Her arrogance made her reckless."

"She knows she made a mistake," she said through clenched teeth.

"She's not allowed to make mistakes, not when there are billions on the line."

"I'll pay double what you did for the shares."

His eyes narrowed for a brief second before he shrugged. "Not interested."

"Of course, you are," she snapped as her nerves stretched to the breaking point.

Seeing him reminded her of all the mistakes she had made. He stirred up so much in her, and none of it was good. She felt as if she couldn't take a full breath, like he was sucking up all the air in the room. She needed to get the hell away from him.

"I have what you want," she said.

"Do you?"

"I do." In that, she had no doubt. What she was offering was nothing to sneer at.

"I'll pass."

He wanted to play hardball. "You haven't asked how much I have."

"It's irrelevant."

She stiffened as he rose. How could she have forgotten how goddamn big he was? He faced her across the length of his desk as he smoothed a hand over his shirt, bringing attention to his body, a body she was intimately familiar with. Their last encounter in her apartment flickered at the edges of her mind, but she resolutely shoved the memories in the dirt where they belonged. She wanted to look away because that probing gaze told her he knew what she was thinking. Fucker.

"Do you know how long I've been waiting for this moment?"

A chill tripped down her spine.

"Revenge. I've heard it's a dish best served cold. Appropriate that winter's coming, hmm?" He slipped his hands into his pockets. "Seven years ago, your father destroyed me, and he had help."

Realization hit. "Oh, my God," she whispered.

"They thought they would teach me a lesson and show me my place."

He drew out the last word, savoring it.

"And now I'm back to put them in theirs."

If he was telling the truth, her sisters were just one of many who he felt deserved punishment. He was about to unleash a tidal wave of terror among the New York elite, and no one was safe. He was unhinged.

He rose and walked around his desk to perch on the front of it. He had always stuck out in a crowd, and it wasn't just his size that drew eyes to him. It was his confidence that assured people he could pull off every venture he proposed. He had always been intimidating, but now he was a step beyond that. The man she married was no more. He was control personified, completely dispassionate and focused on the bottom line.

"My sisters are innocent," she said.

"They owe a debt."

"What debt?"

"Your father's."

Even though she had been expecting something like that to come out of his mouth, she still couldn't believe it. "This is *insane*! You're spending millions to exact revenge on someone who's dead! What's wrong with you?"

"No one gets the best of me, Jasmine."

"But he didn't! You're here." She waved her hands to encompass his grand office and the view. "It doesn't matter what he did to slow you down because you made it despite all of that."

"It's not enough," he said quietly.

"What do you want? Blood?"

He said nothing; he just watched her. She was looking at a complete stranger.

"What are you going to do with Hennessy & Co?"

"I haven't decided yet."

"Liar."

"Your sisters are big girls. They can handle whatever I throw at them."

Her heart sank. "Is that your plan? To humiliate them?"

"Worried, princess?"

Her hand balled at her side. "Don't call me that."

He rose and walked toward her. Her muscles locked against the impulse to run. When he stopped a foot from her, she got a whiff of his cologne. No man as evil as him should smell so appealing. He was the devil incarnate. He should smell of blood and sweat.

"Lyle and Rami will fight you," she said.

He cocked his head to the side. "They haven't been told yet?"

Fuck. He picked up on every detail like a damn bloodhound.

"They told you, but not their husbands? What did they think you could do?"

Her eyes pricked with furious tears. "You won't get away with this."

"Maximus gave me seven years of survival training. I can handle whatever your family throws at me." He reached out and fingered the ends of her hair.

"Fuck you, Roth."

She slapped his hand away and turned to leave. She wasn't going to play his game. As she reached for the door handle, he spoke.

"How much are you willing to sacrifice, Jasmine?"

Her fingers twitched, itching to close around the shiny metal doorknob. Freedom beckoned, but her sisters' faces flashed in her mind. She turned to face him. Why did she feel as if she were being herded into an invisible cage?

"You proved your worth in Colorado. Our time at the cabin reminded me what it's like to have a whore who likes what you're giving her," he said.

She felt the blood drain from her face.

"I may be willing to negotiate if you give me what I want."

She didn't wait to hear what else he had to say. She walked out of his office and closed the door behind her. The security guard stood at the end of the hall near the reception area, which felt like the length of a football field. The guard rode the elevator to the lobby with her and unlocked the front doors of the building. As she stepped onto the sidewalk, the first drops of rain fell. Her guard came forward with an umbrella, which she waved away. She climbed in and stared straight ahead.

"Tuxedo Park," she said and covered her mouth as she fought the urge to be sick. It was okay for a man to be sexual, but the moment a woman reacted just as passionately, she became a whore. Fuck him. She would never let him touch her again.

When she saw a flash, she pulled her phone from her pocket and read Colette's text. *Did you get in touch with him?*

Her trembling fingers hovered over the screen. This was the first time they asked her for something, and she failed. She blinked away tears, so she could type, *I have a meeting with him tomorrow.*

Hopefully, the white lie would give Colette at least one good night of sleep before she broke the news to her. Dread coated her insides. Lyle and Rami would have to be told. Colette was right. Her brothers-in-law were more likely to tell them to bow out of the company than dance to Roth's tune. It wasn't like they needed the money and with both of her sisters having young children, their husbands would love to have them cut down their hours or leave the corporate world completely. But if they did that, Hennessy & Co would be no more.

The way Roth looked at her as if she were a thing and not even a person... Because of her mother, she had always felt the need to downplay her sexuality and femininity. Roth was the first man who had encouraged her to embrace her needs... only to throw it in her face years later. If he aimed to make her feel dirty, he succeeded.

When they pulled up to the front doors of the estate, she went straight to the kitchen. She downed sleeping medicine and something for her stomach and climbed the stairs to her room. She took the time to shower off the layer of invisible filth on her skin. While she dried her hair, she avoided eye contact with her reflection. She turned off the light, slipped beneath the covers, and cried.

CHAPTER 11

FIVE YEARS AGO

*H*er trip to London to surprise Roth was an unmitigated disaster. Five hours ago, she slipped out of a taxi near Hyde Park in front of an impressive glass and concrete monstrosity. She walked into the most beautiful lobby she had ever seen and got a weird feeling in the pit of her stomach. This place screamed wealth. Surely, Roth wasn't doing so well that he lived here, did he?

When she told the concierge that she was married to James Roth, she received blank, inquiring glances in return. The concierge would neither confirm nor deny that Roth lived there. They didn't care that she had flown from the States or that she wanted to surprise him. Even showing her ID granted her no special privileges. She had been forced to sit on the couch in front of a massive waterfall as she tried to get in touch with him. He hadn't responded. As hours passed with no word, her anticipation and excitement began to dwindle away.

Something was very wrong about all of this. How could he afford to live here? He hadn't mentioned that he had recovered financially or that his investments were paying off. He didn't discuss money at all, and she never brought it up since it was such a sensitive topic between them. Once she graduated, she chose a modest apartment. Roth had fought her on it, but had given in when she insisted that it was in a good location and convenient for her. He paid the rent and utilities, even though she offered to help. She assumed his infrequent visits to Philadelphia were due to how tight they were financially, but if this is where he lived... what the fuck?

Her eyes moved over the luxurious lobby made of glass, gray marble, and gold statues. In the five hours she had been waiting, no one had walked through the lobby. Not one person. It was the strangest thing to watch hundreds of people walk past the impressive structure, but no one entered. She had been hoping to catch Roth on his way in, but that hope had died around hour two. A quick glance at the concierge desk told her they were gearing up to boot her. They had been casting her suspicious looks throughout the day, and it seemed they had lost patience. She wasn't used to feeling like an impostor. Being a Hennessy ensured that she was given immediate access to everything she desired. Being a Roth meant nothing, apparently. A month ago, she convinced him to give her his address to send a birthday present. Maybe he had given this address while he stayed with a business associate, and she was wasting her time.

When the manager started toward her, she fiddled with her phone to find a hotel. The manager was a few feet away when the elevator binged. The doors opened to reveal Roth looking spiffy, hot, and all kinds of wonderful. She leaped to her feet and ran to him. She was near tears as she threw herself into his arms and wrapped herself around him.

"Thank God," she breathed. "They wouldn't tell me whether you lived here or not, and I haven't heard from you."

"Mr. Roth, do you need assistance?"

She turned her head to see that the manager had followed and was looking extremely uneasy.

"Assistance?" Roth echoed.

The manager gestured to her, clearly asking Roth if he required assistance in removing her from the premises.

"She's my wife," Roth said coldly. "I assume you made her comfortable while she waited for me?"

The manager's eyes bulged. He glanced at her before he bowed his head and mumbled something unintelligible under his breath.

"L-let me grab her luggage," the manager said and ran to her abandoned suitcase.

When she looked up, she found Roth wearing a fierce scowl.

"What are you doing here?" he asked.

"You couldn't come home to celebrate your birthday, so I thought..." The relief she felt when she saw him began to wane as quickly as it had come. He wasn't himself. He was angry and distant, and the way he was looking at her made her unwrap herself from him and take a step back.

"This isn't a good time," he said shortly.

"But..." She gave him a tentative smile and spread her arms wide. "Aren't you even a little excited to see me? It's been three months."

He stared at her for a long moment before he switched his attention to the manager, who came over at a fast trot.

"I can take it from here," Roth said as he reached for her luggage.

"But Mr. Roth, please allow me to—" the manager groveled.

"You're dismissed."

The manager relinquished her luggage and bowed before he backed away slowly. When Roth stalked to the elevator, she stayed where she was. She felt more lost than ever.

He held the door and glared at her. "Get in."

She entered the elevator and clasped her hands in front of her as he typed in a code. A moment later, the doors closed.

"I was hoping I could catch you as you walked through the lobby," she said.

"There's a basement garage for the residents, so we don't have to be seen."

"What is this place?"

"An exclusive residence for the wealthiest people in the world."

"But, how can you afford this?"

The elevator opened into an entry hall that was just as impressive

138

as the lobby. He strode in with her suitcase, leaving her to follow in stunned silence. The feeling of disquiet she had been experiencing since she arrived began to spread. She wrapped her arms around herself as her sneakers squeaked on polished marble. The penthouse was completely furnished. There were books on the shelves and a vase with orchids on a high table littered with papers. The penthouse was modern, chic, extravagant, and clearly lived in.

"I don't understand," she said faintly.

He strode to the wet bar. "What?"

"This has to be worth millions."

"Yes."

He tipped his head back as he downed a drink. She stared at his rigid back and tried to get her exhausted mind to function. She had been riding high on being reunited with her husband, but that had long since faded. Now, she was jet-lagged and fatigued and had a sinking feeling in her stomach that she was about to step off the edge of a cliff.

"I thought you weren't doing well," she said carefully.

He didn't respond.

"You said my dad ruined you."

He turned with a half-filled glass in hand. She had never seen him drink before, so seeing the generous amount of liquor made her feel even more unsettled. She felt as if she was staring at a stranger rather than her husband of two years. Roth tended to be more on the reserved side, but his expression was far from impassive. The lines of his face were set in hard lines, and something about his stare made her stomach jitter.

"He did ruin me."

"But...?" She waved her hand at their surroundings.

"He did severe damage to my American assets to the point that it wasn't worth rebuilding. He wasn't able to wreck the investments I made here in the UK. This is one of them that has panned out."

"You were an investor for this property?"

He nodded and took a sip of his drink without taking his eyes from her. "What are you doing here, Jasmine?"

"I..." Her voice sounded small and tentative to her own ears. "I thought you couldn't come home because of money, so I used my own to come and surprise you."

They stared at one another across the expanse of the great room. The silence pulsed with something awful and ugly. She wanted to go to him, to soothe away whatever was eating at him, but she stayed where she was. She had no idea how to handle him in this mood. Whenever he came home to Philadelphia, he acted as if he couldn't get enough of her, but now... He hadn't even kissed her and was treating her like an unwelcome visitor.

"Why...?" She swallowed and gathered herself. "Why didn't you tell me you were doing well?"

A muscle clenched in his jaw. "I have a long way to go."

"But..." She tried to tread carefully. "How much do you need?"

"Enough to pay your father back."

She blinked. "I'm sorry?"

"A deal fell through today," he said as he rocked the liquid in his glass from side to side.

She had an inkling of what he was going to say and steeled herself.

"Your dad's still fucking with me."

Her heart sank. "I'm sorry, Roth. Maybe... maybe I can talk to him—"

"Don't."

Her mouth snapped shut at his vicious hiss.

"He's retired and sick, but still manages to find time to fuck with me any chance he gets."

She raked her brains for a solution. "I kept in touch with some friends from college who are doing wonderful things in the tech industry. If you're looking to invest, they would be—"

"I don't need your help." His lip curled. "You rich people with all your connections. You don't have to earn them. You're clustered with future politicians, tech moguls, CEOs, and trust fund babies in your private schools. You make every connection you'll ever need before you graduate. The rest of us have to hustle and pay our dues."

"I'm not rich," she said quietly. "I have some investments and my writing money. That's it."

"You're my wife." His voice was as dead as his expression. "That makes you rich."

"But I didn't even know you were doing well!"

"I'm nowhere near Hennessy rich, but I will be."

She rubbed her throbbing temples. "I don't care about that, Roth. I never did."

"I care."

He turned from her and faced the floor-to-ceiling windows. His view of Knightsbridge lit up at night was a beautiful sight.

"For two fucking years, he's been a thorn in my side. Everything I build, he tries to tear down. Every business connection I make, he tries to undermine."

He drained his glass. The penthouse was so quiet that she heard him swallow.

"I don't know if this is worth it."

Something sharp and cold speared her heart and began to spread through her chest.

"Maximus won't be satisfied until he's stripped me of everything. He'll never let me get where I want to be."

She opened her mouth to say something, but her mind felt like a snowy white TV screen. Panic and fear tumbled around inside her, and she took a step toward him with her hand outstretched to stop this from advancing any further.

"Some days, I wish I never laid eyes on you."

She stopped in her tracks and dropped her hand as his words slammed into her. He turned to face her. His rage blanketed the room and made it hard for her to breathe.

"I'm going to make your father pay for everything he's done to me."

The way he was looking at her made her want to back away, but her legs wouldn't move.

He shrugged back his sleeve to glance at his watch. "I'm late for a meeting. You should have told me you were coming. I would have told you not to bother. I'm busy."

He strode past her to the entrance hall, but his words carried back to her.

"Stay in Philadelphia. I'll visit when I want you."

She listened to him board the elevator, leaving her in suffocating silence. She was too stunned to move, to even crumple to the ground. She stood like a statue as her mind tried to process what had happened.

She thought she was going against the grain by marrying Roth, but she married a man just as driven and ruthless as her father. For men like them, nothing came before success and wealth. Instead of her name aiding Roth, it was holding him back, so he wanted to be rid of her. She no longer held any value for him. He had used her.

As the full impact of the ramifications hit her, her knees buckled. She grasped the back of the couch for balance. She stared at the beautiful penthouse through a haze of wet she refused to let fall. Despite her father's interference, Roth was doing well. Better than, but he didn't see it that way. Her father's obsession with him probably had less to do with her and more to do with bringing Roth to heel, which would never happen. Roth wouldn't give up. Her father and husband were locked in a battle that had nothing to do with her... and she wanted no part of it.

I'll visit when I want you.

She flinched as his words cut through her mind. He didn't treat her like a wife. Was that the only reason he visited her? Sex? Originally, he left her in Philadelphia to finish her degree. Yet, it had been a whole year since she graduated, and he never once invited her to London. His excuse was that he was working and traveling. She understood that he was trying to recover financially, so to discover him living so lavishly was a shock. He owned a multimillion-dollar penthouse, and she had no idea. What else didn't she know? It was abundantly clear that he didn't see her as a partner. She had no idea what kind of life he was living in London. He didn't confide in her and didn't want to share a home with her. Her gaze focused on the flowers on the table.

Hiding other women from her would be easy. He lived his life the way he wanted with no input from her. She was a side note, a prop that wasn't aiding him, so he ignored her.

She was a fucking idiot. She spun away from the great room and ran to the elevator. Thankfully, no code was needed to leave the penthouse. She wrapped her arms around herself as she began to shake. When she walked through the lobby, her focus was on the doors that led out to the street.

"Mrs. Roth!"

She flinched but didn't stop.

"Mrs. Roth!"

The manager skidded into view. She averted her face, but that didn't deter him.

"I'm so sorry, ma'am, for our treatment of you earlier. We had no idea Mr. Roth was married."

He wouldn't be much longer. "Don't worry about it."

"Is there any way I can make up for our mistake?"

"A car."

"Of course. Immediately, Mrs. Roth."

CHAPTER 12

*J*asmine lay on the couch under her weighted blanket and watched sunlight play over the surface of the lake. She avoided her phone as she forced herself to eat and then collapsed on the couch in the library where she had been for hours. While she slipped in and out of sleep, she tried to figure out what to tell her sisters. Maybe she should lie and say she hadn't been able to meet with him at all... Or be honest and tell them to brace for the worst.

Whore. She buried her face in the pillow and drew her legs up to her chest as she curled into the fetal position. He was a master at making her feel worthless, and the fact that she had cried on his chest in Colorado made her sick. She had trusted him to comfort her, while he just saw it as an opportunity to get off and make her feel cheap and sullied.

She didn't write. She didn't try to do anything. Keeping the doors to the library closed made her feel insulated and safe. The princess was locked in her castle, and she didn't want anything to do with the outside world. She imagined Dad sitting at his desk. She could almost hear the pages turning as he read. She missed him so goddamn bad, she couldn't stand it. He would know what to do. He would be able to handle Roth, but she and her sisters weren't a match for him. Would he go for Lyle's and Rami's companies as well? She pulled the blankets over her head and drifted off again.

When she woke, the sun was setting. Time to dash her sisters' hopes. Still lying on her side, she reached for her phone on the side table and turned it on. She would tell them the truth. They had to watch their backs. Roth would do whatever it took to annihilate them. She listened to the beeps of voicemails and texts before she glanced at the screen. The excessive messages under the sister group text got her attention. She read a few and leaped to her feet.

"Fuck, fuck, fuck," she chanted as she dialed Ariana.

"Where have you been?"

"Is she okay?" Jasmine demanded.

"For the moment. She's in premature labor. Lyle's on his way back from Australia. I—"

She was only half listening as she raced out of the library and grabbed the keys to the Land Rover. There was no time to call Sunny for an escort.

"Kye is sick, so I've been home with the kids. Rami won't be back for another two days. She's at the hospital alone."

"I'll be there in forty minutes," she said as she revved the engine. "If anything changes, let me know."

She slammed her foot on the gas as she barreled down the gravel drive. Colette's sky-high stress levels sent her into premature labor. Dammit. She prayed under her breath as she made her way into the city. The traffic added twenty minutes to her commute. When she reached the hospital, it took a few minutes to locate her sister. Colette's housekeeper and two assistants stood outside her hospital room. She walked in and found Colette in bed with an oxygen mask over her mouth and an IV in her arm. Her sister's blond hair was dark with sweat, and she was as white as the sheets. The moment Colette saw her, her eyes bulged, and she held up a hand. She rounded the bed and took it.

"Are you okay?" she asked.

"Your sister's blood pressure needs to come down immediately," the nurse said briskly. "She has preeclampsia, which can be fatal to the mother and child if we don't monitor her."

"Roth?" Colette asked behind her mask.

Jasmine ignored her and focused on the nurse. "What does she need?"

The nurse gave Colette a stern look. "To remain calm and relax."

"Roth," Colette said urgently.

"Where's the father?" the nurse demanded.

"Out of the country. He should be here soon."

"I'll be back," the nurse said and left the room.

Colette squeezed her hand. "Roth!"

"I heard you," Jasmine said and rubbed her prominent belly. "The last thing you should be thinking about is business."

"Did you talk to him?" Colette asked.

"I did."

"And?"

She took in Colette's hopeful expression and felt Polara move beneath her palm. Her heart swelled with emotion, and her throat began to close.

"Minnie?"

Her eyes filled with tears as she whispered, "He's willing to negotiate." And she would do whatever it took to make sure it was in their favor.

Colette's mouth trembled. "Really?"

"Yes," she said and gave her a tremulous smile.

Colette slumped against the pillows. "Minnie, you're a lifesaver. I knew you could get through to him. Hennessy & Co is my everything. I would die if I lost it."

"I know," she whispered as her insides writhed. "You rest and prepare for Polara. You can talk to him after the baby is born."

"But..."

"Rest," she ordered. "Or else."

Colette nodded and took a deep breath. "I know it must have been hard to talk to him. Thank you. I owe you." She shifted and let out a sharp gasp.

"What's wrong?"

"Another contraction," Colette gritted.

After the contraction passed, she went to find the nurse. An hour later, Lyle arrived.

"You don't look good," Lyle said as they watched Colette sleep. "Get some rest. I'll let you know if anything changes."

She gave him a hug before she left the room. Once she was back in the Land Rover, she sat in the driver's seat and stared straight ahead.

She was going to sell her soul to the devil. Panic engulfed her. She tipped her head back as she gasped for air. When the anxiety attack passed, she rested her forehead against the steering wheel and tried to get her thoughts together.

The price to negotiate with Roth was sex. Could she really let him touch her after all he'd done? Her mind told her no, but her body had other ideas. As he pointed out, she had played the whore before. If a couple of fucks with Roth ensured Hennessy & Co would survive and that Colette could have Polara in peace, that was worth it. It would kill something inside her, but did she have a choice? If she hadn't chosen Roth over Ford, none of this would have happened. Her family shouldn't pay the price for her mistakes. She would finish this once and for all.

She pulled out her phone. Her thumb hesitated over his name before she pressed down. The phone rang once, twice, three times. She didn't wait for it to go to voicemail. She hung up and jumped out of the car. She paced with her hands on her hips as a steady stream of vehicles drove in and out of the parking garage. Her stomach lurched when she heard her phone ringing. She approached cautiously and peered at the screen. Roth. She strode away and swiped at the cold sweat on her face as the phone quieted. She was playing Russian roulette with her phone. Once she answered, her life was over. She tensed as the phone blared. Again, she let it go to voicemail. On his third call, she picked up.

"Why haven't you answered your phone?" he barked.

"I..." Her throat closed.

"Jasmine?"

She shook her head. "There has to be another way."

"There isn't."

"But the money—"

"That's not the deal on the table. Yes or no? I don't have time for this."

She lifted her chin. "I have conditions."

"You're not in any position to negotiate."

Her already heavy heart sank to her toes. She didn't have anything to negotiate because she didn't have anything he wanted aside from pussy on demand. She pulled the phone away from her ear and stared at it. He wanted to punish her for leaving him. It was in his words and the way he looked at her. Could she really do this? She could hear the buzz of his voice, but she wasn't listening. Maybe she—

"Jasmine!"

She put the phone back to her ear. "Never mind. I don't think—"

"What are your conditions?"

"It doesn't matter," she said thickly.

"Tell me."

She put a hand over her face as her head swam. "You... I don't think I can do this. You ask too much."

"What are your conditions?"

His voice was uncharacteristically gentle, but that could have been her imagination.

She took a calming breath. "You give my sisters a controlling share of Hennessy & Co."

He said nothing.

"And when we're finished, you can't go after them again."

Still nothing, but that didn't stop her.

"H-how long do I have to...?" She struggled to find the right words and came up blank. "How long?"

"How long what?"

"How long do I have to whore myself out?" When he didn't

respond, she asked, "Do you have a number in mind or is it over a certain period?" God, it couldn't be long. She wouldn't last.

"Where are you?" he asked.

"In a parking garage. Do you agree?"

"What parking garage?"

"Do you agree or not?"

"Give your sisters a controlling share, and I can't go after them in the future. Those are your conditions?"

She must be missing something else. "And you can't come after my writing business either."

"I have no interest in it."

She didn't believe that for a minute. Tires squealed as a car raced past. "How many times, Roth?"

"I'm not talking about this over the phone," he snapped.

And she wasn't going to be around him until it was settled. "Just answer me."

"It won't be a set number of times."

"So, I'm just supposed to hang around until you get tired of me?"

"I'll send Mo to pick you up."

"I'm busy."

"Your time is now my time."

"Not until I see a contract."

"You're pushing me," he said in an icy voice.

"Whores always make sure they get paid first."

He didn't respond. She wasn't sure what his silence meant, but she felt as if she had scored a point against him.

"Send me a contract promising to sell back the shares and that you won't come after them again," she said in a rush as she started to lose her nerve. "And I want in writing how long I'm supposed to put up with you. I'll send you my email address."

She hung up and sagged against the car. When the phone began to ring again, she declined the call and sent him her email address. He texted her immediately. *Pick up your phone.*

She blocked his number again. He wouldn't be able to get a contract together until tomorrow at the earliest. She didn't want to talk to him any more than she had to, and she needed time to come to terms with what she'd done.

There was no way she could drive back to Tuxedo Park in the state she was in. Instead, she checked into a hotel and asked room service for cold medicine, a notebook, and soup. As soon as she entered the room, she went to the bathroom and filled the tub with steaming water. She soaked and tried to find a shred of peace in the midst of her emotional turmoil. She had just wrapped herself in a robe when room service arrived. She ignored the food and medicine and grabbed the notebook. She flopped on the bed and paused to admire the fancy hotel pen before she began to write.

For an hour, the only sound in the room was that of pen scratching paper. Writing was a defense mechanism she had developed as a child. Whenever things got rough in real life, she retreated into her imaginary world. Instead of dwelling on her choices and the future consequences of her actions, she switched gears and focused on work. She caught a glimpse of a potential storyline for book five and leaped on it. All of a sudden, rearranging words on a page didn't seem so difficult. This she could control. This made sense. The real world didn't.

When her fingers cramped, she ate the soup and popped pills before she went back to the page. She contemplated asking room service to buy her a computer, but discarded that thought almost immediately. She was wary of interrupting her flow, and there was something about going old school with pen and paper that freed up a different part of her brain. When she finally stopped for the night, she had over twelve pages of dialogue and her forearm was aching. As the meds did their thing, she slid beneath the covers, and floated in the mind of her character, not her own. The character's voices echoed in her ears as she drifted off to sleep. She clung to them, desperately wishing to be a part of their world instead of her own.

JASMINE WOKE AT NOON. Before she got out of bed, she checked her emails, but didn't see anything from Roth. She didn't know whether that was a good or a bad thing, but decided to view it as a stay of execution. Maybe he was going to take his time getting the contract together. That was fine with her as long as he didn't do anything to Hennessy & Co in the meantime. She was tempted to unblock his number to see if she had any texts or voicemails, but she didn't want to discuss it further. This was a straightforward business transaction, nothing more. Sex to atone for her sins and ensure her family's legacy. Not complicated and a rich man cliché. Talking would only make things worse. And if they had to negotiate, they could do so through lawyers.

She called Lyle. "How's Colette?"

"They're monitoring her."

"Do you want me to come by?"

"Nothing to do here. I'll call if her status changes."

"Okay, love you guys."

"Same."

She called room service for a meal and requested clothes before she showered and wandered back to her notebook. The moment she set pen to paper, the characters came alive. She began to document the conversation in her mind and was just starting to lose touch with reality when there was a knock on the door. She wheeled in a cart and went back to the notebook. At times like this, when scenes were unfolding in her mind, writing became an adrenaline rush. The pen seemed to move over the page of its own accord, completely independent from her, as if it had a mind of its own. She read the story as it appeared on the page. Most times, she felt more like a transcriber than a creator. She didn't know where the words came from and didn't try to analyze the process too closely.

When hunger took precedence over the story, she took a break. She tried on the jeans and button-up shirt delivered by room service. Her dream world vanished in a puff of smoke when the jeans wouldn't button up all the way, and the shirt gaped over her breasts. She undressed and checked the labels. Apparently, she had put on some weight. She was too embarrassed to call room service again, so she left the top of her jeans unbuttoned and pulled her jacket over the ill-fitted shirt before she left the room.

She got some sideways glances as she walked through the ritzy lobby. The chilly breeze put a spring in her step as she bypassed the line of taxis and made her way to 59th Street and Lexington. Her grasp on her dream world dispersed as the city demanded her undivided attention. Autumn in the city was just as stunning as it was in the country. The splash of red, orange, and yellow trees juxtaposed against the brick, glass, and concrete buildings was stunning. The racing pulse of the city invigorated her, while the stampede of people forced her to keep up. The eye-catching, festive shop windows reminded her that the holidays were approaching at breakneck speed, and she had yet to buy any gifts for her family. She hunched her shoulders against the cold and eyed a woman's plaid overcoat enviously. Fall fashion was in full swing, and everyone around her proudly displayed the colors and trends of the season. She was in dire need of a wardrobe update.

As she stopped at a crosswalk, people congregated around her. No one looked at her twice. She loved being anonymous. After growing up in the spotlight, she cherished being able to get lost in a crowd. Most of the surrounding people would recognize her last name since it was stamped on a good portion of the city. Knowing who her father was would automatically create an image in their minds of who she must be... and she wasn't that person. She never had been. When Roth offered her an out, she took it. She hoped that she would be a better wife than a Hennessy daughter and employee, but she failed at that too, so she became Thalia Crane. She felt more herself as Thalia than she ever had as Jasmine Hennessy. She would never attain the same level of success as her father, and she was okay with that. She didn't want fame or riches. She just wanted to be able to create in peace.

She looked up at the buildings towering overhead. New York never failed to make her feel small. It was scary and liberating at the same time. Her grandfather lived the American dream when he had emigrated from Ireland and made a name for himself. She wasn't sure how he summoned the strength and determination to succeed in the most cutthroat city in the world. Her grandfather had done remarkable things and passed the baton to her father, who had accomplished even greater feats. The level of expectation put on her shoulders at such a young age had been crippling. She hadn't been able to live up to it, but her sisters had. She might not be part of Hennessy & Co, but she could ensure their company didn't end with the third generation.

When the light changed, she crossed the street with the mob. She had to do some fancy footwork to make her way into Bloomingdales. It was busy, hectic, and roused memories of her childhood as she walked on the black and white checkered floor. When she was a child, such a huge emphasis was placed on image that she came to hate shopping. Now that she lived out of the spotlight, she had found a happy medium between her personal style and what would be acceptable if she was caught by a stray paparazzi shot. She wasn't pleased by the media attention since Dad's death, which forced her to be a little more aware of her appearance. Being forced to shop for clothes when her self-esteem was at an all-time low wasn't the best combination, but she had no choice unless she wanted to drive back to Tuxedo Park.

When she walked into the women's section, she went up to a smiling sales clerk, and said, "Help me."

The sales clerk didn't miss a beat. She was cheery, upbeat, and, apparently, knew exactly what she needed. The clerk put her in a changing room and started bringing clothes that suited her body shape. An hour later, she had a whole new lease on life. The too-small jeans, shirt, and dirty sneakers were gone. In its place were thigh-high suede boots, a skirt, and camel-colored coat. She looked chic and fashionable and ready to take on the world. The clerk forwarded her packages to the hotel while she moseyed into the kid and baby sections.

She couldn't resist checking her email again. Nothing from Roth. By the time she sent the second load of packages to the hotel, she was high on retail and eager for more. Desperate for more distractions, she caught a cab to Madison Avenue. The chances of being recognized in this area were higher since her father had a building on this block. She crossed the street to avoid her family's hotel and continued on to the designer shops. Several shop workers recognized her and went out of their way to cater to her. She found some gifts for her sisters before she turned off Madison Avenue and slipped into Black Jade, a high-end boutique.

"Jasmine?"

She stopped in the entrance and pulled off her sunglasses. "Dai?"

Daiyu Wu was the daughter of one of China's largest automakers and a fashion designer who had made a splash during Fashion Week while she was still in college. They had grown up in the same circles and attended the same college for a short time before Dai went to Paris to pursue fashion. Jasmine heard from her sisters that Dai had opened up this boutique, but hadn't been able to visit until now.

The small woman threw herself at Jasmine and gave her a bone-crushing hug.

"Oh my gosh! How are you?" Dai asked.

Before she could answer, Dai pulled back and gripped both of her hands.

"I'm sorry about your father."

"Thank you."

"I've been trying to get in touch with you."

"I've been taking some time for myself."

Dai nodded thoughtfully and then switched her attention to Jasmine's clothes. Without preamble, she spread the coat wide.

"Is this retail?" Dai asked.

"Yes."

Dai's lip curled. "You're wearing *retail*?"

"Yes," she drawled. "I live in the country most of the time. I don't need to wear couture."

"Your father wouldn't approve," Dai said.

She snickered. "Probably not."

"You can do better than this," Dai said, tugging on her shirt.

She slapped her hand. "Hey! I like this outfit, and I got catcalled three times on the way here."

"You can rock it, but this..." She tugged on the hem of the skirt. "If it were an inch longer, it would look better, and if I took it in here"—she pinched the sides and then smacked her butt—"your ass would look spectacular."

Apparently, age hadn't toned down Dai's outrageous personality. "Seriously, Dai?"

"Listen to me. Haven't you heard I'm a genius? It was in this month's *Vogue*, page thirty-six."

"Congratulations. What are you doing in your store? I didn't think you'd actually be here."

"I had a celebrity request, so I came in. I'm going into the wedding market. Did you see?" Dai ushered her toward the mannequin in the middle of the store and gestured to the dress on display. "Isn't she beautiful?"

"It is," she agreed.

The ethereal wedding gown was a mix of traditional and modern, and fit for a princess. Knowing Dai, it was hand-stitched, one of a kind, and cost a fortune. The dreamy tulle skirt rustled as a customer entered the store, bringing in a cold breeze with her.

"You've done well for yourself. I'm proud of you," she said.

"And you? What are you up to?" Dai asked.

She hesitated. Although Dai was a friend, she was also a notorious gossip and thrived on drama. Telling her about her books would be tantamount to putting an article in the newspaper. Like everyone in the billionaire's circle, Dai was well-acquainted with her and Roth's past and would figure out who the series was based on in a snap.

"I'm handling some things for my father," she said.

"Back in the business world, huh?"

She let out a non-committal noise and looked around the boutique. "This is my first time here."

"You're a bad friend," Dai admonished before she went to the entrance and spread her arms wide. "When you come in, I want you to be dazzled and imported into another world. Were you dazzled?"

"Absolutely."

"Good," Dai said crisply as she took two steps forward. "I want to design it all. Edgy street wear all the way to elegant wedding gowns. I don't want to be put into a box. I aim to be everything and nothing, you see?"

Dai embodied the attitude of a New York artist—defiant, vulnerable, poetic, and vibrant. Dai's black shirt was two sizes too big for her and hung off one shoulder. She wore ripped yoga pants and dirty sneakers, with a metallic gold fanny pack as a belt that jutted out on her tiny hip. She had a blunt bob with jagged bangs that hung in her eyes and oversized hoop earrings. Jasmine would bet money that the half-moon spectacles on the edge of Dai's nose weren't prescription.

Black Jade was beautifully done with chandeliers, gleaming floors, and amazing lighting. The large shop windows featured everything from grunge and punk clothes to avant-garde pieces. The clothes were categorized by color, which paired formal pieces beside jackets covered in spikes or fringe.

"Let's get you out of those hideous clothes," Dai said and pushed her toward a riot of color.

"I don't—"

"Yes, you do. That's why you were drawn to my shop. Your fashion sense knew it needed me. Okay, what are you looking for?"

"I'm not—"

"Never mind. You don't know what you need. I do."

Dai walked along the racks and started yanking stuff off at random without looking at sizes.

"I've gained some weight."

Dai looked at her over her half-moon glasses. "Am I a genius or not?"

"Yes?"

"Yes, I am. I know exactly what size you are. Now, get in the dressing room."

She stared at Dai for thirty seconds before she decided to obey. The dressing room at the back of the shop was just as glamorous as the rest of Black Jade. In the middle of four rooms were an oversized ottoman that could seat up to six people and a platform to model clothes in front of a massive three-fold mirror. The luxe dressing room had a unique ottoman covered in white satin and gold studs. She surveyed herself in the mirror. She didn't look *that* bad.

Dai banged the door open and tossed the clothes on the cushion. "Take off that ugly coat. I'm bringing back velvet."

She held up a cranberry coat that Jasmine had to admit looked divine. Unlike Bloomingdales, Dai's clothes were all about the details and texture. Dai brought her a cascade of colors, from an olive corduroy jacket to a cherry-colored vinyl trench coat. Despite Dai's bossiness, she was having a great time and had to admit the clothes looked amazing on her.

"Maybe you are a genius," she mused as she stared at her reflection.

"There's no maybe. I am." Dai tilted her head to the side as she examined her. "You need some dresses."

"I think I'm good."

"You're not. I'll get my measuring tape." Dai ran out of the room, shouted to one of her clerks, and then raced back. "Got it."

As she spread her arms obediently, Dai got to work.

"What's with you and your ex?" Dai asked as she measured Jasmine from crotch to ankle.

"What?"

Dai glanced up. "The ex-hubby."

"What about him?"

"You and he had a little blip in the media a few weeks ago."

"Coincidence. We ran into each other."

Dai raised a brow. "Really? He had dinner with my dad the other night."

Her stomach clenched. "He did?"

"Yep. Dad liked him."

Of course, he did. One ruthless businessman recognized another.

Dai straightened and tapped her lip. "If you know you're going to be photographed with him, I'll do them for free. It'll be excellent publicity for me."

"I'll pay for them," she said with a tight smile.

Dai looked disappointed. "Shame." Her expression turned crafty. "So, you don't mind if I take a crack at him?"

"Roth? Be my guest."

Dai grinned. "He into crazy Chinese girls?"

"You'll have to find out for yourself."

"Maybe I will," Dai said as she skipped out of the dressing room.

Jasmine shook her head and turned to examine the exposed gold zipper on the black patent leather skirt she wore that highlighted the curve of her ass. She had a ridiculously oversized but cozy scarf draped around her neck and a crop top that Dai had somehow talked her into. The crisscross top was somehow holding up her breasts and making them look amazing. The triangle of exposed skin on her abdomen didn't look bad at all. Dai's street style was impeccable. Even her sisters would wear some of these pieces.

After waiting ten minutes, she emerged from the dressing room to see that the boutique was having a little rush. Dai was deep in conversation with two women, and both sales clerks were occupied with customers. Others browsed as they waited to be helped. She took the opportunity to peruse without Dai's guidance. She ran her hands over the truly extraordinary clothes. According to Dai, clothes were supposed to be a multi-sensory experience. Appealing to the eyes and pleasing to the touch—even the scent of leather could uplift one's mood.

She hadn't expected to run into Dai or be hustled into buying a whole new wardrobe, but she couldn't deny that she was glad she came. Dai knew her stuff, and now she was catwalk ready. As she admired a shimmering gold top, she looked over the rack and saw a man standing outside the shop watching her. He had one hand in the pocket of his suit. As she raised a brow at him, his mouth curved. He had a nice smile. He was in his early thirties and from the look on his face, he liked what he was seeing. He beckoned to her. She hadn't decided how to react when another man came up behind him. Her gaze flicked to the other man, and her heart slammed against her ribs. Roth glared at her. Slowly, she backed away from the glass. What the fuck was he doing here? And how had he found her?

As he approached the entrance of Black Jade, she made a beeline for the dressing rooms. Her last encounter with him had left her wounded and bleeding, and she wasn't prepared to see him face to face. She had been doing her best to forget their pending, sordid deal and doing a damn fine job of it before he showed up.

She skidded on suede heels as she entered the dressing room and turned to close the door, but she was too late. He shoved his way in while she desperately tried to get her shields in place.

CHAPTER 13

"What are you doing here?" she hissed.

He locked the door and turned. She considered screaming for help, but pride told her she could handle him... and what could he do to her in a public place?

When he stepped forward, her back hit the mirror. "Get out."

"You like attention, Jasmine?"

His voice made the hair on her nape stand up.

"What?"

"Would you have gone out to meet him?"

She lifted her chin. "I can do whatever the hell I want."

"You think so?" he murmured as he reached out and gripped her jaw.

When she tried to claw his hand, he leaned into her, pinning her to the mirror. His rage beat at her, although nothing showed on his face. He rocked against her, and she went rigid.

"This pussy is mine. Bought and paid for."

She smacked his chest hard enough to make her hand sting. "You're renting it."

His hand moved to her throat and gripped as he pressed his lips against her ear. "I own it."

"I don't see a contract."

"Why haven't you answered your phone?"

"I blocked you."

He stepped back. She felt a moment of relief before he jerked her forward and forced her to bend over the white satin ottoman. Before she could get away, he pulled down the zipper on the back of the skirt, which fell away, leaving her in a thong and thigh-high suede boots. He smacked her ass, nearly sending her face first to the floor. The sharp clapping sound carried into the shop, but was drowned out by the multitude of voices.

"Fuck, Roth, stop!"

"Block me again, and I'll beat your ass," he said quietly as he kept one hand clamped on the back of her neck, keeping her in place while the other caressed her stinging ass.

His eyes stayed on hers in the mirror as he put two fingers in his mouth. She watched in horrified fascination as he retracted them, and they traveled to her ass. The feel of his probing fingers made her come back to her senses. She tried to get away, but that hand around her neck tightened, warning her to stay still. Her thong was no barrier, and his fingers slipped right in. She pranced on her heels and would have kicked back like a donkey if he was behind her, but he stood off to the side, making it impossible for her to cause any damage.

She gripped his pants leg and dug her nails into his thighs. "You can't do this." When he didn't respond and continued to work her, she added, "There are people here."

"Does it look like I care?"

His thumb came into play, and she dropped her head forward. "Roth, stop."

"You like doing it in public. You like the possibility of being caught. It makes you hot, right?"

"With someone else, not you."

He pulled on her hair, forcing her head back and blinding her with the ceiling lights.

"You're going to pay for that, princess," he breathed against her temple. "You have no idea what you signed up for." He rubbed her clit, making her squirm and dig her nails into the stretched satin. "This is mine, and I'm going to use it often. Whenever I say the word, you spread wide. Anytime, anywhere."

"You can't do this," she hissed.

"I'm already doing it. This is what you've been craving, princess. Me. No one else. You're not in control; I am."

When he released her hair, she sagged to her elbows on the ottoman. Her body quivered like a plucked string. Her elevated senses focused on the sucking sound her body was making as it clutched at his fingers. She could hear the chatter and laughter of the women in the shop. She was outraged, horny, and pissed.

"You can't do this to me!" she said, even as her treacherous body rocked against his wicked hand.

"You gave me rights, Jasmine. Rights in Colorado, rights over the phone. You gave yourself back to me, which means you yield."

"Contract," she panted, unable to create coherent sentences at this point.

"If you had answered my calls, we'd be discussing this in my office instead of a dressing room."

She raised her head to glare at him in the mirror through one eye as the other fluttered. He was so fucking good at... She moaned and then bit her lips when she heard someone say, "Did you hear that?"

Roth was completely unfazed by the atmosphere, impending scandal, or potential audience. His moody black eyes told her he didn't give a fuck. Nothing was going to stop him.

"We're not d-discussing," she stammered and grabbed his pant leg again as her mind fractured. "Roth."

She heard the inadvertent plea in her voice and was too far gone to care.

He positioned himself behind her. She heard the clink of his belt before she felt the head of his cock slipping through her wet.

"This is the only way I know how to communicate with you," he said.

His eyes gleamed maniacally in his otherwise expressionless face. The sight of him behind her with his hands on her hips while she felt him impale her made her breasts ache. She shouldn't be aroused. She shouldn't be dripping wet, but she was. She hated this man, but his aggression and arrogance brought out something in her that made her want to submit. Her body didn't care that he was using her. It wanted to be sated and dominated.

Under the unforgiving lights, she could see the ripples in her ass cheeks as he began to thrust. She stiffened as she heard several women enter the dressing room. His eyes dared her to make a sound. As he ground against her, she bared her teeth. Her legs weren't going to hold much longer. She pressed her face against the ottoman, so she didn't have to see him. She blocked out the sound of the women's voices and focused on the sensations instead. It didn't take her long. Her frustration and anger fueled her lust, while the reality of what they were doing and who she was doing it with pushed her over the edge. He felt her tense and planted himself deep as she came. She muffled the worst of her moans into the ottoman. Roth sped up. When she could hear over the dull roaring in her ears, she heard his loud groan. He wasn't trying to be quiet. The female voices abruptly stopped. He was close. His face was tipped up to the ceiling, and he was completely lost in the moment. She got his attention when she tried to rise. He shoved her down and tried to keep fucking her, but she fought until she was on her feet.

She pushed him into the corner and grabbed his cock, which leaked precum. As she stroked him, his hands came out and massaged her breasts while he focused on her lips. When he let out a low groan, she grabbed a handful of his hair and yanked his head down, so she could cover his mouth with hers. She closed her eyes to avoid his probing gaze and kissed him as she worked him. At the last second, he covered her hand with his and pointed his cock at her vagina. She tried to swallow his loud groan as warm cum soaked her thong. When he was done, she stepped back. His eyes followed her as he caught his breath.

"Jasmine? How are you doing?" Dai's overly polite voice came from right outside the dressing room door.

"I'm good. I'll be out in a minute," she called as she glared at Roth.

He zipped his pants, ran his hand through his hair, and looked disgustingly poised. Fucking asshole.

She grit her teeth as she pulled on her dress from Bloomingdales. There was no way she was going to smear cum on Dai's beautiful clothes. She turned to the mirror and wiped off what remained of her lipstick, smoothed her hair, and blinked rapidly in an attempt to make her eyes look less glassy. When she scooped her clothes off the floor and unlocked the door, he didn't try to stop her. A crowd of six women greeted her. More spectators looked on from the shop. This was next level humiliating.

There was a pregnant pause before she said, "I'm ready to check out."

"I bet you are," Dai drawled.

She knew when Roth decided to make his debut, since everyone's attention shifted away from her.

Dai rushed forward with her hand outstretched. "Daiyu Wu, a big fan," she breathed.

"Pleasure," he rumbled.

So, he could be polite and courteous to others, just not to her. She left the dressing room and walked toward the front counter as the shop burst out in whispers.

"I'll take this," she said as she piled her clothes on the counter.

Dai and Roth discussed mutual acquaintances. She couldn't believe the names he spoke of so casually. He was associated with not only New York's biggest players, but on a global scale as well. He had been working overtime to ensure he was well-connected. It was no wonder he had been able to buy out the other shareholders of Hennessy & Co. If that was the pool Roth was playing in, he could do whatever he damn well pleased.

She silently urged the sales clerk to hurry, which was a lost cause since the girl's attention was fixed on Roth.

"You have a beautiful shop," he said as he made his way toward her with Dai at his side.

Dai clasped her hands together and pressed them against her cheek like a little girl. "I'm glad you like it. Anytime either of you needs anything, call me." Dai unzipped her fanny pack and handed over a black card with gold script. "It has my personal numbers on it."

Dai was hitting on Roth even as his cum trickled down her leg. *What. The. Fuck.* Not that she wanted Roth, but didn't Dai care that she had just caught them fucking in her shop or that Roth had a messed-up relationship with his ex-wife? She was torn between giving Dai a shove or raking her nails down Roth's face. Of course, she did neither and watched her total climb with each article of clothing scanned.

"I'll leave that to Jasmine," he said and extended the card to her, a subtle putdown that made her look at him.

His gaze was on her, and as usual, she couldn't read his expression. When she didn't take the business card, he slid it into one of her bags and handed the sales clerk his black credit card.

"No, I..." she began, but his cutting glanced stopped her. If he wanted to spend a fortune on her clothes, fine.

"I'm going to make Jasmine some custom pieces. Do you have any upcoming events?" Dai asked him.

She glared at Dai. "We're not attending any events together."

Roth pressed against her as he bent over to sign the credit slip. She stepped away from him and saw Dai staring at his ass. She waved her hand, and Dai blinked.

"Is that so?" Dai asked casually as she made a V with her fingers and stuck her tongue between it behind Roth's back. Jasmine dragged her finger across her throat. Dai made a thrusting motion with her hips and then jabbed her finger at Jasmine and then him, but her expression cleared when Roth turned.

"Well, I'm available for any occasion," Dai said as she flicked her hoop earring and winked at him.

"Good to know," Roth said.

"Miss Hennessy."

She turned in time to see Mo grab her bags.

"Oh, I got it," she said and held out her hand, but he turned and walked out to a familiar Bentley parked at the curb. "Hey!"

A large hand wrapped around hers. "I'm sure we'll see each other again, Daiyu," Roth said.

"Yes. We should do dinner!"

Before she could respond to that with a, "Hell no," Roth dragged her out of Black Jade. Out of the corner of her eye, she saw three men jostling for position and felt her heart sink. More paparazzi. She held up her hand to block her face and had no choice but to duck into the back seat as Roth rounded the car to get in on the other side.

"You can drop me off at my hotel," she said, and gave Mo the address.

She looked out the window as she pressed her trembling thighs together. She didn't know what the fuck just happened. Bad move, thinking he wouldn't do anything in public. He seriously didn't give a fuck. Well, he hadn't cared from the very start. Why would he change now that he was even more powerful? As she registered their location, she straightened.

"Mo, we're going the wrong way," she said.

When he didn't respond, she turned to Roth, who was doing something on his phone. He ignored her while the car carried her away from the safety of her hotel.

"I need—"

He looked up and speared her with a quelling gaze. "We need to talk."

"I thought we just did," she said through clenched teeth.

His eyes dipped to her breasts and then back to her eyes. "We need to talk more."

"Contract," she hissed, so only he could hear.

"I have it."

"Why didn't you send it to me?"

"We have some things to discuss that I didn't want to speak of over the phone. I'll give it to you once we get there."

"There" turned out to be 432 Park Avenue on Billionaire's Row, not even a block from Hennessy Tower, where her sisters lived. As the doormen came forward, she turned to Roth with wide eyes.

"I can't go in there with you! I thought we were going to your office! I—" She stopped when he climbed out of the car and slammed the door.

"Uh, no, thank you," she said to the man offering to assist her from the car. "Mo, take me to—"

Roth reached in and grabbed her. The attentive staff who were well-versed in the elite of New York couldn't hide their shock as they looked from her to Roth.

Under the guise of kissing her cheek, he warned, "Make a scene, and you'll regret it."

He led her into one of the most exclusive addresses in New York. The impressive lobby was filled with people coming and going. She averted her face in the hopes of somehow going unnoticed, which was ludicrous considering how massive Roth was. They had almost reached the elevators when the worst-case scenario happened. Two wives of her father's business partners stopped dead in their tracks at the sight of them. She tried to brazen out the awkwardness with a smile and wave.

"Hi, Mrs. Pearson, Mrs. O'Leary."

Neither woman responded. She tried to step away from Roth, but he didn't allow it. By the time they were in the elevator, she felt as if she had died a thousand deaths and was near tears. She couldn't say anything with the elevator operator right in front of them, but the moment they stepped into his penthouse, she ripped her hand from his and shoved him with every bit of strength she had.

"Are you crazy?" she shouted. "What the hell do you think you're doing?"

"Calm down," he ordered.

"Fuck calm! You fuck me in a dressing room on Madison Avenue, and then you bring me here! What are you thinking? If my sisters find out, they're going to—"

The elevator opened, revealing Sarai and two bellboys with her packages from Black Jade.

Sarai beamed at her. "Ms. Hennessy, so good to see you again."

She swallowed her ire and nodded because if she opened her mouth, she was going to lose her shit. He was taking over again, steamrolling her, and she couldn't stand it.

"I'll meet you in my office," Roth told Sarai before he tipped the bellboys and grabbed her bags. "Come."

She had no choice but to follow him through the massive penthouse. She fantasized about leaping on his back and putting him in a chokehold as he walked into a master suite with jaw-dropping views. He dropped her bags on the bed and gestured to the connecting bathroom.

"Shower. I have a meeting with Sarai, and then we can talk," he said.

"You can't keep dragging me all over the place."

"It's the only way to put you where you should be."

"Is Kaia here?" she asked, hoping for some backup. She had been wondering about his mother, but didn't dare call her, knowing she was with Roth.

"No, she recovered and went home. She missed her mountains."

At the moment, she would give anything to be anywhere but here, even freezing Colorado. "You're going to ruin my life, aren't you?"

Even in the bright sunlight, his eyes were two pitiless black holes with no hint of brown.

"That depends on you. Shower and then meet me in my office."

He walked out without another word. Autocratic motherfucker. He was cold as ice unless they were fucking. An image of him in the dressing room with his head thrown back in ecstasy slipped through her mind, but she resolutely pushed it away.

The bed and bathroom faced the south. She could pick out the Empire State Building, The Chrysler, and several of her father's signature blue structures. She had been fortunate enough to see the city from some exclusive spots, but this was something else. The dramatic panorama took her breath away. She wasn't afraid of heights, but she was hesitant to approach the wall of glass, which was flush with the side of the building.

In the master bath was an elegant egg-shaped tub where one could take in the views, separate his and her vanities against either wall and a glass shower with double doors that could comfortably fit up to four people. His personal bathroom was stocked like a hotel, with rolled towels and a robe hanging in the closet. When she pried her eyes from the view, she stripped. Multiple shower heads removed all evidence of what they'd done in the dressing room. Steam obliterated her view of the city as the warm water cascaded over her used body.

It seemed like a lifetime ago that she discovered her fetish for doing it in public. They were strolling home, and she was in a frisky mood and had been teasing him throughout dinner. When she "accidentally" grabbed him, he'd had enough and dragged her into an alley and pinned her against a grimy wall. She became the initiator then, telling him in graphic detail exactly what she wanted him to do to her. He'd done everything and more. After, he carried her the last block home because her legs weren't working right. That was shortly after they were married and right before he moved to London. He probably considered that moment rock bottom, since he was in the midst of watching his companies topple. But for her, those were her happiest memories. Being disowned had liberating her. No more expectations, standards, and boring dinner functions. She could be whoever she wanted to be and fuck in an alley if she wanted. She thought she was leaving the upper echelon behind, yet here she was... Back then, it never occurred to her who Roth would become. He was worse than her father and even more powerful. How could she have been so blind?

She pawed through the clothes she bought from Black Jade. Dai didn't have anything as mundane as jeans unless they were ripped to shreds, decorated in crystals, or sporting outrageous fringe. She pulled on a full-length skirt that fit her like a glove and the cropped top (since she didn't need a bra to wear it). To top off the look, she pulled on a black and white coat that made her feel like Cruella de Vil. Her suede shoes didn't match anymore, but the skirt was so long, they only peeked out when she walked.

Blow-drying her shoulder-length hair didn't take long. She fingered the strands. She should visit her hairstylist while she was in the city. When she finished fussing, she grabbed her packages and lugged them back through the hallway to the foyer. She could hear the rumble of Roth's voice coming from some room off another hallway, but she didn't go toward it. Instead, she examined his lair, which was superbly done in light colors that made the already massive space feel even larger. The view of Central Park from this height was stunning. It was a riot of orange right in the middle of the city. Along one wall were cutout window seats that would make an epic reading nook.

For the most part, she preferred the country for the solace and quiet, but this was warm and welcoming. If she had a dig like this, she might stay in the city more. Despite its vastness, it felt safe and insulated—its own world of tranquility, which was ironic considering the owner.

Her father had his hand in real estate, among other things. She knew how much her sisters' penthouses were worth, but this was next level. The space, view, size… This thing had to be upwards of eighty million.

"Jasmine."

She jumped and spun to find him less than six feet away.

"Come."

She followed him down a hallway lined with artwork and entered his office. It was just as grand as the one she visited in the business district.

"Did you use the same designer for both places?" she asked distractedly.

The view from his office was cinematic. She had sweeping views of the Hudson and East River, Central Park, and the city. She was so dazzled, she could barely focus.

"This is beautiful," she said reverently.

"It's an investment."

Her lip curled. It was more than an investment; it was a home, but businessmen never got emotionally attached to anything that could make them money. She walked around his office and admired several interesting pieces.

"Sit."

She stiffened. "I don't know where you get off thinking you can order me around. I didn't sign my life over to you."

"That's what we need to talk about."

He was intractable. Had she expected anything else? Not wanting him to put his hands on her again, she approached the desk and sat on the edge of her seat. Involuntarily, her eyes went back to the view until a loud thump drew her attention back to him. Roth rested his hand on a thick stack of papers. She looked from him to the stack and blanched.

"Is that the contract? Why is it so huge? It's going to take my lawyer a couple of days to go through it."

He said nothing. He just stood there, staring at her.

"What?" she demanded.

He pushed the papers toward her. She gave him a suspicious glare before curiosity got the better of her. She leaned forward, read the title, and almost fell off the chair. *"No."*

He didn't react to her horrified whisper.

"A prenup?" she choked.

She shot to her feet and swiped the stack of papers off the desk. They fell to the carpet with a dull thud.

"How dare you!"

"This is what we need to talk about," he said placidly.

"There's nothing to talk about! Marriage doesn't come into it. This is about sex and protecting my family from you!"

He crossed his arms and perched on the edge of the desk. "And how do you think we can carry on this affair without people noticing?"

"If you hadn't fucked me in Black Jade and paraded me through the lobby, no one would know we're involved!"

"You had paparazzi following you today. That's how I found you. And where the fuck is your security? I don't know what Lyle's think-ing, letting you roam on your own."

"Lyle's not in charge of my security, I am."

"That explains a lot. Security isn't optional. You may be in denial about your status and the public's interest in you, but I'm not. As the daughter who gave up her rights to the Hennessy fortune and who shies away from the spotlight, you are more noteworthy than your sisters. At some point, someone is bound to see us together."

"Why? I spend most of my time at Tuxedo Park, and I'll come into the city every other week or something…"

Her voice trailed off because, for once, she could read his expression clearly. He was staring at her as if she'd lost her mind.

"Every two weeks?" he echoed. "Within twenty-four hours of seeing you, I fucked you five times and jacked off on you twice."

Her body tingled at the memory. She paced restlessly with her arms wrapped around herself. "So?"

"So, I'm not regulating myself to fucking you every other week."

"When we were married, we didn't see each other for months at a time."

"We lived in different countries, and I was working around the clock."

"Don't you still work around the clock?"

"I can afford to take time off to do what I want now."

Her chest tightened. "I can't marry you."

"We're not going to skulk around like we did before. Eventually, people will see us together, including your family. I assume you haven't told your sisters about our deal?" When she shook her head, he said, "If they decide to get protective, it will cause unnecessary drama and media attention. I want us to present a united front. If we marry, they'll accept it, and society will follow their lead." He rose and slipped his hands into his pockets. "It also gives me legal rights over you in case you decide to renege on our deal."

"I wouldn't renege!"

"You've disappeared on me one too many times. If I stick my neck out for your sisters, I'm not accepting half measures from you. I want it all."

He picked up the prenup, set it on the desk, and pushed it toward her.

"Look at it. One year. I give you a generous severance once we separate. I promise not to go after Hennessy & Co, and will even assist Colette out of this rut she's in. I'll direct her toward some solid investments, back her in board meetings, and help restore people's trust in her being at the helm. Once she's on her feet, I'll let her buy me out."

His proposal was very generous but, "A year?" She couldn't wrap her mind around that length of time. "I thought three months at the most... and only on weekends," she said weakly.

He walked toward her and cupped her chin. She was too shocked to smack his hand away as he lifted her face.

"Not enough," he said as his thumb brushed over her bottom lip. "I never lost my taste for you. I figure a year should be enough time to work you out of my system, and in return, your family legacy will continue, and you'll never have to worry about me again."

It was more than she could have hoped for, but... a *year*?

"It won't be like last time."

"It'll be worse," she whispered.

His fingers moved to her hair and began to play with the strands as she tried to process his proposal.

"I want to stay at Tuxedo Park," she whispered.

"No. You'll be with me."

"I need to write," she said desperately.

"I won't interfere."

He would. She couldn't think when he was around. "I need quiet."

"You can write here."

Her gaze went back to the multimillion-dollar view. She couldn't believe she was contemplating this, but did she have a choice? "We keep our assets separate?"

"Yes." His eyes narrowed. "Why do you care about the prenup? You refused to take anything from me the first time."

Seconds ticked by, and then his expression sharpened.

"Daddy left you something, did he?" he asked softly. "Is that what you were going to use to buy back the stocks?" He shook his head. "Your sisters don't deserve you."

"They shouldn't have to pay for my mistakes. If it wasn't for me, you wouldn't have gone after the company."

"Blame Maximus."

"But my father wouldn't have targeted you in the first place if we didn't have an affair."

"Maximus made a lot of enemies, princess. If it wasn't me,

someone else would take my place. Your sisters will pay for the sins of their father in one way or another. You're lucky I intervened." His finger drifted down her cheek. "And I have an incentive to help them instead of letting them drown. You owe them nothing."

"Then I should walk away right now and call this whole thing off," she bluffed.

He leaned down, so their faces were inches apart.

"Even if you don't sign, every time I see you, I'm gonna find a way to get you on your back. At least, this way, you'll get something out of it other than a climax and material for your books."

"You ass!"

Her hand swung but didn't connect with his face since he caught her by the wrist.

"You want me even though you claim to hate me. I fought long and hard for you, and you left me. I want my prize."

"You—" she began, but stopped when she heard the distant ring of her cell phone. Her phone was on do not disturb, which meant the caller had dialed her number twice within five minutes. An emergency. Colette.

CHAPTER 14

She ripped herself out of his grasp and ran down the hallway. She dug through the shopping bags until she found her purse. She answered the call on the last ring.

"Lyle? Is she okay?"

"She's going to have the baby now. Get here," he barked and hung up.

She didn't grab her purse or shopping bags. She ran to the elevator and smacked her hand on the button before she realized nothing was happening.

"Roth!" she roared.

"What's going on?" he asked so close behind her that she jumped.

"Colette's having the baby. I need to be there now! Call the damn elevator."

He keyed some numbers into the keypad as he spoke into his phone, "Bring the car around."

As she boarded the elevator, she texted Ariana, who had left the kids with a nanny and was en route to the hospital. Rami was still out of the country. This time, when she walked through the lobby, she didn't care who saw her. All she cared about was getting there in time. God, it was still too soon…

Mo sat behind the wheel of an SUV this time. She rushed toward the open passenger window and gave the address before she climbed into the back seat. When Roth got in, she stared at him.

"What the hell are you doing?"

"I'm coming."

"No, the fuck you're not."

He leaned forward and tapped the tinted glass partition dividing the front from the back, prompting Mo to pull away from the curb.

"We lay the groundwork now," Roth said as he typed on his phone. "The paparazzi shots will help our story."

"I didn't agree!"

"You will. You'll do anything for your family."

She couldn't believe his self-assuredness. "The only reason I'm even thinking of your stupid deal is because of Colette. She went into premature labor yesterday because of stress, because of *you*! She's so damn worried about Hennessy & Co that she's putting her and the baby's life in danger. If it wasn't for that, I'd tell you to fuck yourself."

His eyes narrowed. "That stress comes from being a CEO, not just from me."

"But you initiated the takeover and then refused to speak to her. What did you think would happen?"

"It's not my job to worry about the opposition. Everyone knows your sister hasn't been putting her best foot forward lately. She's been losing steadily enough that word's gone around."

She slashed her hand through the air. "You can't barge in at a time like this. This is real life. This is my family."

He grabbed her hand. "We present a united front."

She stared at him. "How can you be so heartless?"

"Practice."

She pulled away. "I can't deal with you now. I just want to make sure my sister's okay and Polara's healthy."

"Polara?"

"My niece."

"Interesting name."

When they reached the hospital, she dashed out of the car. Roth kept up with her as they entered the maternity ward. As she got directions to Colette's room, Roth fell back, for which she was grateful. She didn't need him interfering at a time like this. As she approached the room, a medical team filed out. She paused on the threshold and saw Lyle and Ariana on either side of Colette, who was sitting up in bed with a small bundle in her arms. Colette's expression of dazed wonder made Jasmine rush forward.

"She's here?" she whispered and pressed against Ariana's side so she could see.

The bundle in the crook of Colette's arm peered at them through squinted eyes. Polara had a tiny rosebud mouth and not one strand of hair on her perfect head. Jasmine tucked her fists under her chin to stop herself from snatching up her new niece and smothering her with kisses.

"We were thinking of calling her Maxine for Dad," Colette said.

Ariana put a hand over her mouth and nodded because she couldn't speak.

"Polara Maxine," Jasmine said and shook her head. "Holy shit. She sounds like a terror."

"You better believe it," Lyle said as he took his daughter and began to walk around the room.

"It happened so fast," Colette said faintly.

Colette was emotionally shattered and desperately trying to keep her composure. Jasmine bit back a smile and rubbed her arm.

"It's all over now."

Colette took a deep, shaky breath and waved her hand in front of her face as her eyes filled with tears. "I don't know what's wrong with me."

"Hormones," Ariana said sympathetically and handed her a tissue.

Colette's eyes followed her husband for a moment before she said, "Lyle, I want her."

Colette, the cool-headed drill sergeant, was desperately in love, and it was a beautiful sight. Ariana stepped out of the room to take a call. Jasmine watched Lyle hand the baby back to Colette. He pressed his forehead against hers and whispered to her while he stroked her hair. Jasmine's heart clenched with painful happiness. She stepped back to give them a moment.

The past two months had been a roller coaster of trials, but this… This was good and pure. Polara started a clean slate for all of them. She was so caught up in the moment that she didn't realize Ariana was back until she grasped her arm and dragged her out of the room.

"Ariana, what—?"

"He's here. I just saw him," Ariana hissed.

"Who?"

"James Roth!"

The warm feelings in her chest began to dissipate. "He is?" She was hoping he'd left by now.

"What's he doing here?"

She licked her lips. "He… I…" She gave herself a mental bitch slap. "I was on Madison Avenue and ran into him at Black Jade. You know Dai's shop?"

Ariana blinked. "Yes, I know it."

"Dai and I were catching up, and he brought me here when I got the call," she said as casually as possible. She wasn't lying, just messing with the timeline and not accounting for everything in between.

Ariana's brows drew together. "You guys are okay? I thought…"

"Yeah, we're fine," she lied and felt her spurt of joy crumple into a ball and sink to the pit of her stomach. Reality was a fucking bitch. "I didn't know he was still here. I'll tell him to leave."

Ariana grabbed her arm. "Colette told me Roth's willing to talk to us."

"Yes," she said cautiously.

"Maybe I should come with you and see what his terms are."

Her stomach lurched. She hadn't signed the prenup yet. He wouldn't negotiate until she did. "I don't think it's the right time. Besides, Colette would want to be there too."

Ariana hesitated and then nodded. "You're right." She cupped Jasmine's cheek. "Thank you for speaking to him on our behalf. You don't know how much this means to us."

She gave Ariana a weak smile as her sister slipped back into the delivery room. She looked through the window at her family before she walked down the hallway. Roth was in a small waiting room, pacing as he talked on the phone. When he caught sight of her, he stopped in his tracks.

Roth was destructive, selfish, emotionally abusive, and unflinching in the face of unbeatable odds. He wasn't the same man she married. That man had been reserved, but not cold. Had Maximus hardened him, or had he always been like this, and she ignored it? The man watching her through the glass had a detached, Hannibal-like quality that would make any sane person run. Instead, she stayed put while he continued the call, eyes fixed on hers.

They had an unhealthy addiction to one another. It began the moment they met and hadn't let up even now. Back then, she had given herself to him unreservedly, naïvely believing he loved her. She made excuses for him until that night in London forced her to face the truth. She never planned to remarry. Once was enough. She didn't want to set herself up for the pain that came with giving herself to someone and coming up short. She didn't have a filter when it came to those she loved. Case in point, the lengths she was willing to go to for her sisters and what she had given up to be with Roth the first time. She was idiotically loyal and built to protect... but who would protect her from Roth this time?

He got off the phone and slipped it into his coat. He didn't come to her; he just waited. He had orchestrated all of this with the precision of a military colonel. What else did he have up his sleeve? An invisible clock was ticking, forcing her to decide. Could she do this? Put herself at his mercy? Did she have a choice? If she walked away, they'd lose everything their father and grandfather worked so hard for. Life would go on, but they'd never be able to rebuild what took three generations to accomplish. Now that Roth had a foothold in New York, he would use every contact at his disposal to crush her sisters into rubble. He had turned the tables on them, and like last time, she was caught in the middle. One year and it would all be over. She would celebrate her freedom at Polara's first birthday party.

She walked into the waiting room, which had a weird, off-putting smell.

"I need vacation time," she announced.

He frowned. "Excuse me?"

"Vacation time," she said crisply. "Everyone gets vacation while they're working, right? I want a month of vacation."

"If you need a vacation, we'll take it together."

"You? Vacation?" Before he could answer, she waved the questions away. "No, I'm talking about time away from you if I need to... recover."

"Recover?" he repeated with a scowl.

She rolled her hands as she tried to find a polite way to say his presence was suffocating. Not only that, but she was sure she would need time to fortify her walls. "If I need a mental break... or even a physical one if you go overboard." She'd taken painkillers for two days after she got back from Colorado.

"I've never hurt you."

She crossed her arms. That was a fucking lie. He destroyed her five years ago.

"Most work trips you'll come with me, but others I may go alone," he said. "Whatever time you want, you'll need to take around my schedule."

She twisted the sash of her coat as she said quietly, "You can't call me a whore."

That was a hard limit for her. She might be one in the Biblical sense, but repeatedly throwing it in her face... *No.* He had already stomped all over her pride, but she wasn't a punching bag. She was a fucking person, and once upon a time, she had been a real wife (in her mind), and he wasn't allowed to mock her for it.

He nodded.

She twisted her hands together as she tried to think of anything else. "If we say we're dating, we might be able to get away with it. There's no need to get married."

"Exes don't date."

"Maybe we do," she argued, even though he had a point.

"People in families like yours don't date. You date with intention and then marry. Marriage shuts everyone up, and I don't want anyone questioning our relationship. Marriage is clear-cut, legal, and will make everything simpler."

"If you get tired of me before the year is up, if you want out, then what happens?"

His eyes swept over her before he said, "If that happens, you've upheld your end of the deal. I'll fulfill all of my obligations."

"And if you get angry with me," she said tentatively, "you can't lash out or threaten to go after my family."

He closed the distance between and cupped her nape.

"Are you planning to make me angry?"

"No, but I will. There's too much shit between us to live in harmony."

He buried his face in her hair and inhaled. "You used my shampoo."

She gripped his lapel. "Roth, focus."

"Once you sign, we both keep up our ends. No reneging, regardless of what happens in between."

There was a poster on the wall about antibiotics and asthma. She stared at it for a few seconds, but was distracted by his scent. As she turned her face into his neck and inhaled, he stiffened.

"You smell like me," she said and tried to move away, but the hand on her nape stopped her.

"Anything else?"

She stared at his throat as she tried to think.

"I'll make it official," he rumbled. "I'll speak to Colette and make her day even better than it already is."

"You're an arrogant bastard."

"But I'm right, aren't I? Your sister lives and breathes business, same as me. She may be a mother now, but she'll never stop worrying about the company or what people think of her. It weighs on her, having to uphold her reputation as a Hennessy and holding her own against her husband. Maximus chose Lyle to spur her on."

She was stunned by his spot-on analysis.

He massaged her nape as several seconds ticked by. "I know your family better than you think I do. I know how close you are to Lyle, that you used to see him when I was in London. He's going to be the biggest problem. Your sisters will believe you because they want to, but he won't."

She had been so focused on how this would impact her that she overlooked the fact that she would have to convince her family. "Oh my God. This isn't going to work."

"It will," he said. "Do you agree?"

She looked up, her gaze colliding with his devil eyes. "Do I have a choice?"

"No. Do you agree?"

Her heart slammed against her ribs as she fought against her better judgment and whispered, "Yes."

His eyes flicked over her head and came back to hers. "Showtime."

"What the fuck is this?"

She jumped and whirled around. Lyle stood in the doorway, and he looked furious. He advanced into the room and held his hand out to her.

"Minnie, come," he said imperiously.

The hand on her nape tightened, but she didn't need the warning.

"It's okay, Lyle," she said.

He shook his head. "No, it isn't. Roth, let go of her."

Roth leaned down and kissed her temple. "You wanna tell him the good news, princess?"

"Good news?" Lyle spat. "It's not good if it involves you. Minnie, I want to talk to you."

"We're getting married again," Roth announced, and her heart skipped.

"No, the fuck you're not," Lyle snapped.

"You sound like Maximus." Roth sounded amused.

She elbowed him in the side.

Lyle jabbed a finger at him. "Maximus told me if anything happened to him, you'd show up, and here the fuck you are."

"He knew, no matter how long it took, I'd get her back, and she finally agreed," Roth said.

She looked up as he stroked her hair. She didn't know he was such a good actor. Then again, he had duped her before, so why was she surprised?

"Fuck, Minnie, you know he's no good for you," Lyle said.

His worry was easy to read, and she felt like shit. When she would have gone to him, Roth leaned down and nuzzled her temple as he reminded her, "United front."

"When did this happen?" Lyle asked.

"In Colorado, and it's been going on ever since," Roth said bluntly.

She wanted to stomp on his foot. Did he have to tell Lyle everything? God!

"Is that true, Minnie?"

The hand on her nape felt like a noose. "Yes."

Lyle ran a hand through his hair. "When's the wedding?"

"We—" she began, but Roth interrupted her.

"In a couple of weeks."

She jerked, but he covered the movement by bringing her against his body.

"We don't want to wait, do we, princess?" he asked.

She opened and closed her mouth and uttered not one word. *Wedding?*

"We hope Colette will be recovered by then," Roth said smoothly. "We want to include the family this time, and do it right."

What the fuck was he doing? Her family wasn't a part of the deal. They didn't have a wedding the first time—they had a judge—so why would it be any different this time around?

"Min, do your sisters know?" Lyle asked.

She shook her head.

"Why didn't you tell us?"

"I… I knew it was gonna stir up the past, and I wanted to keep it under wraps as long as possible, but…"

"But we're not hiding like last time," Roth finished.

Lyle sighed. "Are you sure about this?"

He couldn't hide his skepticism, and she couldn't blame him. She was in way over her head.

"Yes," she said with a confidence she didn't feel.

Lyle jerked his thumb over his shoulder. "You better tell your sisters. I need to talk to Roth."

"Lyle."

"This is man talk, Min."

When Roth released her, she walked toward her brother-in-law. Lyle stood like a soldier ready for battle.

She wrapped her arms around him. "I didn't want to hurt you," she said quietly.

His arms came around her. "You haven't. I just wish it was anyone else."

Me too, she thought. She walked out of the waiting room, but peered through the glass as she passed. Roth commanded her attention. He didn't care that Lyle was about to rake him over the coals. No matter what he was up against, he always stood tall, and he never wavered. Once upon a time, she had admired him for that trait, but now, it made her stomach churn. He would never stop, never give in. This was the only way to protect her family from him. One year and all of this would be over.

When she entered Colette's room, she found her sisters cooing over Polara who was sound asleep in her mother's arms. She stopped at the foot of the bed and struggled to find the right words.

"Minnie?"

Ariana's concerned tone made her eyes prick with tears. Her sisters were watching her, clearly realizing something was going on. She wanted to confide in them and blurt out her fears and wants and needs, but they wouldn't understand. Her relationship with Roth was a tangle of lust, rage, bitterness, and satisfaction wrapped up in extortion, manipulation, and silence. Even though she hated herself for it, she craved what Roth could give her, and suspected it was the same for him. Neither wanted the other, but they couldn't help themselves. Sex had been a driving force in their relationship right from the start, and seven years later, nothing had changed. Their bodies didn't care about their bad history. For the next year, they would slake their lust for one another, and hopefully, it would fizzle out and die. In return, her family would be safe, and she would never have to deal with him again.

She plastered a smile on her face and raised both arms in a guilty shrug as she announced, "I'm getting married."

"You're what?" Ariana gasped.

The contented smile vanished from Colette's face. "Roth?"

She clasped her hands behind her back as she tried to think of something to say.

"I slept with him in Colorado," she blurted, and instantly wished she could take it back when their eyes flared.

"What?" Colette was clearly scandalized.

She straddled the line between fact and fiction. "We've been seeing each other off and on since then. He's been trying to convince me to give him another chance, but I thought it was too complicated to sort out. I didn't know all of this was happening with Hennessy & Co. He keeps business and personal separate, so when you told me about it, I was pissed. When I met with him, we talked."

"And?" Colette probed.

"He was still focused on paying Dad back for the past even though he's gone," she said with a shrug and tried to act like this was normal behavior when it couldn't be further from the truth.

"Which is what I suspected," Colette said quietly. "Dad shouldn't have gone after his businesses or turned so many people against him."

Jasmine blinked. That was unexpected.

"Now, what does he think?" Colette pushed.

"He realizes he can't have me and still seek his revenge, so… he's going to help."

There was a buzzing silence.

"He'll help you stabilize the company and let you buy him out for some ridiculously inflated price in the future." She clasped her hands behind her back. "I… I think it's a good deal, right?"

Ariana and Colette looked at one another, communicating in their secret language. She couldn't tell whether they were relieved or insulted.

"He's doing this for you?" Ariana sounded dazed. "He must really love you."

Her chest ached from holding in all the things she wanted to say, but couldn't.

"You're really going to work things out? After everything that's happened?"

She nodded.

"Why marriage?" Colette asked.

"He wants to do things right this time," she said hoarsely.

"Wow," Colette said and gave herself a little shake. "If that's what you want, we support you."

Her sister's easy acquiescence was startling. All her life, she longed to hear those words from her family, and when she finally received their support, it was for a sham. A cynical voice in the back of her mind wondered if they would be as accepting if Roth didn't have a controlling share of Hennessy & Co. She pushed the nasty voice away as Ariana gave her a hug.

"Congratulations! We were worried about you living at Tuxedo Park by yourself. I know how close you and Dad were. I hope Roth gives you what you need."

"Me too," she whispered.

"Maybe your books made an impact on him," Ariana mused. "Perhaps he's going to do things differently this time."

He was definitely doing things differently. He was starting with coercion. She was relieved when Polara stirred, distracting them from her impending nuptials. She got a turn with the baby and buried her face against the newborn who smelled like new beginnings and sunshine. She had just handed her back to Colette when the door opened, and Lyle and Roth entered.

Seeing them together was surreal. Aside from the function where they first met, she had never seen Roth with her family members. Her worlds were colliding, and she didn't like it.

Lyle's jaw was clenched, and his eyes were fixed on Roth, who showed no outward signs of anger or distress.

"Congratulations," Roth said to Colette, who managed to look regal even an hour after giving birth. Her back was ramrod straight, and even without makeup, she was a knockout.

"Thank you," Colette said and glanced at Jasmine as she said, "It sounds like congratulations are in order for you as well."

"Thank you."

Their awkward, overly polite chitchat made her want to squirm. Roth showed no signs that he was uncomfortable with the tension in the room. He walked toward her. He didn't try to get a look at the baby or even fake interest in Polara. Men, in general, weren't known to fuss over babies, but now she knew Roth didn't care for children at all. It was an unfortunate moment for her to remember his vasectomy when he held a hand out to her. Bastard.

She ignored his outstretched hand and went to Colette's side as Polara yawned. When she glanced up, she saw Lyle and Colette watching her closely, and inwardly cursed. She reached back. Instantly, Roth's beefy hand closed around hers.

His other hand ran down her back before he gripped her hip. "We have to get going. We have some details to iron out for the wedding, but we'll keep you posted."

Colette nodded. "Yes, please do."

"Auntie's gonna see you later this week, okay?" she cooed to Polara before she hugged Colette and Ariana.

"Call if you need anything," Lyle said as she kissed his cheek.

She nodded and inwardly bristled when Roth grasped her hand and led her to the hallway, away from the prying eyes of her family. He called Mo and told him to bring the car around. Even though the hallways were crowded, Roth easily cleared a path. She walked by his side, staring straight ahead. It was done. She had agreed, and her family was on board. A heavy weight settled on her chest. It was the same sensation she had after her father died.

"What did your sisters say?" he rumbled.

"You were right. They asked some questions, but they wanted to believe, so they did."

"Good."

"You're good at predicting people's reactions," she said.

"It's part of my job."

"You knew I'd agree," she said.

"Yes."

When she tried to slip her hand from his, he tightened his hold.

"Let me go, Roth."

"No."

He led her out of the hospital. Reliable Mo was at the curb. He paused in the act of getting out of the driver's seat when Roth opened the door for her. She climbed in and watched him come around to the opposite side. Why didn't he sit in the front?

"Park Avenue," he said to Mo before he closed the door.

"I want to be dropped off at my hotel," she said. She needed a dark room and to slip under the covers and forget what she had agreed to.

"No."

She whipped her head around. "You can't tell me no. I still have a few weeks of freedom left."

"You agreed verbally, but you haven't signed the prenup."

"Not until my attorney looks at it."

"Give me their info. We'll fax it over."

Her stomach roiled as she pulled up her attorney's information on her phone. Roth called Sarai to have the prenup faxed, forcing her to call her attorney and explain what the fuck was going on.

"I want to go back to my hotel," she said again after she finished her call.

"Your things have been transferred to Park Avenue."

Her mouth dropped. "What? Why?"

"You agreed."

"Twenty minutes ago! When did you issue that order?"

"Before I went to fetch you from Madison Avenue."

"I hadn't agreed!"

"I knew you would."

He was such an arrogant fuck! "I still need to go to the hotel. My car's there."

"You don't need a car. Either Mo or Johan will drive you where you have to go."

"It'll take my attorney a couple of days to review it, maybe a whole week—"

"It's done, Jasmine. Stop fighting me."

"I need some time before—"

"You had time. Five years of it."

The walls were closing in around her. "Give me one more night."

"No. You have a habit of disappearing." His eyes strayed to her lips before they came back to her eyes. "That's not going to happen again."

"I need my things from Tuxedo Park. Once my attorney looks over the prenup, I'll come back to New York and sign."

"No."

"I need my laptop!"

He shrugged back his sleeve to check his watch before he rolled down the partition to say, "Tuxedo Park."

"I don't need you to come with me," she said as the partition clicked back into place. "You have meetings to attend, don't you?"

"I have time."

He had never made time for her in the past, so why now? Three hundred and sixty-five days with her ex-husband. How was she going to keep up the charade? "Why did you tell them we're having a wedding?"

"Because we are."

"Why?"

"Marriages always impact business, and this one is going to send a shockwave across the globe. We'll take pictures at our wedding to show everyone the feud's over, and we're allies."

Just like last time, he was mixing business with their personal lives and would benefit from this alliance in more ways than one. Business-wise, if he helped her sisters turn the company around, he would profit when they bought him out for more than what he paid for the shares. Being associated with the Hennessy's would give him access to their extensive contacts. Combine that with Rami and Lyle, and Roth had a whole new arena to play in and would be indestructible. Not to mention, he had her in his bed... There was no downside for him, but there was a shit ton for her.

"How does this work?" she asked.

"What?"

Her nails dug into her thighs as she tried to suppress her emotions. "Us. How far are we going with this? Where's the line?"

"There's no line."

"There has to be a line. Rules..."

He reached over and grabbed her hand. "Breathe."

She twisted her hand out of his. "Rules, Roth."

"Look at me."

She didn't want to. She didn't want him touching her, either. She didn't know which direction he was going to shove her in next. He switched from psychotic asshole to polite gentleman in the blink of an eye. He was a chameleon, adapting to those around him with ease, while herding her into a gilded cage. The fact that he had so easily taken over her life in a few short days freaked her out. What did he want from her?

"Jasmine."

"Just tell me."

He tugged on her hair, a playful move that surprised her into looking at him. Black eyes speared into hazel.

"You'll fulfill all roles as my wife. You attend functions with me, you travel with me, you fuck me." He cupped her chin as he leaned in. "No other men. If I even see you look at another man, I'll..."

He brushed his thumb over her bottom lip and shook his head.

"Just, don't."

Fingers stroked along her jaw and then down her throat.

"We have history, most of it bad, but that's in the past. We start from here."

"Start what?" she asked.

"What we would have had if Maximus hadn't ripped us apart."

"Dad didn't make me leave you," she said quietly. "You did."

A muscle jumped in his jaw, but his caress remained light.

"I was pissed at your father, and I took it out on you. It won't happen again."

She didn't believe him. "Boundaries, Roth."

"One thing neither of us likes is rules," he said thoughtfully. "Your dad gave you an ultimatum, and you bucked against him. People tell me no, and I react the same way. You and I are more similar than you think."

"How far are we supposed to take this act?"

His eyes narrowed. "Act?"

"The PDA. What you were doing in the hospital." She swatted his wandering hand. "What you're doing now."

"You think it's an act?"

"What else is it? You weren't like this before."

He leaned in. She balled her fists in her lap as she resisted the urge to scoot back.

"I spent five years without you, and then you gave me the green light in Colorado. You're better than I remember. One taste, and I'm addicted, worse than before."

His hand landed on her breast with unerring accuracy. She fell back to get away from him, and he followed, pinning her against the door. His dark eyes were burning and hungry.

"Been jacking off to the thought of you for three weeks." His hand clenched painfully around her breast. "You want to know why marriage? I want legal rights over you. I want you at my mercy. I want everyone to know I'm fucking the Hennessy princess. I want those frat boys to know they'll never be where I am. I want Maximus to turn in his grave."

"Get off me!"

"You want me, too. You admitted it. You have wet dreams about me."

"Shut up!"

"You like how I give it to you. You like when I take over, when I force you to bend. You were made for me. No one fits me like you."

His head dipped down, and when she turned her face away, he

forced her still for his kiss. His tongue demanded entry and danced with hers. When he pulled back to survey her with heavy-lidded eyes, she panted for breath.

He dropped his forehead on hers and inhaled. "A year of you. That's my price to stop me from claiming my vengeance. Your father made me a slave for seven years. You'll be mine for one." He pressed a chaste kiss against her throbbing lips. "Surely, that's fair?"

"It isn't."

He clucked his tongue. "Life isn't fair, princess. You should know that by now."

"Let me up," she whispered.

His weight disappeared. She stayed in place, trying to find the strength to move her heavy limbs.

"I'm not your enemy," he said as he adjusted her in her seat and belted her in. "I'm the only thing standing between your sisters and the wolves who would like a chance to knock them off their throne."

As she tried to think of something to say, he reached into his pocket for his phone and answered, even though she hadn't heard it ring.

"Roth," he said and paused. "You have the figures for me?"

She stared out the window without seeing a damn thing. How could he switch from sex to business in a heartbeat? Why couldn't she be like that? Her heartbeat wasn't back to normal, and he was spitting out numbers as if he had a sheet of them in front of him.

She heard her father mention Roth once in passing before she met him. Roth made his first million before he graduated from college. He was a whiz with money and had a knack for choosing the right companies to invest in. He was a mathematical genius with a photographic memory. Being raised around her father, who had a similar set of skills, she knew what to expect. Their minds were always turning over some problem, always researching and analyzing. Frequent calls, endless meetings, not mentally present. The more they worked, the more energy they had. Her father had a hard time in relationships, evidenced by his two failed marriages and three baby mamas. Men like them didn't know how to slow down and tired of things quickly. Roth was no different. She suspected part of her appeal still stemmed from a need to get one up on her father by reclaiming the daughter of his enemy. Maybe once they had been married for a few months, the novelty of having her back would wear off, and she'd be free.

CHAPTER 15

hen they reached the estate, she left Roth in the car. She lost count of how many calls he'd taken. How he managed to retain all that information without jotting down a single thing was a mystery.

Her hands trembled as she packed a suitcase. *This isn't the end of the world,* she told herself. This was temporary, not a big deal. After she lugged her suitcase downstairs, she entered the library. She averted her face as she passed her father's desk. She could imagine his fury if he knew she was breaking her promise to him. Not only had she laid eyes on Roth, she had also fucked him, and now she was legally binding herself to him once more. Roth was right. Her father was probably turning in his grave, but what choice did she have?

She was at her desk when Roth entered the library. Seeing him cross the threshold into the sanctuary she shared with her father felt like he was desecrating holy ground.

"I'm almost finished," she said curtly.

He ignored her and looked around. The way he was sizing up the place got her back up. She could imagine him tallying up what he could get for the estate. There was no way in hell he would ever get his hands on her castle. She would make sure the prenuptial agreement protected her assets.

He walked toward the massive windows and stared out at Tuxedo Lake as she finished packing her notebooks and favorite pens.

"I'm ready."

When he didn't move, she checked the end tables to see if she had left anything there. Thea had obviously been by to clean since the used tissues and water bottles were gone.

"This isn't what I expected," he said.

She wasn't sure what he meant by that. "It's home," she said simply.

"I can see that."

Some tension eased out of her. "It's a special place."

"We should have the ceremony here."

She stiffened. "No."

"Why not?"

"Because." After they divorced, she would come back here. She didn't want it cluttered with thoughts of him or their fake wedding.

"Why?" he pushed.

"I'm sure we can find somewhere in the city," she said.

He examined her for a long moment. "You don't like me in your space, do you?"

Obviously.

The corner of his mouth curved. "Too fucking bad, princess."

She let out a growl when he kissed her forehead and slung her laptop bag over his shoulder.

"We're not having it here, Roth!" she shouted as he strode out of the library.

When he didn't reply, she hurried after him. He snatched her luggage on his way out the door before handing it off to Mo, who put everything in the trunk.

"Is that all?" Roth asked her.

"For now, but—"

"Get in."

She opened her mouth to argue, but he didn't wait around to

listen. He got in the car and slammed the door. She rushed around to her side and climbed in.

"We shouldn't have a wedding. Dad just passed and now this? It's gonna look..." She searched for the right word. "Tacky!"

"Getting cold feet, Jasmine?"

She twisted her hands in her lap. "I don't want to make a fuss about this."

"You never liked being the center of attention, did you?" He shook his head. "You have no choice. We're having a wedding, and your family will be present. You'll wear a gown fit for a Hennessy, and the backdrop will be one only the elite would recognize. Tuxedo Park... Old money, exclusive, private. A picture is worth a thousand words, and our wedding photo will be better than any statement either of us could give."

She understood, even though she wished she didn't. Her mind skittered in a dozen directions.

"Get Daiyu to make your dress."

Her mouth sagged open.

"She said she'd be willing to dress you for any event."

Instantly, her mind went to the dreamy gown on the mannequin. It was breathtaking, but not for her. It wouldn't be right to claim that dress for a fake wedding... "I'll find something."

"If you don't call her, I will."

She scowled. "Don't I get to pick my own dress?"

"Not if you're going to wear black."

She looked out the window.

"Do it, Jasmine."

"She's busy, and her shit costs a fortune," she muttered.

"Money's no object."

He wasn't satisfied with gaining access to her body. No, he wanted legal ties, and he was still pushing for more. A ceremony with her family present, a wedding gown... Her stomach tightened.

"Lyle wanted to know if there's a prenup," he said quietly.

"Of course, he did." She turned back to him. "What did you say?"

"I have no interest in what Maximus left you." He cocked his head. "How much did Daddy leave you, Jasmine?"

She said nothing.

"Your assets have to be disclosed in the prenup. If you don't tell me now, I'll find out later."

She debated for a moment before she revealed, "His remaining assets, which include real estate and some stocks worth upwards of three hundred million." She raised a brow. "Would that have bought back the stocks?"

He shrugged. "Maybe."

"You interested in selling?"

His hand landed on her thigh. "No."

She smacked his hand, but he didn't retract it. "It's a lot of money."

He examined her for a moment before he said, "For every hundred million you have, I'll match you ten billion."

"What?"

"Working like a dog pays off," he said quietly. "Your attorney will advise you to ask for a bigger settlement."

She closed her eyes and slumped against the seat as the magnitude of the power he wielded hit her. She was so fucking screwed. "I won't ask for anything."

"You'll receive one hundred million at the end of the year."

Her eyes flew open. "What? Why?"

"It's expected."

"I don't need it!"

"You'll take it."

"I'll donate it to charity."

"Do what you want with it. In the meantime, don't touch your inheritance. While you're with me, I pay your way."

"Keep your money, Roth. You're going to need it for the next woman you buy."

"We'll see if you're this brave tonight."

His hand smoothed down her thigh and then came back up to rest far too close to her crotch for comfort.

"I haven't signed the prenup yet."

"In Colorado, there was no contract, and you spread wide for me."

"That was before I remembered what an asshole you are."

"I can be," he agreed. "Being nice hasn't gotten me anywhere in life."

She opened her mouth to snap, but his next words stopped her.

"But I have everything I want now, so I'll try."

She was relieved when he took another call, so she could fortify her shields. She couldn't let him get to her. He was a bully and willing to topple companies with tens of thousands of employees out of his petty need for vengeance. He might play the nice guy at times, but she wouldn't allow herself to forget that he had destroyed her once.

Desperate for a distraction, she retreated into her fictional world. The new plot she uncovered last night still pulsed with life, but it was getting dimmer by the second. Too much real-life shit. If she didn't find the time to write, her idea would slip away, and she'd be lost again. She wanted her laptop, noise-canceling earphones, and a couple of hours to make some progress.

She tried to explore her plot, but she couldn't think without a pen in her hand. She didn't realize she was scribbling on her leg with her finger until Roth dropped a small booklet and pen on her lap. He seemed absorbed in his phone call, but the notebook and pen suggested differently. *This means nothing*, she told herself as she eagerly flipped past pages filled with figures, acronyms, and names. His notes looked like math formulas from a mad scientist. When she found a fresh page, she began to write.

By the time they pulled up to 432 Park Avenue, she was completely immersed in her story. She stepped out of the SUV and was pulled to a stop by Roth.

"I have a meeting in Boston," he said.

"Okay," she said distractedly.

"There are multiple restaurants in the building, or you can order from the on-call five-star chef for dinner. I don't know when I'll be back."

When she tried to walk away, he wrapped an arm around her waist and drew her against him.

"Kiss me," he ordered.

She looked up, eyes narrowed. "You can't just demand—"

He covered her mouth with his, ripping her out of her fictional world and slamming her back into the real one with such speed that she felt dizzy. When he detached his mouth from hers, she was aroused and annoyed, knowing he wasn't going to do anything about it.

"Don't bother wearing anything to bed," he said before he slipped back into the SUV.

She watched it drive away before she turned and found Johan and a small crowd watching her. She cleared her throat and marched into the lobby. Johan followed, weighed down by all her belongings. Fucking Roth. He was trying to mess with her head.

Johan didn't say a word as he rode the elevator with her. When they reached the penthouse, she walked into the massive living room and was entranced by the sunset.

"Ms. Hennessy?" Johan said.

"Jasmine," she said quietly.

"Jasmine, is there anything you need from me?"

She turned and saw her bags were missing. "Where's my stuff?"

"I put them in the master bedroom. The housekeeper already unpacked your things we brought from the hotel." When she grimaced, he took a step toward the hallway. "Should I...?"

"No, that's fine. I'll move them. Thank you."

He pointed at a phone. "My number is on the notepad along with the restaurant. Press zero if you want to order anything, and two for the housekeeper. She has an apartment in the building and is ready to assist you in whatever you need."

She nodded. "Thank you."

He inclined his head and boarded the elevator. She perched on the window seat and watched the sun go down. One day made a world of difference. Polara had been born, and she was now engaged to her ex-husband. She pulled her phone out of her pocket and called Colette.

"How are you doing?" she asked.

"I'm exhausted. I can't wait to get out of here," Colette said wearily.

"How's the dynamo?"

"Docile," Colette said. "I'm pleasantly surprised."

"She's faking."

Colette snickered. "So, Ariana keeps telling me." She paused. "How are you doing?"

"Fine. We're gonna be neighbors."

"We are?"

"Roth lives at 432 Park Avenue."

A pause and then, "Damn."

"One of the top floors. I thought I'd seen the best of New York, but this view is worth whatever ridiculous price he paid for it."

Colette's voice dropped to a whisper. "Are you sure, Minnie? Marriage?"

Roth could be a first-class asshole and was definitely bad for her mental and emotional well-being, but she could do this. "Yes."

"Lyle's not happy."

"I know."

Colette sighed. "He'll get over it."

"I hope so. I just wanted to check in. How's your blood pressure?"

"They may keep me for another day."

"Okay, well, keep me posted and send me pics of Polara."

"Will do."

She hung up and went into the master suite. Roth's closet was as large as most people's apartments and designed with custom nooks and crannies. The clothes she had bought from Bloomingdale's and Black Jade hung on the opposite side of the closet from a rack of Roth's suits. They were all relentless black and hung with military precision. He had a drawer of ties and watches and an army of polished shoes. Daiyu's colorful pieces were a burst of color in the otherwise monochrome closet. The notebook from the hotel where she had sketched her latest idea was on a glass shelf. She tucked the notebook under her arm before she grabbed the things she had brought from Tuxedo Park and put them in the guest bedroom. After she grabbed her laptop, she headed to the kitchen, which had the best lighting.

She sat at the massive island on a cushioned stool and propped her notebook against a bowl of fruit as she began to type what she'd written last night. When she finished, she went to the fridge and selected a lime soda water and picked up the landline phone and dialed zero.

"Ms. Hennessy, what can I do for you?"

The sexless, cool voice on the other end of the line made her jump. The phone didn't even ring.

"Hello?"

"Ms. Hennessy, yes, what can I do for you? Mr. Roth said you'd be calling for dinner. What can we prepare?"

She looked around. "I don't see a menu, so I'm not sure what you have."

"Anything you want, we will make, Ms. Hennessy."

She pursed her lips. "Okay, can I have grilled salmon with mashed potatoes and Brussels sprouts?"

"It'll be sent up as soon as it's ready. Any desserts?"

"Um, no, that's okay. Thank you."

"Our pleasure, Ms. Hennessy."

She set the phone back in its cradle and stared at it for a moment. 432 Park Avenue was doing it right. She had been treated to excellent service before, but this was next level. While she was waiting for her food to arrive, she showered and changed.

As she padded back into the main living area, once again, she was drawn to the view. Night had fallen, and New York City spread out beneath her. She was so used to being among the maze of buildings that looking down at them from this height was unsettling.

She jolted when the elevator dinged. A woman dressed in a white uniform walked out of the elevator with a silver trolley.

She smiled. "Ms. Hennessy?"

Jasmine nodded.

"I have your dinner. If you need anything, we're available around the clock."

"Thank you."

"Enjoy."

And that quickly, the woman stepped into the elevator and was gone. Jasmine shook her head. She could get used to this. She felt guilty asking Thea to cook for just one person, but this was perfect. She pushed the trolley into the kitchen and uncovered her meal. It was so artfully plated that she had to take a picture before she dug in. Between bites of fish that melted on her tongue, she dictated the notes she had made during the car ride and then got to work.

She tentatively punched the keys. Her gaze wandered around the kitchen and then to the magnificent view before she tapped some more. The more she wrote, the better she felt until all of her emotions drained away, leaving her pleasantly empty. When her vision blurred and her neck cramped from hunching over her laptop, she glanced at the time. Two in the morning.

She closed her laptop and tottered down the hallway. She didn't feel like searching for toothpaste, so she went into Roth's bathroom and used his. She didn't need to turn on any lights when she had the city as a nightlight.

She padded over the heated floors to the guest room and slid beneath the covers. The duvet was so heavy, it felt like her weighted blanket at Tuxedo Park. The sheets smelled citrusy and sweet. She inhaled deeply and smiled as she got comfy.

HER WORLD TURNED UPSIDE DOWN. She screamed and put her hands out to brace herself, but they pedaled through empty air.

"Didn't I tell you not to wear anything to bed?"

Her cloudy mind barely had time to deduce who that deep rumble belonged to before she was falling again. She let out a stifled shriek as she landed on something soft. Large hands grasped the ankles of her sweats and dragged them off her legs. She moaned as her warm flesh touched the cool sheets. A damp body crawled over her and gripped the front of her shirt. The silver glow of city lights bounced off Roth's stark features.

"Don't—" she began a moment before he yanked and buttons flew in every direction. "Dammit, Roth!"

He buried his face against her neck, and she hissed in annoyance. "You're wet!"

"Just stepped out of the shower," he said as he sucked on her neck.

"What time is it?"

"Time to fuck."

He didn't give her time to prepare. He slid inside her and didn't stop when she cried out and dragged her nails down his back. He purred and brushed kisses over her face as she cussed him out. He rocked slowly in and out of her until she quieted. He stared at her as he fucked her, commanding her attention without saying a word. Desire blossomed inside her, and her hands slid up his arms to his damp hair. Drunk on lust and still half asleep, she grabbed a handful of his hair and tugged until he dipped his head. Their mouths fused together. He planted his fists on either side of her as his rhythm changed. She moaned, urging him on. He began to move faster, rougher. She whispered what she needed against his lips, and he gave it to her, nudging her into a climax. He forced her legs to wrap high around his waist as he took his fill, making her ass bounce on the soft mattress until he came, shouting her name into the sheets and flooding her with cum. She nuzzled his neck as he slumped over her. He tipped to the side and adjusted her against him. He said something as he brushed her hair back from her face, but she was already slipping back to sleep.

JASMINE SQUINTED AT HER SURROUNDINGS. The gauzy white curtains were no hindrance to the blazing sunlight. She moaned and rolled. Her disgruntled gaze took in the room. She was in Roth's master suite. She sat up and looked at her naked body. Fragments of their sexual encounter slid through her mind.

On her way to the bathroom, she saw her ripped shirt on the ground. Roth wasn't here. Maybe he'd already gone to work. If this was how the year was going to be, she could definitely deal. What girl wouldn't be happy with room service, a great fuck, and excellent Wi-Fi? She showered and slipped into a robe because she was too lazy to dig through her things. Her story was front and center in her mind. All she wanted was coffee and her laptop. She was digging through the kitchen cabinets looking for coffee and filters when someone said her name.

"Jasmine."

She leaped a foot and whirled with a scream to find Roth standing in the doorway, dressed in a suit with a navy silk tie. She pressed a hand to her chest and slumped against the counter.

"You almost gave me a heart attack!"

As he approached, she eyed him warily. She blinked when he kissed her.

"Morning."

"Hello," she said awkwardly, and pressed against his chest to get some breathing room. "What are you doing here?"

"I live here."

She scowled. "Don't you live at your office? What time did you come back last night?"

"You sound like a wife already."

She turned away from him. "I'm looking for coffee."

"Call room service."

She made the call. Once again, that sexless voice greeted her. It was only when the operator asked if she wanted breakfast that she ordered oatmeal. Since Roth was standing there, she asked if he wanted something. He shook his head. When she hung up, she said, "These people are remarkable."

"Amazing's what I pay for." He shrugged back his sleeve to look at his watch. "My plane leaves in two hours. Pack a bag. I have business in Germany, and I want you with me."

She stared at him. "You can't be serious."

"Do I look like I'm joking?"

"But… I haven't even unpacked."

"Good. You don't need to. And why were you sleeping in the guest bedroom?"

"We need our own space."

He gestured around them. "This isn't enough space?"

"It is! But why use the same bedroom when there are so many?"

"We won't give the staff anything to talk about. We'll share the same room."

"Okay, but I can't go to Germany."

"Why?"

She pointed at her laptop. "I'm in flow! Finally!"

"You can write while I work."

She grappled for more excuses. "I want to see Polara, and my attorney could call for me to sign." When he still didn't look convinced, she added, "And don't you want me to call Dai about the dress thing?"

He raised a brow. "Dress thing?"

She grimaced and waved a hand. "You know..." She wanted to avoid saying "wedding" because it would make it too real. Currently, her mind was allowing her to float partly in reality and partly in fiction, so she was neither here nor there, and that was how she wanted to stay.

He cocked his head as he surveyed her. "You're different today."

"I wrote last night."

His eyes drifted to her laptop. "Book five is coming along?"

She tensed. "Yes."

"You figure out what happens to my character yet?"

She leaned against the island and crossed her arms. "A knife-wielding hooker cuts off your penis, and you bleed to death in a dirty motel in Vietnam?"

He strolled toward her and leaned down to whisper in her ear, "You don't want to disappoint your fans, do you?"

She shoved him. "This is my book, not yours!"

He patted her ass. "I'll be home soon. Don't get used to staying behind. In the future, you'll travel with me."

"Yeah, sure, whatever."

He clutched her ass. "Next time I come home, I want you naked in my bed, got me?"

"Yeah."

She winced as he let go of her.

"Call Dai. Let me know if you have any questions about the prenup. Do you need anything from me?"

When she shook her head, he tipped her chin up for a deep kiss.

"I'll be in touch."

With that, he boarded the elevator. She stood there for several seconds before she pushed all the buzzing questions to the side and checked her phone. There was an update from Colette who was being kept at the hospital for one more day and numerous adorable photos of Polara. When breakfast was delivered, she sat at the island, which was fast becoming her favorite place.

The morning passed in a blur as she wrote fast and furious, determined to continue her streak. When she took a break, she checked her email and took care of some business. When she couldn't put it off any longer, she called Dai.

The phone rang once, and then she heard, "Finally."

"Dai?"

"I've left you at least three voicemails."

"You did? Why?"

"Why?" Dai echoed dangerously. "You have the nerve to fuck in my shop and then don't even call me to give me the dirty details? That's the least you could do, especially since he's not interested in crazy Chinese chicks."

She rolled her eyes as she paced around the kitchen. "I have a job for you."

"Don't try to distract me! You tell me you're done with that gorgeous ex of yours, and then you fuck him in *my* dressing room." Dai took a deep breath and then let it out. "I could come just remembering what he sounded like. I love a man who makes noise. Tell me he's cut like Brad Pitt in *Troy*. Or if he isn't, lie to me. Or better yet, tell me he can't get enough of you and fucks you all over New York."

"Dai," she said sharply. "Snap out of it. I want to talk business."

"And I want to talk about sex."

"That wedding gown in the shop, is it the only one you have?"

There was a pause and then, "Shut the fuck up."

She frowned, pulled the phone away from her ear, and then put it back. "Excuse me?"

"Shut *up!*"

"I just asked—"

"You're getting *remarried?*"

She rubbed her temples. "Is that the only dress you have or not?"

"What does it matter? I can make you a custom one."

"I don't have time."

Another pause. "Are you pregnant?"

"No, and don't you dare spread that rumor."

"But you *are* getting married?"

"Do you have more gowns or not?" she snapped.

"That's the only one that's complete. How soon are we talking?"

"Weeks."

"Stop it," Dai said flatly.

She tapped her fingers on the counter as she debated what to order for lunch.

"Please tell me you're joking." Dai sounded shaken.

"What?"

"Get your ass here now."

She frowned. "But I—"

"*Now!*"

The line went dead. She stared at the phone for a moment and then sighed. All she wanted to do was write, but now she had to get fitted for a fake wedding dress for fake wedding pictures. Ugh.

She dialed Johan, who picked up on the first ring. "I need to get to Black Jade on Madi—"

"I'm on my way up," he said.

"I can meet you in the lobby."

"I'll be up in a minute," he insisted.

She slipped on black jeans and a top and added Dai's cherry-colored vinyl trench coat, which made her feel like a badass. When she walked into the living area, Johan was standing in front of the elevator.

"I could have met you downstairs," she said.

"No need, Ms. Hennessy," he said as he typed on the keypad.

"Roth didn't give me the code. What is it?"

The elevator doors opened, and he gestured her inside. "Mo's bringing the car around, ma'am."

She stepped in and then narrowed her eyes at him. "The code, Johan."

He stared straight ahead. "What's the address we're taking you to?"

When she invaded his space, he stiffened. "You're seriously not going to tell me the code?"

"Ms. Hennessy, I think this is something you need to speak to Mr. Roth about."

Oh, she would. He hadn't given her the code, so she couldn't leave. What an ass. What did he think she was going to do? As the elevator opened into the lobby, she texted Roth. *What's the code for the elevator?*

Johan opened the door to the Bentley, and she slipped into the back. She stared at the two guards in the front seat.

"You're both assigned to me?" she asked.

"Yes, Ms. Hennessy," Mo said.

"Who's with Roth?"

"The others."

"How many of you are there?"

"As many as he needs."

She sat back with a shake of her head and checked her messages. Her voicemail was full, and she left it that way. She texted Colette, who said she was resting and not feeling great. Her social media was out of control, but she did her best to respond to messages and thank the readers who were enjoying her work as Mo pulled up to the curb in front of Black Jade. She finished her correspondence as she ambled up to the store, grasped the door handle, and pulled. Nothing happened. She looked up from her phone and saw that the store was dark. What the hell? She was about to step back when she saw movement inside. Dai blitzed toward her. Today, she was dressed in black silk overalls and a skintight white long sleeve with five strands of pearls around her neck. Dai threw the door open, grabbed her arm, and towed her through the dark shop.

"What's going on?" she asked.

"What's going on," Dai growled as she shoved her onto the pedestal in the middle of the dressing rooms, "is you're giving me mere weeks to make you bride-ready."

"But why's the shop closed?" she asked as Dai's assistant closed off the dressing room from the rest of the shop and began to undress her.

"The shop's closed because I don't want to be distracted," Dai said curtly. "Now, let's see if this fits."

Jasmine stared at the beautiful dress the assistants were holding, so she could climb into it. "I wasn't asking for this dress in particular. I was just wondering—"

"Just shut up and get in," Dai ordered.

She gave her friend a quelling glance, but did as she was told. She braced her hands on the women's shoulders, stepped into the dress, and sucked in a breath as they pulled it up. Dai stood in front of her, hands pressed together in prayer as she watched. Carefully, Jasmine slipped her arms into the delicate lace sleeves and watched Dai's face as the assistants did up the back and then backed away.

Jasmine looked at her reflection and felt her stomach ice over. The gown had been breathtaking on the mannequin, but on a living body, the dress came to life. Rhinestones shimmered as she sucked in a breath. The intricate lace pattern on the long sleeves and high neck made her look regal and elegant. The tulle skirt fell around her in soft waves and… it was all wrong.

"This isn't the right dress," she said flatly.

"But it's perfect," one of the assistants said.

She shook her head and tried to step off the pedestal, but Dai shoved her back onto it.

"This isn't it, Dai!"

This dress was special. It was made with love and care and so beautiful, she couldn't bear to look at it. This dress was what little girl's dreams were made of. It would be disrespectful to steal someone's dream to promote a business arrangement with a time limit on it.

"This dress is too much. I need something simple and—"

"You're kidding me, right?" Dai snapped her fingers. "You're a Hennessy, and he's the guy from the other side of the tracks who made it big in the business world. You give up everything for him, divorce him for some reason I'd like to know, and then you magically get back together? This dress screams fairy tale, and that's what you're living, biotch."

"It's too small for me."

Dai pulled a measuring tape out of her pocket. "It's snug around the bust and can be taken in at the waist. I can fix that."

"I want to try on something else."

"When it's right, it's right. The dress picks the princess, Ms. Jasmine. You ever heard that one?"

She snorted. "No."

"Well, now you have."

Her phone rang, and she waved to the assistants. "Can someone please get that? I've been waiting for a call."

Coming to Dai was a mistake. Dai would force her to walk down the aisle in what she saw fit, and nothing would dissuade her.

When the assistant brought the phone to her, she saw Ariana's name. She answered with, "Ariana, is it an emergency?"

"Um, no, I was just—" Ariana began when the phone was snatched from her.

"Ari," Dai said in a no-nonsense tone. "It's Daiyu. Uh-huh. Yeah. Tell me why your sister is here by herself trying on wedding gowns. Of course, it's my gown! Where are you? At work? You need to take a break. You have to see this, and I want the lowdown on what the heck is going on with Jas and Roth. She's being stingy and not telling me shit. Okay, see ya."

When Dai offered the phone, she grabbed it and saw that Ariana had hung up. "She's coming?"

"Of course, she is. Her sister's getting married. She won't want to miss this, especially since the second time's a charm, right?"

She grit her teeth. "I want to see another dress."

"You're not getting one," Dai said crisply. "Now, tell me everything."

"About what?"

Dai looked up with three pins in her mouth. "If you don't start talking, I'm gonna stab you with one of these."

This was hell. She didn't want to discuss her and Roth. There *was* no her and Roth, and when it was over, she would look like an ass for making the same mistake twice. But she couldn't let anyone catch on that she was selling her body so...

"We never got over each other." She grimaced at herself in the mirror and was glad everyone was focused on the dress and not her.

"I heard that for myself," Dai muttered. "So, he chases you down yesterday and fucks you in the dressing room and proposes?"

That sounded insane, but what else could she say? "Yeah."

"And now you're getting married in a couple of weeks?"

"Yes."

"What does your family think?" Dai asked as she measured her bust.

"They're willing to give him a chance."

"Times have changed," Dai said sardonically.

"Yes. This needs to be kept under wraps. We're keeping everything quiet for now."

"Sure."

Dai's easy agreement made her suspicious. "I'm serious, Dai."

"I heard you."

She watched Dai in the mirror as the smaller woman moved around her. "How many people did you call after I left yesterday?"

Dai gave her a salacious smile. "Just a few of my besties."

Dai's "besties" could be anyone. She wanted to ask, but decided it was best that she didn't know. "I'd appreciate it if you didn't tell anyone else."

"I heard you. What do you think I am?"

"One of the biggest gossips on the planet."

"I'm offended," Dai said, sounding anything but.

Ariana arrived shortly after. She pushed through the curtains to the dressing room and stopped dead. Jasmine's heart sank as Ariana raised her hands to her mouth and her eyes filled with tears.

"Oh, my gosh. You're beautiful," Ariana breathed.

"See?" Dai said snidely.

She did see, and she didn't like it. "I want something simpler. Roth wants to have it at Tuxedo Park. This is too much."

"This is precisely what you need," Dai declared. "Just because you're having a wedding in the country doesn't mean you have to be simple. You need to stand out, and in this dress, you shine."

She didn't want to fucking shine. "I was thinking..."

"Leave it up to me," Dai ordered and pushed Ariana onto the satin ottoman. "Isn't she gorgeous?"

"She is," Ariana said and gave her a shaky smile. "It's perfect."

She didn't know what to say, so she stayed quiet as Dai and Ariana caught up on life. She endured Dai's poking and prodding and mentally distanced herself from what was happening by focusing on the book. She jumped when Dai smacked her balled up fist.

"Chill!" Dai ordered.

She unfurled her hand and did her best to ignore the heavy weight on her chest. She was relieved to step out of the dress and put on her regular clothes.

"Come back in two days," Dai ordered as she air kissed her cheeks.

She grunted as Ariana slipped her arm through hers.

"This coat looks great on you," Ariana said.

"It's Dai's."

Ariana looked around the shop as they approached the door. "I may need to check this place out."

They stepped onto the sidewalk.

"You didn't have to leave work for this," she said.

"Of course, I did. We're turning over a new leaf to be there for each other. That gown is perfect for you," Ariana said.

She nodded as Johan approached. "Can we give you a ride?"

"Sure."

They slipped into the Bentley. She was relieved when Ariana got a call that lasted all the way to the business district.

"Everything okay with you and Roth?" Ariana asked.

She blinked. "Yes. Why?"

"Just checking." Ariana gave her an overly bright smile. "Call me if you need anything, okay?"

Jasmine watched her sister rush into the building and glanced across the street at Roth's. Ariana was worried. Fuck. She glanced at the phone and saw Roth hadn't answered her text. *Probably still in the air*, she thought.

"Home," she told Mo, and mentally screeched to a halt. 432 Park wasn't home. It was a place she was staying for a while. She couldn't forget that.

CHAPTER 16

"*M*r. Roth's offer is more than generous."

She eyed Roth's attorney, Mason, an aggressive bulldog who had interjected multiple times during her meeting with her attorney to discuss the terms of the prenup. His slick hair, pinstriped suit, and air of arrogant authority made her hackles rise.

According to her attorney, the prenup was straightforward. Their assets would remain separate and if (when) they divorced, she would receive one hundred million dollars in the settlement. Aside from the exorbitant figures being discussed, there were no surprises.

When she picked up the pen to sign, she hesitated. She had verbally agreed, but this was legally binding, a declaration that she intended to marry him again. One year with Roth...

"What's the holdup?" Mason asked, his voice tinged with impatience. "Are you holding out for a bigger settlement?"

Henry, her seventy-two-year-old attorney, bristled at her side. "Mr. White, if Ms. Hennessy has any further questions, we'll contact your office."

Mason ignored him and kept his gaze fixed on her. He spun his phone on the table and said, "Mr. Roth made it clear he wants this wrapped up today. If you want to negotiate, I need to know what you want, so I can call him and get this taken care of."

So, Roth would pick up his attorney's call, but couldn't shoot her a text with the elevator code. Typical. She regarded Mason as she tipped the pen from side to side on the prenup, which was clearly getting on his nerves. Apparently, he felt she was wasting his time and wasn't happy about it.

"Considering the fact that Mr. Roth now owns a controlling share of Hennessy & Co, don't you think it's wise that you tread carefully?" Mason asked.

Outwardly, she didn't react, but her stomach clenched.

"That has nothing to do with this," Henry said with heavy disapproval.

Once again, Mason ignored him. Sensing her discomfiture, he went in for the kill.

"Mr. Roth made it clear that this is a fair settlement," Mason drawled, "considering your past record."

Henry stiffened, and her pen stopped tapping.

"I was the one who initiated our first divorce, and I took nothing," she said quietly. "What makes you think I'm holding out for a larger settlement?"

"You have no one to run to anymore now that Maximus is gone," Mason said bluntly. "And your sisters aren't doing too well, either."

"You can—" Henry began hotly, but fell silent when she touched his sleeve.

"Mr. Roth's a busy man," Mason continued, unfazed by Henry's outburst. "You don't want to test his patience by asking for more now, do you? My advice is to take what he offers and be grateful."

She dropped the pen on the prenup and got to her feet. She looked at her attorney who was flushed and visibly upset by Mason's insults. She squeezed his shoulder. "Thanks, Henry. I'll be in touch."

Mason shot to his feet. "You're not going to sign? He told me he wants this taken care of."

"When he asks why I didn't sign, tell him it was because I didn't like being insulted or told I'm not worth a larger settlement by a pushy attorney who doesn't know his place."

She had the satisfaction of seeing the blood drain from his face before she walked out of the room. It felt good to make a dramatic exit. She had no intention of asking for a larger settlement or backing out of their deal, but she would let Mason sweat thinking he had screwed up Roth's plans. Served him right. Who did he think he was talking to? If this was how Roth conducted business, he was going to make countless enemies. She was in too deep to pull back, but she wasn't going to let anyone talk to her that way. Fuck him. The prenup could wait until her wedding day. If Roth gave Mason orders to intimidate her, he was way off base. Mason's snide insults only made her more determined to give him a hard time.

Mo materialized by her side as she caught the elevator to the first floor. As she slipped into the Bentley, her phone rang. Roth's name appeared on the screen. Screw him. She wasn't in the mood to listen to his threats. Mason had already done an exemplary job of pointing out how little power she had. She put her phone on silent and stared out the window as they headed back to the penthouse.

"Ms. Hennessy."

Mo was turned in the front seat, holding out his phone. She didn't take it.

"It's Mr. Roth," Mo said, extending the phone, so it was inches from her face.

"I'll call him back," she said, knowing full well Roth could hear her.

"Ma'am, I don't think—"

She reached out and pressed the button to end the call. Mo's eyes bulged.

"I don't want to talk to him," she said firmly.

When they pulled up to 432 Park Avenue, Mo accompanied her to the elevator and typed in the code while purposely blocking the keypad, so she couldn't see. Roth made it abundantly clear that he didn't trust her. She was a temporary asset that wouldn't be given free rein.

Mo pulled his phone out of his pocket and glanced at her before he put it away without answering. She walked out of the elevator, tossed her coat on the couch, and headed to her computer, so she could erase the bad taste in her mouth. As she pulled up her manuscript, text messages from her phone appeared on the screen.

Roth: *How much?*

She turned off her messages, put on her earphones, and got to work.

SHE WAS TRYING to enter La-La Land, but real-life crap filled her mind. She had just returned from her final fitting with Dai, which left her completely drained. The dress was sublime. If that wasn't bad enough, Dai insisted on a veil... and that was when all hell broke loose. She panicked and almost ripped the dress in her haste to get out of it. This sent Dai into an epic meltdown caused by days of little sleep to complete the gown that she was convinced would catapult her to the top of the bridal market. It took two hours to calm the distraught designer. The only thing that would appease Dai was Jasmine's promise that she would wear the veil. Both items now hung in the guest bedroom closet.

There were words to write, but she couldn't focus. Mason had called several times since she walked out of the meeting. Her voice-mail was full, so he couldn't leave a message. He sent her a few text messages. His tone had significantly changed, but she wasn't buying it. Roth also sent texts ordering her to call, but she didn't. Mason's words kept knocking around in her head. The fact that he had brought up Roth taking over Hennessy & Co niggled at the back of her mind. Would people assume she was marrying him out of gratitude for saving their company, or that she was in dire need of funds and groveled to be his wife again? Even as she told herself it didn't matter what others thought, she stewed on it.

She had visited Colette numerous times in the past week and spent hours cuddled up with Polara while Colette napped. The only downside was running into Lyle, who wasn't buying into her engagement.

He was suspicious and determined to have her spill what was really going on, but she stonewalled the fuck out of him. Her brother-in-law was a successful and formidable man in his arena, but Roth's assets were diverse, and he didn't play fair. Not only that, he had built up an impressive network that could endanger Lyle and Rami's companies. It wasn't worth it. The easiest course of action was to go along with the charade. One year and all of them would be free of his machinations.

She rapped her fingers on the counter as she contemplated her computer screen, and froze when she heard the elevator ding, announcing someone's arrival into the penthouse. She watched the kitchen entrance warily, expecting Roth to charge in and grab her by the throat.

"Ms. Hennessy?"

The soft, feminine voice was the last thing she expected. She slipped off the stool and found Sarai in the living room with a stylish workbag slung over one shoulder.

"Congratulations!" she said with such exuberance that Jasmine took a step back.

"I'm sorry?"

"On your engagement." Sarai bounced up and down in her heels and clapped her hands. "I knew the books would bring you two back together."

She hid her clenched fist behind her back. She couldn't beat up her own fan now, could she? "Can I help you with something?"

"Yes, I need information," Sarai said promptly and perched on the edge of the couch and brandished her iPad. "What theme did you have in mind?"

"Theme?" she echoed, completely at sea.

"For the wedding."

It took a concentrated effort to stop her lip from curling. "What do we need a theme for?"

Sarai blinked. "Your bouquet? The cake? We want them to match, right?"

She pursed her lips to stop herself from saying she didn't give a rat's ass about a theme for her fake wedding. This was getting worse and worse. It was bad enough that he had spent a ridiculous amount on a dress, but now he sent Sarai to ask her about *themes?*

"How about modern fall colors?" Sarai said. "Plum and soft pinks? What do you think of that?"

When she nodded, Sarai began to scribble.

"Great. I already have the photographer booked…" Sarai said absently.

"For what date?"

Sarai waved her hand. "Not sure yet. Roth's schedule is still in flux. They're on standby." She looked up and pointed at her. "Don't you worry about the details. That's my job."

Good because she wasn't going to fuss over any of this.

"I have a minister," Sarai continued. "Aside from your family, is there anyone else you'd like to invite?"

"No," she said, and then amended, "Kaia."

"Great, great," Sarai said as she made more notes. "Preference for the menu?"

"Menu?"

"A little spread after the ceremony." Sarai glanced up, saw her expression, and waved a hand. "I'll take care of it. Do you have your dress?"

"Yes."

"Goodie." Sarai made a notation on the iPad. "I'm sure it's *gorgeous.* Daiyu Wu is a genius."

"So *Vogue* says," she muttered.

Sarai grinned. "*Vogue* doesn't lie."

"Don't you normally travel with Roth?" she asked, belatedly realizing they were normally joined at the hip.

"Yes," Sarai said absently as she continued to scribble. "I just got back. I had some other things to take care of here. He'll be back soon. What's your favorite flower?"

"Jasmine."

Sarai winked. "Gotcha. Is there anything else that you want me to organize for your big day?"

"Um, no. Thank you."

Sarai rose and tucked her iPad away. "I'm so happy for you two."

She didn't have the energy to smile, so she nodded. "Thank you."

Sarai examined her for a moment before her expression softened. "Are you okay?"

"Of course."

"I know this is a lot, and you've had a rough few months, but I think this is a step in the right direction. If what you wrote is true, you guys had something special. You don't want to let that go. You're getting a second chance, and that's a beautiful thing."

Sarai radiated sincerity. She didn't have the heart to shatter her illusions.

"Roth holds everything close to his chest, but he's a good man," Sarai continued as she shouldered her bag. "No one can force him to do anything. He knows what he wants, and he doesn't stop until he obtains it." She cocked her head to the side. "He's different with you."

She said nothing.

"Have you been settling in well?" Sarai asked, tactfully changing the subject.

"Yes." She waved vaguely. "I've been spending a lot of time in the kitchen."

"You're a cook?"

"No. I've been working in there."

Sarai's eyes lit up. "You're writing?"

"Trying to, but there's a lot going on."

Sarai gave her a sympathetic look. "I bet. Maybe after the wedding, you can really get to work. Are you writing book five?"

"Yes."

Sarai put a hand on her chest and took a deep breath. "I can't wait to see how you wrap this all up. If you ever need anyone to read for you, call me, okay?"

She nodded. "I will. Thank you."

Sarai checked her watch. "I'll get everything sorted. In the meantime, you need anything, I'm your girl."

Sarai walked to the elevator. Was it a coincidence that Sarai blocked the keypad, or was she being paranoid? And how the fuck did Sarai have a code, and she didn't? Jasmine ground her teeth.

"By the way, Roth said to call him when you get a chance," Sarai said over her shoulder as she boarded the elevator.

Fuck him.

CHAPTER 17

SEVEN YEARS AGO

*S*he was walking across campus when she saw him. He was standing beneath a tree, hands in pockets, and getting a lot of attention from the girls passing by. He wore dark glasses, jeans, a light blue button-up, and a gray sports coat. He made college boys look like they were going through puberty. The sight of him made her already heavy heart sink to her toes. He shouldn't be here.

For a moment, she considered ignoring him. She should. It was over, and any other interactions with him would only lead to more pain, but she didn't walk away. She stood rooted to the spot with students rushing around her. He didn't come to her; he just watched her steadily, waiting for her to come to him. He exuded confidence. It was something he had in spades and something she lacked. She wanted to throw herself into his arms and cry, but she had done too much of that lately. What was he doing here? Had he come to say goodbye? Even as the thought filled her with dread, she lurched into motion because she was a glutton for punishment. She stopped several feet away, drinking him in and trying to imprint this image of him in her mental bank to drool over later.

"We need to talk," he said.

She blinked. That wasn't what she was expecting. "That's not a good idea."

"I'm not asking."

She frowned. "Didn't you get my text?"

"My father knows," he quoted. "I can't see you anymore. I'm sorry."

"So, what are you doing here?"

"I need more than that."

He grabbed her arm and propelled her in the direction of her apartment, which was a block away.

"I have class!"

"You can make it up."

"Someone's going to *see!*" she hissed as she tried to pull away.

"Let them."

He sounded supremely unconcerned.

"We need to stop this," she whispered desperately. "My father will destroy you."

"Let me worry about your father."

"He said he'll cut you out of the Langdon deal if I don't—"

"He already did it."

"But..." She felt ill. "But I broke it off with you."

He glanced at her, but she couldn't read his expression since he had his shades on.

"I'm sorry, Roth. You worked so hard to get in on that deal."

He dragged her into her apartment building and didn't release her even when they got a sidelong glance from the couple in the elevator. Her stomach rocked as she stared straight ahead. Her father followed through on his threat, even though she had complied with his wishes. The Langdon deal was supposed to take Roth to the next level, and now it was gone.

Her hand trembled as she pulled the keys out of her backpack. Roth pulled them from her grasp and unlocked the door. She preceded him into the apartment, set her bag on the floor, and strode to the windows.

"I'm so sorry," she said thickly. "He promised he wouldn't..."

He pulled her around to face him. "Tell me what happened."

She dropped her face as her eyes filled with tears. She took two uneasy steps back and shrugged, eyes downcast. "I'm sure you can guess."

"I want to hear it."

She swallowed hard and wrapped her arms around her middle. "He told me to come to New York." She stared at his shoes as she tried to think of a way to make this as painless as possible. "He knew."

She dragged her shoe on the carpet, attempting to focus on the pattern she was making rather than the insults that had been hurled at her. She had never seen her father like that before. He was enraged and disgusted at the sight of her. She had been such a fool. For two blissful months, she had suspended reality, and for the first time in her life, she did what she wanted. She fell for a man and indulged to the hilt. She convinced herself that Philadelphia was worlds away from New York, and their affair would remain between them. She was wrong.

"I don't know who told him," she said, and acted like she was brushing back her hair, so she could surreptitiously swipe away a tear. "He told me he would go after your businesses if I didn't break it off."

"And?" he prompted when she went quiet.

She covered her mouth as it began to tremble. When he took a step toward her, she held up a hand and stumbled back. "No."

She couldn't let him touch her. She was hanging on by a thread. One touch and she would shatter.

"Tell me what he said."

A tear slid down her cheek, and she wiped it away with her sleeve. "It doesn't matter."

"It does."

She flinched as her father's voice sliced through her. *You really are your mother's daughter.* She had always known she was a disappointment, but the things Maximus hurled at her destroyed the alternate reality she had been living in. He laid into her, reviling her. Every word out of his mouth felt like a physical blow, and she stayed in bed for days after. He didn't stop even though she begged him to. She promised she would never do anything like this again, but he wouldn't listen. No apology would be enough to repair what she'd done. What had she been thinking to start an affair with another man when she was engaged to Ford?

A hand slid over her hair. She wrenched away and held both hands up.

"Don't, Roth," she whispered.

"What did he say, princess?"

"Don't call me that," she said harshly as she covered her face with both hands. "I'm not a princess."

"You are to me." He pulled her hands down, and when she tried to turn her face away, he cupped her wet cheeks. "Look at me."

"No."

She trembled as she tried to keep it all in.

"It's okay."

"No, it's not. We shouldn't have… and you lost your deal."

"There will be other deals."

"No, there won't. You don't know my dad."

"Don't worry about me."

His calm voice soothed her frazzled nerves. He wiped away her tears with the sleeve of his coat and brushed her hair back from her face.

"Don't be nice to me," she said raggedly.

"Why?"

"I don't deserve it."

He jerked her chin up, forcing her to look at him. The anger he didn't allow to leak into his voice was in his eyes. The black pools were swimming with dark emotions.

"Don't listen to him," he said.

She gave a weak laugh as more tears slid down her face. "That's not possible."

"What do you want, Jasmine?" he asked as his thumb brushed over her bottom lip.

She stepped back as a bolt of heat chased away the guilt and sadness. She touched her pulsing lip, which begged to be kissed. "What are you talking about?"

"This is about Ford, right?"

She twisted her hands together. "He doesn't know yet."

"Do you want to marry him?"

Her brows drew together. "We're engaged."

"That's not what I asked."

She searched his face. "I don't understand."

"Do you want to marry him?"

"I…"

"If you wanted him, you wouldn't have slept with me."

She jerked. "I don't—"

"Be honest, Jasmine."

She threw up her hands and paced. "My relationship with Ford isn't like that!"

"You don't have a relationship with him. You see him once a month for dinner with his family. It's all business."

"It's what my sisters have."

"You aren't them."

"How do you know?"

"You aren't built like them." He gestured to her bookshelf. "You're an artist. You should be writing, not going to school for business and economics. It's why you have such a hard time in your classes. Your heart isn't in it."

She stiffened. "I'm trying."

"You shouldn't. You're no good at it. Your family is trying to fit you into their mold, and you don't fit."

Her eyes filled with tears. "I want to fit."

"There are other molds. You don't have to fit into theirs."

She stared at him. "What are you saying?"

"I'm saying you can choose another path."

"Which is?"

"Me."

Her heart stopped.

"I don't have the money your family does, but I work hard. I'll marry you."

She shook her head, eyes wide.

"Is that a no?"

"My father's going to ruin you and disown me," she whispered.

"I have money."

"But..." Her mind was buzzing. "My father..."

"Leave him to me."

She shook her head. "You don't know him like I do."

"I know how he works."

"But he means it. He'll destroy you."

"Don't worry about that. Do you want to marry Ford?"

Before she met Roth, she thought she wanted Ford. Now she wasn't sure. She hovered on the precipice.

Roth brought out a side of her she didn't know existed. She didn't have to put on an act. He liked her for who she was. For the first time in her life, she truly understood what it meant to be happy. All her life, she followed the path her father plotted out for her. She'd been content because she didn't know anything existed beyond her father's outline, and then she met Roth. She loved the way he made her feel—empowered, desirable, strong. He listened to her and asked for her opinion. He made her yearn for a different path. With Ford, she already knew what her life would look like and where it ended. With Roth, the possibilities were endless. She had no idea how he felt about her, but he was offering marriage. Maybe he did love her.

"Jasmine."

His voice was terse and impatient.

"What?"

"Stop thinking about what others want for you. Do you want him or not?"

As she struggled to answer, he closed the distance between them.

"You don't want him. You want me."

Her lip trembled as she tried to keep her emotions contained.

"You want me, don't you?"

With everything in her. "We can't."

"Why not?" he asked gently.

"My father's going to…"

"What do *you* want?"

She hesitated.

"Come on," he coaxed.

"I… I want you," she said in a rush. "But I can't have you!"

He caged her against him. "You can."

He was willing to risk his livelihood for her? She couldn't believe it. "No."

"Don't worry about your father or what people will say."

A tear slipped down her cheek. "I don't want you to regret this."

"I won't."

"Promise?"

"Promise." He stroked her cheek. "Are you going to marry me?"

All the wounds her father inflicted instantly began to mend. Her heart swelled so large, she couldn't take a breath. "Are you… Are you sure?"

She wanted to leap off the cliff, wanted it so desperately she could taste it. Freedom. That was what he was offering. She was lightheaded with terror and hope. She hadn't realized she was in a cage until she met him. He was her knight in shining armor, willing to slay dragons for her.

His eyes moved over her face before he said, "Yes, I'm sure."

"I-I won't have money for college."

"Drop out. Be a writer."

"No. I'm so close to getting my degree." She bit her lower lip. "Maybe… maybe I can get a job and do school…"

"I'll pay for it."

"You can't do that!"

"And the apartment."

"Roth—"

He kissed her. "Say yes."

"But ..."

"Say it."

Her face was streaming with tears as she smiled. "Yes."

"Your father will come around," he said as he kissed her and backed her toward the bed. "Don't worry. I'll take care of everything."

CHAPTER 18

*J*asmine opened her eyes with Roth's assurance echoing in her ears. Even as she lay in bed, staring up at the ceiling, she could feel his hands moving over her. He consummated their engagement by fucking her until she screamed. Even as she indulged in the graphic memories she couldn't forget, her inner critic began to point out all the things she had overlooked. He hadn't given a clear reason for wanting to marry her. He had proposed (sort of) and she had agreed. She had been so desperate for love that she took a chance on him and jumped. Stupid girl. She had uttered the L word many times over the two years they were married. He never had. Roth assumed Maximus would come around. He hadn't, so he considered giving her up because she was bad for business.

She rolled out of bed, walked into the bathroom, and splashed water on her face. The best thing that came from her relationship with Roth was her writing career. He had encouraged her to invest in her dream instead of going into the business world to get pummeled and constantly sabotaged by her father. Roth paid the bills while she wrote the Thalia Crane books that later helped her build a life without him. Writing helped her cope with her demons, gave her purpose, and a community of people who gave her the support she never had in real life. And she couldn't let them down now. Her personal life might be in ruins, but she still had writing.

She trudged into the dark kitchen and started the coffee maker she had requested. Once she had a steaming cup with just the right amount of creamer, she perched on the window seat with a notebook balanced on her knee. Her mind was a stress ball of anxieties. As the sun rose, she listed every fear plaguing her. It went on for pages, but once she had it on paper, the sharp tip of the imaginary knife pressed against her throat disappeared.

Roth made her feel trapped, vulnerable, needy... He made her feel like that insecure college girl again, and she hated him for it. She owned her own business and had more money than she could spend in this lifetime, but she still couldn't win in a fight against him.

A seething mass of grief, fury, and lust pulsed inside her. Her father's passing combined with Roth's relentless siege was taking its toll. On top of that were professional worries. Everyone was waiting for book five. The brief burst of inspiration had long since lost its shine, and she was adrift again. She had to bring the story to a solid and satisfying conclusion. Everyone expected the story to be epic. What did that mean? Between both pen names, she had almost twenty books under her belt, yet she still didn't know why some books hit, and others didn't. Thousands of messages poured in, giving her advice on how her story should end. Before her success, it was just her and the characters. Now, tens of thousands were chiming in and everyone wanted something different. She couldn't write for them; she had to write for herself. She watched many authors crack under pressure, and she was feeling it now. The knowledge that Sarai, Roth, and even her sisters would read the book paralyzed her. She tried to tell herself they were just words. Her job wasn't rocket science, but still... They weren't just words, just as music wasn't just noise. Stories were meant to transport people to a different world and make them feel. To accomplish that feat, every word and paragraph had to be laid down with purpose, precision, and care.

She left the window seat, refilled her cup, and booted up her laptop. She put her hands on the keys, closed her eyes, and took a calming breath. There was a direct connection between her emotional state and her writing. Whatever she was feeling, whatever was going on in her real life affected the actions/decisions/thought processes of the characters. The reason the Thalia Crane books had been so successful was because there was no filter between her and the character. They were one and the same. Readers could feel her pain and related to her struggles. The readers were rooting for her. She thought she had moved on with a bang (well, many bangs), but life had thrown her a curveball and she didn't know how to pivot and get her mind back in the game. Her past was right in her fucking face, forcing her to realize that she hadn't overcome it, she had avoided it. How could she give her character the closure she needed when she was back at the beginning?

She stared at the blinking cursor. She had nothing to offer the book right now but her own heartache and confusion. It would have to do. Life wasn't an upwards trajectory. There were ups, downs, and long plateaus. There was only one way to write the book, and it was going to fucking hurt.

People thought writing was fun. Sometimes, it was. But the books that moved a reader emotionally were the ones where a writer sewed pieces of their soul into the work and dripped their blood on the page to give the characters' life. Great writers sliced open their scars, sifted through their pain, and transcribed it on paper for the world to read and judge. Her job was to blend fact and fiction so seamlessly, no one could tell one from the other. It was brutal, draining work, but if done right, it could heal others and give them hope.

Her fingers tapped on the keys. *The fucker was back.* She bit her bottom lip and then shut off the judgmental voice in the back of her mind and continued. *The years in between turned him into a stranger.*

As the sun rose and filled the kitchen with light, silver flecks in the quartz countertops shimmered around her laptop. She chose to believe they were magical sparkles, and she was being anointed for a great writing day. Words filled the screen, not in a steady stream, but in choppy spurts as she grappled with the story. Things she didn't allow herself to dwell on in real life filtered into the heroine. She gave herself up to the characters and let them mold her as they would. Hours passed. She took a break and decided to order food. She took some notes, checked social media, and then lost two hours talking to fans and thanking them for their well-wishes. She reassured them she was working as she munched on a salad and side of fries. Having her heroine kick Roth's ass on the page was therapeutic and raised her dragging spirits. In the story, the heroine gave him the middle finger as she drove away, leaving him stranded. God, if she could have done that in Colorado, that would have been the best thing ever. It didn't matter that he fucked like a god or that she liked his craggy face or even his facade of calm that vanished if she provoked him. He was such a bully.

Now what?

She tried a few scenarios, none of which panned out. Her fingers fell on an empty plate. She had finished all the fries, so she picked up the fork and stabbed a crouton. Out of the corner of her eye, she saw her phone light up. She didn't get up to see who was calling. She returned her attention back to the screen and read over what she wrote. She changed some things and jumped around, prodding ideas to see if they had any life. More hours passed. She paced, checked her email, and delved once more onto social media, reposting hilarious memes before she hopped off again. She tugged on a story thread, following the path before she slammed into a wall. Her fingers stopped their tap dance over the keys.

A man stood by the lake. As she approached, he turned. Her father didn't smile. He couldn't anymore, but he held his hand out to her in invitation.

"Come, daughter, tell me a story."

She retracted her hands. They dropped like lead weights onto her lap. The fantasy world fell away, leaving her with no protection from the pain. Maximus hadn't been a perfect father or even an admirable one, but he was hers. She fanned her face as the tears came and when that did nothing, she went to the large double sink and splashed her face with cold water. She braced her hands on the counter as she tried to control her roiling emotions, but writing had opened the floodgates, allowing grief to take over.

She sagged to the floor and put her hands over her face as she sobbed. She could still hear the heart machine, smell the sterile scent of his hospital room, and feel his hand growing cold in hers. She rocked, trying to soothe herself, but knew it would do no good. Guilt savaged her insides. His voice whispered in her ears, which made her cry harder. She had her ups and downs with her father, but he was the only parent she'd ever known, and in the end, he was there when she needed him most. Their time together was a gift, but it had been too brief.

When the storm had passed, she forced herself up and hobbled out of the kitchen. She stole a duvet from one of the bedrooms and dragged it into the living room. She lay on the couch facing the windows and let out a shaky sigh. At this height, no buildings obstructed her view. She was a part of the endless blue. She could be anywhere in the world. No one would believe she was in the heart of the city. She buried her face in the pillow as another wave of sorrow crept up on her. She cried until her eyes were swollen shut, and she was limp.

When she was disowned, it hurt, but it was nothing compared to this. Not talking to her sisters and father wasn't an impossible feat because they didn't have a relationship, but now... Now, she knew what she was missing—support, guidance, love... It was all gone, just like that. Losing Maximus was a cruel blow that knocked her to her knees. The Thalia Crane series was intrinsically intertwined with her life, which meant she would have to relive her father's death on the page. The readers would think it was a cruel plot twist. If only they knew it wasn't fiction. Her father was a fan favorite with all of his flaws proudly on display. The readers would mourn him with her. Maximus had been an extreme father, but what did one expect from a man who had been raised to excel at everything he did? He wanted what was best for her and assumed that he knew what that was. Maybe he did. Perhaps marrying Ford would have led her down a more contented path. She wouldn't be a writer, but maybe she would have found joy in her children or some other hobby. Who knew?

The sky turned to gold as the sun began to set. Drawn to the beauty, she left her position on the couch and curled up on the window seat and watched the clouds creep in, concealing the city below. If she could get through this window, she would fall right into heaven… She splayed her hand on the glass, wanting to be a part of something stunning and tranquil, instead of being herself. She preferred to be in an alternate universe because she didn't fit in the one she had been born into. Roth was the one person who made living in the now worth it, and he had damaged her so badly that a part of her was still trying to piece herself back together. For a short time, she had her father, and now she was alone again.

Her hand dropped from the window. A tear slipped out of the corner of her eye as she rested her head on her arm and tucked herself as close to the glass as possible. She closed her eyes and imagined the soft brush of central air were clouds caressing her face.

The ding of the elevator interrupted her snooze. It was dark now, and as the lights came on, the window reflected a large figure entering the penthouse. Roth was back. She willed him to go to his office or the bedroom, but he came straight toward her. She closed her eyes and tried to even out her breathing. He brushed the duvet down.

"Jasmine."

The sound of his soft murmur nearly broke her. To cover the fresh burn of tears, she made a grunting noise and pressed herself against the glass to hide her face. He wasn't having it. He gripped her shoulder and pulled, so she rolled into his arms. She kept her eyes closed as he picked her up with the duvet still wrapped around her. *Leave me alone*, she chanted in her head. She had turned to him in Colorado, but she would never do so again. She wouldn't give him the opportunity to fling her pain back in her face when he felt like it. No matter how considerate he appeared at times, it was only skin deep. He didn't really feel anything for her. It was a painful lesson she had finally learned.

He settled her on the couch and hovered over her. What the hell was he looking for? Her breath stuttered when he brushed his finger against her damp eyelash. What the fuck? She felt a whoosh of air as he walked away. She relaxed and tried to think of what to do when she heard his footsteps coming back. She jostled when he sat beside her. She heard a familiar whirring sound as his laptop booted.

"Yeah?"

When she jerked, his hand rested on her hair.

"Yeah," he said again.

Oh, he was on the phone. The person on the other end sounded like Mickey Mouse. His hand disappeared as he typed and then returned to play with her tangled hair.

"Mm. Get back to me."

She heard a thump as he set the phone on the table. That was how he ended his calls? She played dead as she felt his eyes skim over her. Ten seconds later, she heard him tapping keys.

His presence diluted the pain, and thoughts of her father began to dissipate as her mind focused on the rhythm of his typing. She didn't know how to get out of this. If she opened her eyes, he'd see how swollen and bloodshot they were. There would be no hiding the fact that she had a crying fest. Her thoughts drifted as he worked, taking two more phone calls and giving one-word answers. She wasn't sure if that was how he normally talked or if he was trying to be considerate. Between phone calls, he worked on his laptop and occasionally stroked her hair.

When she calculated that thirty minutes had passed, she fake-stirred. Instantly, the typing stopped.

"Jasmine?"

She shifted the duvet to cover her face. "You're back."

Once more, his hand landed on her hair. "A little while ago."

She pulled away and sat up with her face turned away from him. "I'm going to shower."

Before she could stand, she was dragged onto his lap.

"Let me go, Roth," she said and kept her eyes closed.

He clasped her face. "Look at me."

She ducked her head as her eyes burned. "Why?"

He forced her face around. She reached out blindly to push him away.

"You had a hard day," he murmured.

With all the attention he had paid her, she had begun to suspect he knew, but the confirmation made her swallow hard.

"How?" she whispered.

"Security cameras."

"Johan and Mo watch me?"

"No."

Her eyes opened. She stared at him as a tear trickled down her cheek. "*You* watch me?"

He regarded her for a moment before he brushed away her tear. "It's the only way I can find out what's going on with you. You won't take my calls."

She tried to slip off his lap, but his hands gripped her hips, keeping her in place. She looked away from those probing eyes.

"You really loved him, didn't you?"

Another tear slipped down her cheek. "Yes."

"He hurt you."

"I forgave him for that."

"And he acknowledged you as his own by giving you your inheritance," he said quietly.

Her mouth trembled. "I'd give it all up for one more day—no, I need at least a month. I needed more time..." She shook her head and swiped at her eyes. "He left letters for Colette and Ariana. I would rather have a goodbye than the money he left. I don't understand."

"No one understood that man."

She stiffened and dropped her hand to glare at him. "He changed, unlike you! You're still an ass. You buy a controlling share in Hennessy & Co and then coerce me—"

His hand slid into her hair and gripped a moment before his mouth landed on hers. She tried to pull away, but he held her still as he ravished her. She wrapped her hand in his suit and twisted it as more tears leaked from her eyes. He gentled the kiss and ran his hand up and down her back before he pulled away. She buried her face in his shoulder as her breath hitched.

"I'm not sorry for pressuring you. I have you where I want you."

"I can't do this," she said hoarsely.

"You can," he said as he lifted her.

He walked somewhere, she didn't care where. When he set her down, she opened her eyes and found they were in the shower. When he reached for her top, she gave his hand a weak smack he ignored. He undressed her and then himself and pushed her under the spray. She hung her head as the warm water washed away her tears. Roth squeezed shampoo into his palm and massaged her aching scalp. She braced her hand on his stomach and felt the muscles bunch beneath her fingers. He was aroused, but not acting on it. She watched him from beneath lowered lashes as he lathered up a cloth and began to wipe her down like a car. She pursed her lips to stop them from curving. He was such a *guy*. He cleaned her the way he did everything —*thoroughly*. He lifted her breasts to slide the cloth beneath and grabbed her hand and cleaned each finger individually. He continued down her body, but paused when he reached her pussy.

"Here," she said, and held out her hand for the washcloth.

"I got it," he growled. "Spread."

More out of curiosity than anything else, she did as she was told. He had never bathed her, not even in the honeymoon phase of their relationship. Watching her breakdown today must have made an impact on him.

She expected him to seduce her, but he remained all business, even though his jaw locked. He seemed almost relieved to move onto the rest of her body. She had to brace a hand on his back as he bent over and cleaned the bottom of her feet like horse hooves. She was sad, incredulous, and amused. When he straightened, he pushed her beneath the water again and ran his hands over her to make sure she rinsed off well, even spreading her ass and thighs.

"Do you have OCD?" she asked.

He scowled. "Why do you ask?"

She raised her brows. "No reason."

He grunted and began to clean himself. "If you're going to do a task, you should do it right."

She stood there for a moment, watching water slide over him. His body was far from perfect. There was a large scar on his thigh and others scattered over his arms and back. His body was powerful, but it was nothing compared to his mind, which didn't work like everyone else's. He saw opportunity where no one else did, and could make the impossible happen through sheer force of will.

She watched him soap his penis efficiently before moving on. He acted like his erection was a common occurrence, and it was clear he wasn't going to jerk off to relieve it. Was it because she was here? She pictured herself kneeling in front of him, sucking him off. Warmth spread in her belly, but she turned away. This was a business arrangement, not a romantic affair.

She toweled off before she dressed in comfy, sexless pajamas and went back into the bathroom to begin her nighttime routine.

"What do you want to eat?" he asked.

"I'm not hungry." She looked away from her reflection with its puffy, bloodshot eyes.

"You should eat something."

She shook her head. "I just want to sleep."

"All you ate was a salad and French fries hours ago."

She examined him in the mirror as he wrapped a towel around his waist. "Don't you have better things to do than watch me eat a salad?"

"It was a long flight."

After she brushed her teeth, she slipped into bed. She hugged a pillow to her chest and stared out the window at the starry sky. The only source of light was the silver glow from the city and moon.

When the mattress dipped, she stiffened. A massive arm dragged her back against him. Her curves fit into the hard planes of his body. Minutes passed, but neither of them spoke. She found herself trying to copy his steady breathing. The moon highlighted clouds as they drifted lazily past.

"I'm fine," she said quietly.

He said nothing.

As her mind inevitably circled back to her father, she attempted to hide her sniffle. The arm around her waist tightened.

"It'll pass," she whispered.

She buried her face in the pillow, closed her eyes, and gave into her heartache.

———

SHE CLASPED her father's hand in both of hers, and silently begged him to wake up as the doctor coached her on what was about to happen. Her father looked like he was sleeping. He was still warm, he was still here, but they told her it was suspended animation and not really him. Dad didn't want this half-life, but selfishly, she had held on to him for several days as she grappled with this decision. It felt so wrong.

Her heart raced as the doctor approached the ventilator. She had to stop herself from attacking him. She was lightheaded with panic as the doctor flipped the switch on the machine. Her mind floated out of her body as she tried to distance herself from what was happening. She stared at her father as his breathing paused. She stopped too, but then his chest began to move again, and she almost lost it.

The nurses said something to her, but she didn't look at them. She couldn't. Her eyes were locked on her father. When they left her alone, she sank onto the chair beside the bed.

"I'm here, Dad. Can you hear me?" She pressed her cheek against his warm skin. "Can you feel me?"

He collected tears in the palm of his hand as she began to tell him a story. It was a game they had developed. She would begin a story, and he would try to guess the sequence of events. She had to throw in as many misdirects as possible so he couldn't guess the ending. This time, there were no interruptions, predictions, or critiques at the end, only the sound of his rapid breathing. She finished the story and launched into another, convinced that he could hear her and just maybe, he would shock them all and make a miraculous comeback.

She was in the middle of the third story when she noticed that his skin had changed color, and his lips had a bluish tinge. Her voice faltered. She desperately tried to control her wavering voice so he could hear the end, but she never made it.

"He's gone."

She didn't react other than to rub his cold hand between both of hers.

"Ms. Hennessy, he's gone."

She stopped her ministrations and nodded, acknowledging the doctor. He backed off. She should say something meaningful and poignant, but nothing came to mind. More time passed. She didn't move.

"We have to take him, ma'am," someone said.

She nodded but didn't release him.

"You need to let him go," the nurse said gently.

"I don't know how," she whispered.

The nurse put her hand over theirs. "Honey, is there anyone I can call?"

"No," she whispered.

She counted to ten, taking deep, shaky breaths as she did so. On the tenth, she released his hand and placed it on the bed. She got to her feet and kissed his forehead before she stepped back with tears slipping down her face.

The nurse patted her back. "You're going to be okay."

SHE REACHED for her father to touch him one last time. Her fingers landed on warm, muscled flesh. She opened her eyes and stared up at Roth.

He stroked her wet cheek. "Wake up, princess."

She stared at him as her heart broke all over again. "He never heard the end of the story," she said raggedly.

"It's okay, Jasmine."

She shook her head as she gulped down tears.

"I miss him so much. I don't have anyone," she whispered forlornly.

"You have me," he murmured as he brushed kisses over her face.

"I never had you."

His kissed the corner of her mouth. She gripped his hair and held him still as she kissed him, pouring her sorrow into him. He let her set the pace as she gorged on him. When she pushed against his shoulders, he tipped on his side. She shoved him onto his back. There was no need to undress him since he was naked. She closed her mouth around his penis. He hissed, and his limbs jerked.

"Jasmine."

She ignored him as she worked him the way she should have done in the shower. He would have fucked her into a dreamless sleep, and she wouldn't have relived that memory. She didn't want to think, didn't want to dwell on the pain. When he was ready for her, she yanked off her pants and crawled up his body until she was straddling his face. She didn't need to tell him what to do. He ate her as she yanked off her top, popping off buttons in her haste to get it off. She grabbed the headboard as she rode him. When she needed cock, she slid down his body and slipped him inside her.

He bared his teeth as she moved, eyes glittering as he let her use him. The sound of her low moans filled the room as she reached for ecstasy. A hand wrapped in her hair and yanked her down. His mouth closed over hers. The kiss was carnal and disrupted her rhythm. She tried to pull away, but he wouldn't allow it. A heavy hand flattened her over him as he began to thrust. She thought she was in control because she was on top, but it was just an illusion he allowed her to believe. He surged beneath her, slamming into her with eye-rolling force. His arms banded around her waist, keeping her in place.

"Roth," she panted.

"You with me?" he asked roughly.

"I'm always with you, even when I don't want to be," she said as she stared at his face, half of which was cast in darkness.

"This is where you belong."

He whispered filthy things in her ear. It didn't take long for either of them. He roared loud enough to make her ears ring when he climaxed. When she collapsed on top of him, he patted her ass.

"You have me," he declared.

When she didn't answer, he clutched her ass hard enough to make her moan.

"You hear me?"

He sounded like a pissed-off drill sergeant instead of a man comforting his distraught lover.

"Yes," she murmured as she listened to his rapid heartbeat.

"Say it," he ordered.

"I have you."

He swept his hand up her spine and clasped the back of her neck. "You always did."

CHAPTER 19

*S*he woke with a weight on her chest. Literally. Roth slept facedown with her partially buried beneath him. The remnants of yesterday's grief hung over her head, along with a feeling of impending doom. She felt like Meredith Grey in that *Grey's Anatomy* episode where she doesn't want to go to work. *"I need a reason to go on, I need some hope. And in the absence of hope, I need to stay in bed and feel like I might die today."* That was how she felt. Of course, unlike Meredith, when she went to work, she wouldn't be in danger of being blown up.

But she couldn't stay in bed and block out the world. She had shit to write. She examined what she could see of Roth's face. Even in slumber, he looked angry. She tried to think back to when they were married. He had never been one to snuggle. If she remembered correctly, he had always been quick to disengage after sex. So, what was with this spooning shit?

He didn't stir when she slipped out from under him. She showered and pat eye cream on her swollen eyes before she dressed. She brewed fresh coffee and leaned against the counter as she watched the dark drops trickle into the pot. Despite the bucket of tears she shed yesterday, she still didn't feel right. The midnight fuck and Roth's attempts to comfort her weren't a magic elixir that banished the melancholy. The pain was going to linger, and she was going to have to deal with that.

She sat in front of her laptop and pulled up her mangled manuscript. She didn't want to poke the beast again, so she jumped to another scene and left the one with her father unfinished. When she was stronger, she would breathe life into it, but today wasn't that day. It wouldn't take much to topple her into another round of inconsolable sobbing.

As she did most days, she prayed for guidance because she didn't know what the hell she was doing. She nudged words around on the screen and waited for the caffeine to do its thing, hoping the muse would show up since she was being a good disciple.

She was so deep in her words that she didn't hear Roth enter the kitchen. When he tossed a stack of papers onto the counter beside her, she almost fell off her stool. She eyed the prenup, shot him a lethal glare, and returned her attention to her computer, even though she was now thoroughly distracted. He wore sweatpants and nothing else. The morning light turned his dark complexion into a warm hue that made him look like the god he thought he was. Ass.

"How much?" he asked.

Couldn't he wait until she had finished her first cup of coffee before he started talking about money? She erased one word and replaced it with another.

"Two hundred million?"

When she reached for her mug, he grabbed it. She looked up in time to see him take a sip and then grimace. He wasn't one for sweet beverages. No, he liked things bitter like him.

"Serves you right," she muttered.

"Tell me how much you want."

She let out an irritated huff and grabbed her teal-colored pen and signed where all the tabs were. She didn't allow herself to overanalyze. This was only skin deep. A year and then she could move on. When she finished signing, she looked back at her manuscript.

"Why hold out if you didn't want more money?"

She kept her attention welded to her computer screen. He pressed against her side and tugged on her hair. When she still didn't look at him, he grabbed her face and turned it toward him. Before she could snap, he covered her mouth with his. She wasn't prepared for his gentleness. When he pulled away, she gripped the bottom of the stool for support.

"I don't like being ignored," he said.

"I don't like being interrupted," she countered.

"Tell me why you didn't sign."

She crossed her arms. "The next time you feel like putting me in my place, do it in private instead of making your attorney do the dirty work."

The hand on her face tensed before he released her. When she would have gone back to her laptop, he closed it and forced her around so she was facing him.

"Explain," he ordered.

"You don't need to keep throwing your weight around, telling me I have no choices. I know I have no power, but you—"

"What did Mason say?"

"He assumed I was looking for a larger settlement since Dad is gone and my sisters aren't doing well. He also pointed out that your offer was generous, considering my track record." She jabbed his bare chest with her finger. "Screw you, Roth. You act like I took off because I found someone else and—"

"He's fired."

She pulled back. "What?"

"I told him to make sure you signed. That's it."

She searched his eyes. "But he brought up Hennessy & Co."

"That's public knowledge. I didn't discuss that with him. I told Mason I wanted the prenup signed as soon as possible. It's his job to know which tactics to use with his opponent. He miscalculated with you. He should have known better. You're a Hennessy."

"So?"

"You were raised by Maximus. Coercion and threats won't work."

"Then why the hell am I in this position?" she demanded.

"Because I play dirty. You didn't stand a chance against me."

She shoved at his chest. "You're annoying."

"I'll fire him today."

She shrugged. "What's done is done."

"It's not done. He riled you up and made me think you were going to back out. I don't need that shit. I need you sweet, not hostile."

She made a face. "Sweet?"

"Sweet like last night. That's how I want you all the time."

Her pussy pulsed. "Not gonna happen."

"We'll see about that."

He kissed her slow and deep, savoring her. Everything else faded away as he dragged her under a tide of sensation.

"Sweet," he confirmed against her lips.

"I'm not sweet."

"You can't help it," he said as he raised his head and looked down at her. "I have some calls to make."

"What?"

"You gotta let me go."

She'd been so sunk in him that she wrapped her arms and legs around him. Horrified, she jerked back while he gave her a satisfied smirk.

She bared her teeth at him. "Don't read anything into this. I hate you."

He chucked her under the chin. "You can't resist me."

She tried to bite him, but he retracted his hand. Her teeth clicked in midair as he grabbed the prenup and started out of the kitchen.

"I have somewhere to be," she said. She needed to get the hell away from him.

He stopped in the doorway. "We have an excursion today."

"I have plans," she lied and then snapped, "Why the hell won't you give me the elevator code, jackass?"

"I'll give it to you tomorrow."

"Why tomorrow?"

"You'll be legally bound to me then."

She felt the blood drain out of her face. "Excuse me?"

"We're getting married this afternoon at Tuxedo Park."

"What? *Why?* I thought Sarai said there was no set date."

"I was giving you time."

She tripped off her stool. "Time? Time for what?"

"To get used to the idea."

"You lied to me?"

He raised one brow. "Can you blame me?"

"Yes, I can! I can't do it today! Nothing's ready! Rami and Lyle aren't in town. I can't get married without them there. You wanted us to look like a big, happy family. If they're not there, people will wonder—"

"Rami flew in this morning, and Lyle caught a ride back with me last night."

Her mouth dropped. Lyle and Roth? Hell had just frozen over. That feeling of impending doom was getting stronger. "You're buddies now?"

"We're civil."

This couldn't be happening. "What about the photographer? What about Kaia? I want her there."

"Everybody knew the real date except you, including Daiyu. I contacted her to make sure she finished the dress on time. The only thing that wasn't settled was this prenup."

Her eyes went to the papers under his arm. "And if I hadn't signed?"

"You'll never know."

Fuck! "I-I think we should do this on another day."

"No."

He had deliberately kept the wedding date from her, knowing she would freak out. It was one thing to agree, another to sign the prenup, and quite another to go through with the sham of a wedding. "I need more time."

"You don't."

"What about my hair? Look at my face! My eyes are swollen!"

"Colette's bringing someone to do your hair and makeup."

He'd taken care of everything with her family's help and blocked every excuse she could think of.

"We'll leave in an hour. Pack a bag. We'll spend the weekend there," he said as he left her standing there in complete shock.

She should have stayed in bed today. She should have claimed she was deathly ill, but *nooooo*, she got dressed and started working, giving him the impression that she was a fully functioning human being, which she wasn't. Her mind skittered in a million different directions, but it was no use. She had signed the prenup. All that was left was the ceremony, but it was what she had been dreading the most. If a judge married them, it would be all business, but dressing up as a bride and having her family involved made it personal. Seven years ago, she would have done anything to have her family and Roth in the same room, but now the thought of everyone coming together to witness the ceremony made her sick.

She saved her manuscript before she cleaned up the kitchen. It was a beautiful day in New York without a cloud in the sky. She wished it was fucking storming. As she left the kitchen, she heard the rumble of Roth's voice as he talked on the phone. How did he have the time to run an empire and box her in so neatly? Fucker.

The only thing she needed to pack were toiletries, since she had clothes at Tuxedo Park. She focused on the positive. This was the beginning of the end. The sooner this shit went down, the sooner it would end. She was happy to take a break from the city and stay in the country for a while. She was going to see Kaia. It would be great to see her recovered from surgery.

She was on her knees in the closet fussing with her bag when Roth walked in.

"Why is your stuff on the ground?"

"I haven't had time to sort through everything," she muttered as he stripped off his sweatpants and reached for his slacks. Out of the corner of her eye, she admired his sculpted ass.

"You don't have to do it. That's the housekeeper's job."

"I..." To keep herself occupied, she double-checked that the lids on her products were on extra tight. "I don't want anyone coming in while I'm working. It's distracting."

"She can unpack while we're gone," he said as he zipped up his pants.

"I'd rather do it myself."

"You're still resisting," he said quietly.

She waved her hand at her toiletries. "Does it look like I'm resisting?"

"You resist in your mind."

Of course, she was. What was she supposed to do? Give herself to him so when he got rid of her a year from now, she'd be a wreck again? Fuck that.

She fetched her wedding dress and veil from the guest bedroom and piled everything near the elevator before she went to the kitchen to pack her work bag. Once she finished, she found Johan near the elevator with her garment bags and suitcase. Roth came out of the room with a small bag over his shoulder. He was talking on the phone and held his hand out to her. A glance at his face told her this wasn't the time to test him. She let his fingers engulf hers and boarded the elevator.

She kept her head high as they walked through the lobby. Like the other times she had passed through, it was busy and teeming with people. There was a slight din in the noise level as they strode through, but Roth couldn't care less. He was still on his call with her hand held securely in his. She kept her eyes trained straight ahead.

Mo was at the curb. She climbed into the back seat with Roth and saw the partition was already up. She looked out the window as Roth ended one call and took another. Just another day, which turned out to be her wedding day. No biggie, right? People got married all the time. Some even married the same person twice, like she was about to do. The real question was, did they divorce the same person twice?

They left the city behind and cruised through the country. Orange and yellow leaves still decorated the trees. *At least the pictures will be nice*, she mused.

She jolted when Roth grasped her wrist. She turned her head, saw the ring in his hand, and tried to pull away.

"No," she said firmly.

"It's expected."

"But—"

"Don't argue."

She attempted to curl her fingers into a fist, but he flattened her hand and threaded the massive ring onto her finger. It was a flawless cushion cut diamond on a delicate band encrusted with more flawless diamonds. It was massive and ridiculous and so beautiful that her already heavy heart sank to her toes. The ring dominated her hand. It was a declaration, one that no one would overlook.

"It's too much," she said faintly.

"It's perfect." He tilted her hand from side to side, making it sparkle. "It suits you."

He was going all in on this charade. "This must have cost a fortune."

"Don't worry about it."

"Dai said you picked up the tab for the gown as well."

"I'm looking forward to fucking you in it tonight."

Her gaze whipped up to his. While she had been studying their hands, he'd been watching her. His eyelids lowered over hungry eyes. Her skin tingled as his thumb brushed over her skin.

"I decided in Germany that I have a bride fantasy," he said quietly as his finger nudged the diamond ring. "You're going to make it come true."

She tried to untangle her hand from his. "Cocky."

"Cocky describes someone who *thinks* they're a boss. I *am* the fucking boss."

"You're not the boss of me," she snapped.

"We'll see."

His eyes dipped to his crotch, and hers automatically followed. He was aroused.

"I want to see you fisting me with my ring on your finger."

"You've had too much time to daydream on your trip." She tried to sound lofty, but it came out sounding breathy instead.

"That's why you'll travel with me in the future. I won't have to fantasize because I'll get to act them out immediately."

"You've been sexually deprived, Roth?"

His gaze was fixed on her mouth as he said, "I've never been one to take what's offered just because it's free."

"You'd rather pay and have an unwilling partner?" she asked caustically.

"I pay for the best, princess," he said softly. "And you only fight me because you think you should. I allow it because it makes my victory that much sweeter."

She wrenched her hand from his. "You're such a—"

"Looks like my mom made it before us."

They passed through the front gates of the estate without her noticing. As they approached the house, she saw a rental car parked in front. Roth answered his phone as Mo pulled up to the front door. She slipped out of the SUV and headed inside to find Thea and Kaia in the foyer.

"You are getting married, miss?" Thea asked with wide eyes.

She hoped neither of them noticed the hitch in her step. "Yes, I am. I'm sorry I didn't warn you."

"A woman, I think her name was Sarai? She called me an hour ago to let me know you'd be coming today and to make sure I was here to welcome the caterer and guests. Who else is coming?" Thea asked.

"My sisters and their families. I'm so sorry, Thea. I should have given you a heads-up." Well, she would have if she'd known she was getting married today.

"Are you all staying the night?" Thea asked.

"I believe so."

"I'm going to freshen up the rooms," Thea said and hurried upstairs.

She hugged Kaia, who was dressed casually in jeans and jacket. "I'm glad you're here. How are you feeling?" She pulled back to find

Kaia regarding her with a strange expression on her face. "Are you all right?"

Kaia looked behind her. "Where is he?"

"Roth? He's outside taking a call."

Kaia gripped her hand. "I need to talk to you."

"Okay," she said, and went along willingly as Kaia led her into the library. "Did something happen on the flight?"

"It's not that." Kaia stopped in the middle of the room and turned to her. "I need you to answer me honestly."

A trill of foreboding trickled down her spine. "Okay."

"Are you marrying him of your own free will, or is he forcing you in some way?"

She felt the blood drain from her face. "I'm sorry?"

"I knew it." Kaia paced away and tugged on her braid as she mumbled under her breath. "This is all my fault. I should have let you leave when you had the chance."

"What are you talking about?" she demanded.

Kaia turned back to her with an expression that was almost fearful.

"You can't marry him, Jasmine. He'll ruin you."

Her heart stuttered. "What?"

"He's my son. I should love him, but..."

Should love him? What the hell? "Kaia, what are you talking about?"

"I should have known once he saw you again, he wouldn't let you go. The way he watches you..." Kaia shuddered. "He's a master strategist, always one step ahead of everyone else. He'll wait years before he makes a move, and when he executes, he never makes a mistake. The psychologist says he lacks empathy. It allows him to focus on his goals without letting emotion get in his way. He's always been cold, even as a child. Once he starts on a path, nothing can stop him."

"Psychologist?" she whispered.

Kaia cocked her head to the side. "You don't know?"

"Mom."

They both jumped. Roth stood in the entrance of the library. His expression was as inscrutable as always, but something was wrong with his eyes. They glittered like black diamonds in his otherwise still face.

"You're done," he said in a soft voice that made her stomach flip.

"She doesn't know, does she?" Kaia managed to sound defiant and nervous at the same time.

"That doesn't concern her."

"You haven't changed," Kaia whispered.

"Neither have you," he said coolly.

"You're holding something over her. She's not willing," Kaia said.

His eyes cut to her. She felt as if she were receiving tiny paper cuts all over her body. The low-key anxiety she had been nursing on the ride here turned into full-blown panic.

"You know nothing about my relationship with Jasmine. Johan." A second later, the guard appeared at his side. "My mom needs a ride back to the airport."

She stepped protectively in front of Kaia. "No, Roth!"

"It's fine, Jasmine," Kaia said.

"No, it's not. I don't understand what's—"

She didn't realize Roth had moved until it was too late. He yanked her away from Kaia, who backed away from her son as if afraid he was going to get physical with her.

"Wait, Roth, you can't let her leave!"

Kaia paused at the door and opened her mouth to say something, but after her eyes flicked to Roth, she hastily looked away. When Johan gestured to the door, she walked out.

"Wait!" Jasmine shouted, but Johan closed the door, bouncing her scream right back in her face.

Roth cupped her chin. "What did she say to you?"

"What the hell is wrong with you?"

If she wasn't plastered against him, she might have missed the way he tensed.

"What do you mean?" he asked in a voice devoid of all emotion.

"She said you're going to ruin me."

His eyes moved over her face as he considered her words. The fact that he didn't immediately contradict Kaia made her heart slam against her ribs.

"What are you going to do to me?" she whispered.

"I'm not going to hurt you."

She didn't believe him. "Back off."

"She was your one request, so I allowed her to come. I knew better," he said mildly, as if she wasn't struggling with every ounce of strength she had to get away from him. "Don't listen to her."

"Your mother told me not to marry you!"

"Your father told you the same thing, but you did it anyway."

"That was different."

"How so?" His eyes were black holes that led into the abyss. "I'm the same man."

No, the fuck he wasn't. "You're hurting me."

Instantly, his touched gentled, as if he didn't recognize his own strength.

"Don't believe her," he said.

She couldn't look at him, not with Kaia's warning ringing in her ears. "I need…" She tried to think of an excuse, anything to get away from him. "I need to…"

"You're safe with me."

He was standing so close, she couldn't breathe. There was activity in his eyes, lots of it. More than she had ever seen. She felt as if she was standing on the edge of the cliff, and he was trying to coax her off the ledge. She wasn't convinced he was the safer option.

"My mother and I have never seen eye to eye."

"You need to let me go."

His expression hardened. "There's no going back."

There was a cursory knock before the door opened. That quickly, he was beside her, hand clasped in hers as Ariana came into the library with Kye on her hip.

"There you are! I have the makeup and hairstylist with me!" Ariana said gaily.

When she started toward her sister, Roth pulled her to a halt.

"Give us a minute, will you?" he asked so courteously that Ariana

MIA KNIGHT

left without a murmur of protest. Clearly, Ariana didn't realize she was leaving her sister with a psycho. Jasmine was encouraged by the fact that Ariana didn't close the door on her way out.

"Whatever my mom said, forget it," Roth said.

She nodded, but couldn't meet his gaze. Her mind raced as she tried to think of all the ways he could screw her over.

"Jasmine."

"Mm-hmm?"

"Look at me."

She mentally braced as she obeyed. His expression was dispassionate, but something vicious lurked in the inky depths of his eyes.

"You know me," he said in a low voice vibrating with some emotion she couldn't define.

"What the hell are you two doing?" Lyle asked brusquely, breaking their staring contest.

She stepped away from Roth, and this time, he let her go. She walked up to her brother-in-law and gave him a hug. When he put her at arm's length, he frowned.

"What's wrong?"

She might have just made the second biggest mistake of her life with the same man.

"You sure about this?" Lyle asked as his gaze flicked over her shoulder.

She sensed Roth draw near a second before he said, "Of course she is."

His hand brushed the small of her back, reminding her he was watching, listening, waiting.

"I'm glad you're here," she said hoarsely.

"You never invited me to the first one," Lyle said, eyes on Roth. His finger bumped against her new engagement ring. He raised her hand and gave Roth an arch look. "You couldn't get a bigger one?"

"No," Roth said.

Lyle pushed her toward the door. "Get ready. Roth and I have things to discuss."

She left the room without looking back. The foyer was filled with people. Kye dashed through the legs of the caterers. Rami held Polara in one arm while he shouted at his son, and Ariana tried to console Bailey, who was crying over a broken headband.

"Today's the day!" Colette gave her a side hug. "Are you ready?"

Jasmine glanced at Mo who stood casually in front of the door, but she had a feeling he would do something if she tried to go through it.

"Come on, Min." Ariana looped their arms together. "We need to get this show on the road!"

Her sisters ushered her into a guest room, where the hair and makeup artist had taken over.

"Congratulations, Ms. Hennessy. What look are we going for on this special day?" the makeup artist asked.

She tried to think of something, but her mind was blank.

"What color is your bouquet?" the makeup artist prompted.

"Do... do I have a bouquet? I don't even know." Her heart thudded in her ears as they all stared at her. She looked to her sisters for help.

Colette stepped forward. "Her bouquet has dark purples, soft pinks, and white. Let's put her hair up. She has a high-necked gown, and you can see the veil there." She pointed at one of the garment bags. "As for the makeup, let's keep it light and classic with a bold lip. Minnie?"

She nodded, and everyone lurched into action. The hairstylist tugged on her hair while the makeup artist caked her face and told her to tilt her head this way and that. Her sisters sat on the bed with the kids to watch. The mood in the room was light and festive while she sat there, paralyzed with shock. Hysteria spread with every second that ticked past. She felt detached from everything that was taking place around her. Kye and Bailey perched on her lap, but she didn't hear a word they said. When the makeup and hair stylist stepped back so she could see the full effect of their work, she didn't react for several seconds.

"What do you think, Ms. Hennessy?"

The makeup artist was so skilled that there was no trace of fear on her face. The cold sweat had been powdered away, and the soft blush on her cheeks gave the impression that she was joyful and excited rather than panicked and ready to lose her shit. Her hair was sleek and shiny, and the beautiful veil fell around her in soft waves. She had an unusually dark purple matte lip, a personal touch that made her feel more like Jasmine and less like a Barbie playing dress up.

"You did a fantastic job," she said. "Thank you."

As the hair and makeup artists packed up their things, she turned to Colette, who sat on the bed breastfeeding Polara.

"Are you excited?" Colette asked, but her attention was on the hair and makeup artist as they filed out of the room. As soon as the door closed, she turned back to Jasmine. "I started," she confided.

Jasmine blinked. "I'm sorry?"

"Your books."

"Oh." She didn't feel the normal rush of nerves or insecurity over her work. She didn't feel anything.

"They're very steamy," Colette said and shifted uncomfortably.

"I told you they would be."

"Is all that real?" Colette asked.

"Is what real?"

"The main character. How she feels about him? Is that how you felt about Roth?"

She wanted to lie, but there was no use. "Yes."

Colette nodded. "I can see why you left Ford if that's how you felt about him. Lyle and I don't have that." She rocked Polara and stared pensively out at the lake. "I don't know if I'd want to have that, honestly. The way he looks at you…"

"How does he look at me?" she asked sharply.

Colette waved her hand. "You know."

No, she didn't know. "How?"

"He's…" Colette cleared her throat. "Completely focused on you, watching every expression that crosses your face. He's really intense. I don't know if I could handle a man being that attached to me."

Attached? For most of their marriage, they lived apart.

"I don't know how you function with someone who feels like that about you. It takes you over, doesn't it?"

She nodded. The last time she had played this game with Roth, she walked away in pieces.

"I'm glad you two are getting this second chance," Colette continued. "Ariana's been working with him. He went to Germany to close a deal and let us in on it."

"Wait, what?"

"You didn't know?"

She didn't know a lot of shit, apparently. "No."

Colette gave a one-shoulder shrug. "That's probably best to keep business and personal separate. When you mix it together, bad stuff happens. That's why I'm glad we sorted this without Lyle getting involved."

"You're supposed to be on maternity leave," she reminded her.

"I am!" Colette gestured to the breastfeeding Polara. "Ariana's handling everything and doing an excellent job. I've been eating, sleeping, and reading about my sister's love affair. The company's turning around, and Polara's gorgeous. It's all working out."

Ariana came in and shut the door on her kid's screaming. "Come on, let's get you into this dress."

After Colette burped Polara, her sisters helped her into her gown. They chattered excitedly as they did up the buttons and fluffed her skirt. As the tulle settled around her, she took in the finished product and felt her stomach lurch. This was all kinds of wrong.

Ariana flapped a hand in front of her face. "Oh my God."

Colette brushed away a tear and pulled out a handkerchief embroidered with her initials. "These damn hormones."

"We're having the ceremony in front of the lake," Ariana said, peering through the windows. "Thea said she'd watch Polara, and then we'll bring her out for pictures. The light's perfect right now."

"I..." She cleared her throat. "Can I have a minute?"

"Of course."

Her sisters smiled at her as they withdrew and closed the door. She stared at herself in the mirror. She looked like a bride. Between the ring and the gown, she estimated she was wearing over a million dollars. If she had planned it, she couldn't look any better, but it was all a façade for his gain.

You can't marry him, Jasmine.

Her hands crept up to the high neck of her gown as her throat began to close. She felt like a rabbit looking over its shoulder for the wolf. Could she really do this? His mother had warned her not to marry him. If she was looking for a sign, that was it, right?

He'll ruin you.

Her fingers trailed over the scalloped neckline. She brushed her fingers over the delicate lace before she gripped and prepared to pull.

A soft knock interrupted her dark reverie. Before she could call out, the door opened to admit Thea, who looked harried after running around to accommodate them.

"I'm sorry, miss, but I had to see you…"

Thea fell silent when Roth appeared beside her. He was in a tuxedo with a dark purple rose pinned to his pocket.

"I need a word with my bride."

Thea immediately dropped her head and backed out of the room. "Of course, sir."

As Roth closed the door and locked it, she dropped her hand from the neckline of her gown.

"You look beautiful." His shoes clicked on the wood floors as he walked toward her. "Your sisters tried to stop me from seeing you. They say it's bad luck to see the bride before the wedding."

He stopped behind her, so close she got a whiff of his cologne.

"I don't believe in luck. I believe you make your own destiny." There was a taut pause and then, "Having second thoughts, Jasmine?"

Her eyes collided with his in the mirror.

"Bad girl," he murmured as he brushed her veil to the side and pressed a kiss on her exposed nape. "Everything is in place. All I need is you." He held her still with a grip on her hips when she tried to step away. "There's nowhere you can hide from me. I'd hunt you down."

Her chest was so tight, she could barely breathe.

"You think you have a choice, but you don't," he whispered as one hand splayed over her tummy. "Everything's already in motion. You're in too fucking deep, princess."

"Roth, she said—"

"I don't give a fuck what she said." His hand slid down, probing layers of tulle. "She's poison."

She grabbed his wrist. "What are you doing?"

"Reminding you what matters."

Her grip didn't stop him as his fingers burrowed into the layered skirt and found the heart of her.

"Spread for me."

"Fuck you."

"I will if you want me to. I'll open that door and let your family watch."

She clenched her teeth and widened her stance. "I hate you."

He rubbed the coarse tulle against her. The sun beamed down on the wicked scene. She, the proper and classic bride with the debauched fiancé copping a feel before the ceremony. His eyes bored into hers in the mirror as he expertly roused her, burying her fear and anxieties beneath a tidal wave of sensation.

She clenched her teeth to hold back a moan. "Stop, Roth."

"I need you to say two words for me, and it'll all be over. You can do that for me, can't you?"

She shuddered as he worked her roughly. Her mind went white as she focused on the crest just out of reach.

"Do you know why you ran from me?" he asked harshly.

She gripped his wrist to hold him still so she could fuck herself on his fingers. His arm came around her waist and held her still as he ground himself against her ass.

"It's because you know you belong to me. You crave what I give you. You're not strong enough to fight me, so you ran. That fucking ends now."

His fingers scissored, and she let out a ragged moan.

"You have no idea what I've done to bring us here. No one comes between us. Our parents don't get a say."

Her breath hitched as she felt her orgasm coming. "Jamie."

"Yes, Jamie," he crooned in her ear. "Are you with me, Jasmine?"

"Yes," she moaned.

His hand disappeared, and she tipped forward. He caught her before she fell and turned her to face him. She stood there, throbbing and aching, as he smoothed down the bunched-up tulle and fixed her veil with a poise that made her want to rake her nails down his face.

He met her seething gaze. "Tonight," he promised and held out his hand.

There was so much to say, but he was right about one thing. She was in too deep, and there was no going back. Kaia's warning had come too late.

"Take my hand," he ordered.

She took a deep breath and stepped off the cliff. She put her hand in his.

CHAPTER 20

*C*hen they walked out of the room, a flash went off in her face. As her vision cleared, she saw a woman in a white pantsuit holding a camera.

"The photographer will be taking candid shots as well," Roth said.

"Are we all set?" Lyle asked as he walked up.

"Yes."

Ariana handed her a beautiful bouquet with deep purple, blush, and white roses with jasmine. Before she could admire it, Roth led her outside with everyone trooping behind them. She picked up the front of her dress and was glad her shoes had a square heel, so it didn't sink into the soft ground. A man stood beside the lake as the sun began to set, streaking the sky with color. As they stopped before the minister, the photographer positioned them to face one another and took a round of shots. She stared at Roth as the cold crept into her bones. His eyes were steady on hers. The sound of Bailey's and Kye's happy voices was a jarring contrast to the heavy conflict going on inside her.

Once the photographer was satisfied, Jasmine handed her bouquet to Ariana, and the minister began to speak, his voice carrying easily in the hushed quiet. Her nerves began to fray as the minister's words began to penetrate her daze. Her fingers dug into Roth's flesh, but he didn't react as he began to speak. She couldn't hear his words, not over the sound of her heart thudding in her ears. She was dimly aware of the photographer hopping around and the occasional blinding flashes, but she didn't look away from him.

"Ms. Hennessy," the minister prompted.

She blinked and saw Lyle holding a ring out to her. As she took the platinum band, Roth extended his hand. She threaded it on his finger, wondering why he had gone to the trouble when he hadn't worn one the first time around.

"Now, Ms. Hennessy, repeat after me."

The knowledge that her family was witnessing this union and the photographer was capturing the most dramatic shots for the world to see made her voice falter a few times, but Roth's eyes commanded her to soldier on. When the time came, Roth produced a delicate diamond band to compliment the already stunning engagement ring.

"You may kiss the bride!" the minister declared with a smile.

Roth draped her veil back, tipped her chin up, and then his mouth was on hers. It was a brief, hard kiss, a reminder of who she belonged to. She was Mrs. James Roth once more. He received a congratulatory pat on the back from Rami, and her sisters cheered while Lyle watched through narrow eyes. It was clear he still had mixed feelings about Roth. He wasn't alone on that point.

"Pictures, quickly! The sky is perfect!" the photographer shouted.

Her sisters' families flanked them on either side. Kye leaned into her and clutched her skirts.

"Aunty?" Kye called.

"Yes?"

"You're married?"

She placed her hand on his head. "Yeah."

"Are you gonna have babies?"

She kept her voice light as Roth's hand tightened on her waist. "Not everyone has babies, Kye."

"Aunt Col did," he said.

"Not now, Kye," Ariana said as the photographer jumped up and down to get the kids to look at her.

"And now some shots of the happy couple," the photographer said.

"Food!" Bailey shouted as she pulled Lyle toward the house. "Come on, Uncle! They have cake!"

"Okay, you two face one another," the photographer said.

They did as she asked.

"You just got married," the photographer said as she stalked them like a sniper. "You're so happy. Smile, smile, smile. Or... don't. You can do that too. Okay, look out at the lake. Soft face, soft eyes. Think of your new life together. Chin up, darling. Yes! There you go."

She was trembling. She wasn't sure whether it was from the low temperature or the fact that she was now legally bound to him again.

"You've taken this too far," she said.

"It's necessary," he murmured.

"Happy faces!" the photographer barked.

Both of their faces eased into expressions appropriate for wedding photos.

"What's going to happen to Kaia?" she asked as the photographer jockeyed for the right angle.

His hand flexed around hers. "Nothing."

"You promise?"

"Negotiations are over."

She shook her head, but stopped when the photographer cursed. She tried to clear her expression as the woman fussed with her veil and even draped it over Roth to give the impression they were in their own world.

"Okay, look at one another and *smile*," the photographer called.

That was beyond her at the moment, and Roth only smiled when he was making money, so their expressions stayed neutral but intense.

"Okay, I think we got it!" the photographer announced and high-tailed it to the house.

Roth untangled himself from the veil and held her troubled gaze.

"She had no right to interfere," he said.

"I don't understand."

"You don't need to." He twined their hands together. "Let's go inside. You're cold."

"Roth."

He squeezed her hand. "It's over."

She wanted to argue that point, but she saw Thea watching them from the window and shut her mouth. Time to dust off her acting chops.

The formal dining room they never used was set with china that Thea had unearthed from God knew where. They sat around the table as the food was served, but eventually migrated to the kitchen, where they sat on stools. She wasn't comfortable with the personal, candid shots the photographer continued to take.

"She knows what she's doing," Roth assured her.

When she sat, Bailey immediately climbed onto her lap. "You look like a princess."

"Thank you."

"Can I keep your bouquet?"

"Of course, you can."

Bailey peeked at Roth, who stood a few feet away talking to Rami. "He's your husband now?"

Her stomach clenched. "Yes."

"Is he nice?"

"Yes." He better be nice to her nieces and nephew.

"Aunty?"

She refocused. "Yes?"

"I love you."

She hugged her. "I love you too."

Things might be fucked up between her and Roth, but everyone seemed to be having a good time. Lyle was being civil, and her sisters looked more relaxed than she had ever seen them. They might be bosses, but her intuition told her they were relieved Roth had stepped in. They were grateful for his assistance and guidance. Roth had done his part. Now, she had to do hers.

She stole Polara from her parents. She couldn't get enough of her niece's brilliant blue eyes. Sarai had done an excellent job with the catered food and cake, which was decorated with sugar flowers that matched her bouquet. Jasmine talked to her family, ate, and allowed

Roth to hold her hand, pull her on his lap, and let him feed her a slice of wedding cake. She smiled for the cameras while her insides remained frozen.

Night fell and all too soon the kids were ready for bed. The caterers packed up, and the photographer bid them farewell. She received hugs from her sisters and brothers-in-law who went to one wing of the house while she went to hers. Roth stayed downstairs to make some calls.

She found Thea in her bedroom. The room was decorated with a blanket of white rose petals, the fireplace was going, and candles flickered around the room.

"Oh my gosh, Thea."

"It's the least I could do."

"What would I do without you?" she asked as she gave her a tight hug.

"There's something I've been meaning to—" Thea began, but stopped and focused on something over her shoulder. "Mr. Roth."

He entered the room, taking in the flowers and candles. If he said something nasty, she was going to—

"Thank you for your help today," he said.

Thea couldn't hide her surprise. "Of course, sir. Anything." She gave Jasmine a kiss on the cheek. "Congratulations, my dear."

Roth looked around her bedroom room, which was a clash of child and adulthood. She had everything from Susan Cooper and Harry Potter to Stephen King, Stephanie Laurens, Kristen Ashley, and Charlaine Harris on her shelves. She was a sucker for trinkets, especially glass ones, which meant she had a collection of random paperweights and snow globes. Chinese cats waved at her as other whimsical items she picked up on her travels gleamed in the firelight.

As the door closed behind Thea, she kicked off her heels and stood in front of the fireplace. She stared at a painting of Rapunzel lounging in a window of her tower, hair cascading down to an imaginary prince who wasn't in frame. Life was no fairy tale. She understood that concept before she turned five. She should have thrown the painting out ages ago.

She closed her eyes and let the heat chase the chill away. The smell of the burning wood and the white noise soothed her, but that expression on Kaia's face before she left niggled at her. What would cause a mother to look at her son that way? She thought back to Colorado and that staring contest Roth and Kaia had in the hospital room. At the time, she assumed Kaia had been shocked because she hadn't seen him in years, but now she wasn't so sure.

She heard the rustle of clothing and curled her toes in the blanket of rose petals as she sensed him come up behind her. She waited for him to speak, but he stayed quiet. *Waiting for her to make the first move,* she thought cynically.

"Tell me about Kaia," she said.

"No."

When she would have turned to face him, he wrapped his arms around her and pulled her firmly against him.

"You can't tell me no," she hissed. "Not after that."

"That's between her and me."

"Apparently not, since she felt the need to warn me. She said you're going to ruin me. What the hell, Roth?"

He buried his face in her hair and inhaled. "I've done things she doesn't approve of."

"*What* things?"

"This isn't about her. It's about us. *This.*" His hands splayed on her stomach before they swept up to her breasts and squeezed as he pressed against her from behind. "This is all that matters."

"Sex doesn't solve anything!"

He found that spot on her neck and lapped at it with his tongue.

"There's nothing to solve. You're back where you belong, and everything's as it should be."

Her eyes fluttered shut against her will. "This is wrong."

"For the first time in years, everything is right. You know it, but you keep fighting it, fighting me." His teeth scraped over her nape, and she shivered. "You can fight all you want. You won't win."

She fought his spell and stared at the flames as she asked, "When we were in Colorado, were you already pursuing Hennessy & Co?"

"Yes."

Rage trumped desire. She stomped his shoe with the heel of her foot. He hissed, and a second later, lifted her high against his chest so her feet were dangling in the air.

"Behave," he hissed against her ear.

"I've been *behaving* all fucking day. You've been pulling the strings for weeks, manipulating me, boxing me in. You took over my life, threatened my family, threatened *me*. I'm done. Let me go."

"No."

When she tried to bruise his shin, he carried her to the bed and threw her on top of it. As she floundered in a sea of skirts, he flipped her onto her back and yanked her to the edge of the bed. As she struggled to sit up, he spread her thighs. She froze when he pressed his crotch against hers.

"You want to kick off our wedding night with me spanking your ass?" he asked as he loomed over her.

"This isn't a real wedding night. It's an expensive charade so you can solidify your rule of New York by showing you have my family's support."

"Is that what you think?"

"Yes. This is about revenge."

"A part of it."

"And the other parts?"

His eyes dropped to where he was pressed intimately against her. "You know the rest."

He pulled her into a sitting position. She tensed, ready to punch his dick. He disarmed her by tunneling his hands into her hair and gently tugging the bobby pins out. She closed her eyes as she fought the surge of pleasure caused by the simple action. This was far more seductive than sexual fondling. She swayed toward him before she caught herself.

She had grown up without hugs or kisses. Affection was something she received in small doses from Thea when her father wasn't looking. Everyone kept her at arm's length, afraid of inciting her father's wrath. In boarding school, the teachers pushed them hard, knowing their jobs would be forfeit if the students didn't excel. When she was engaged to Ford, she was giddy over hand-holding and pecks on the cheek. She was starved for touch. Roth seemed to sense that and used it to bind her to him. Did he remember? Was that why he sifted his hand through her hair slowly, soothing her when she wanted to fight? When she tried to pull away, he pressed her face against his abdomen and massaged her nape, coaxing her to relax. How could she hold out against him? She didn't know how to battle his tender onslaught.

He's going to ruin you.

Her eyes opened as Kaia's words echoed in her mind. "Why does she think you'll ruin me?"

"Why would I do that?"

"To punish me for leaving you?"

"Does this feel like punishment?"

She swallowed hard. "I don't know how to do this."

She didn't know how to compartmentalize when it came to him. They had history, so he wasn't a faceless fuck. Once upon a time, he had been her best friend and savior, and now... She had no fucking idea what they were. Enemies? Partners? It was only hours into day one, and he had her all fucked up.

"You don't have to do anything."

She closed her eyes as he tipped her face up to his. He defused her tension even more by covering her face in kisses.

"Stop," she said, eyes burning.

His fingers traveled down her throat. "Did my mom tell you she calls me a monster?"

Her eyes flew open and clashed with his. "What?"

"My mom thinks something's wrong with me. She used to take me to psychologists in the hopes of getting me institutionalized." He leaned down and pressed a kiss over her hammering pulse. "Maybe she's right."

She clutched a handful of his suit. "Roth."

"I'm not what she wanted in a son. That's something you and I have in common. We never fit in with our families." He sucked on her neck and smiled against her skin when her breath hitched. He followed the tendon in her neck to her jaw and then her ear. "You're a Hennessy, heir to one of the largest empires in the country. You were engaged to a Baldwin, a golden boy who grew up like you. On the outside, your life was perfect, but you were looking for something. You found it in me." He raised his head and looked down at her. "You gave me what no one else has."

"What?"

His hand circled her throat. "You accepted me for who I am. You chose me when no one else did."

When she tried to draw away, his hand tightened on her throat.

"You gave me everything. How can anyone compare to that?"

"Stop it, Roth." He was slicing open old scars that had never completely healed.

"If you remarried, I would have destroyed him."

She could see he meant that.

"If I had the names of the men in your books, the men you used to forget me, I'd fuck them up." His eyes traveled over her face. "Be careful who you bring between us."

"You said—"

His hand flexed, cutting off her words.

"You forgave your father. Why not me?"

"He loved me."

His eyes moved over her face. "Do you want me to love you?"

"No."

"Why not?" he asked as his thumb stroked her pulse.

"I want to be free."

"I'm a wealthy man."

"Money doesn't equal freedom, and you... you'll never be satisfied with what you have. I already know what road you're on. I've already lived that life. I don't want any part of it."

"I'm not like everyone else."

"I want *freedom*," she said fiercely. "I grew wings after I left you. I soared without you."

"I'll burn your fucking wings."

"You have me for a year. After that—"

His mouth closing over hers swallowed her voice. He gripped her hair, angling her face for him. Her mind went blank as he swamped her senses with him—his taste, his touch, his will. There was darkness in Roth that drew her like a moth to a flame. Ford's impeccable manners hadn't done it for her. It was Roth's aggression and rough edges that drew her in. She wanted authenticity, a rare commodity in her world. People were constantly hedging their bets or kissing someone's ass for a favor. Roth hadn't bowed to her father's decrees. He wanted to get to the top through hard work. Back then, he made it clear that he desired her and never made any false promises. That was why she believed him in London. He never lied.

His hand went between her legs. Her underwear was no barrier. She gripped his jacket and pulled him against her. She didn't know how to feel about him, but the bitter heat he ignited overruled her anger and hurt. He was right. This was all that mattered. She just prayed it burned out before she got singed.

He groaned when he discovered how wet she was. When she rocked her hips against his hand, he cursed and fumbled with his pants. He freed his penis and sank into her, as if he couldn't bear to be apart from her a moment longer. He detached their mouths and pressed his forehead against hers.

"Look at me."

She opened her eyes. He glared at her as he slid in to the hilt. The layers of her skirt were a crumpled mess between them.

"No one but me," he growled.

She stroked his beard and fingered the scar on his neck. "I know."

His hand came over hers and brushed over the massive ring. She saw the dark flash of satisfaction in his eyes.

"You're mine."

And he was hers. They had changed roles. Now he was the one who was sought after and admired. He was an eligible bachelor that any of her friends would love to claim. As Dai's reaction to him slid through her mind, her nails sank into the back of his neck. He was the bad boy who fucked like a god and would give it to them dirty.

Women sensed it instinctively and would do anything for a taste. That was why Dai had hit on him minutes after he fucked her. They wanted a man to wreck them… For the next year, this beast was hers.

He wrapped his hand around her throat and pinned her on her back. He loomed over her, bearing down to force himself as deep as possible. She gasped, limbs jerking as she processed the pain and pleasure.

"Say you're mine," he demanded.

The turbulence in his black eyes told her his control was in shreds. His façade was cracking, as it always did in the bedroom. After weeks of playing his game, she wasn't about to wave the white flag. She might wear his ring and bear his name, but she wasn't going to give him everything.

"Jasmine," he said raggedly as he thrust into her, face screwing up with pleasure as she flexed her inner muscles to torture him.

She yanked on his shirt and was pleased when the buttons popped free. Her hand skimmed over his hot flesh before that hand on her neck forced her down again.

"You're mine," he said again.

When she raised her brows at him, deliberately not repeating his demand, he froze. She hissed as he planted himself deep.

"You want to play games?" he asked as he nibbled on her bottom lip before he bit.

When she didn't tap out, his hand landed on her clit and applied pressure, making her squirm. When he released her, she swiped her tongue over her lip, sure he had broken the skin. He hadn't, but it hurt like a bitch.

"Say you're mine before I fuck your mouth."

"That's a threat?" she scoffed. She didn't sound as tough as she wanted to because she was panting like a bitch in heat.

He hauled her off the bed and carried her to the fireplace, where he settled her on her knees on a bed of white rose petals. As she looked up at him, he twisted one hand in her hair.

"Hands behind your back," he ordered.

She did as she was told. He paused for a moment, but she didn't balk. She held his eyes and saw something shift in the black abyss before he said, "Open."

Once more, she obeyed. He held her head steady with both hands as he slid into her mouth.

"Ever since I saw you wearing this color, this is all I could think of." His lips peeled back from his teeth as he sank into her moist cavern. "Those purple lips wrapped around my cock. Yes."

She kept eye contact as he pulled back and slid in again. He seemed mesmerized by the sight of his cock disappearing into her mouth. When he tried to pull back again, she leaned forward, taking him deep in her throat. Roth tipped his head back and let out a tormented groan as she choked and then withdrew.

"Jasmine, *fuck*."

He didn't take his eyes off her as she took over. The stinging grip in her hair turned into pets as she sucked him as if her life depended on it. His eyes closed, and he yanked away, hissing through his teeth. Knowing he was close to orgasm, she chased him.

"Fuck! You don't know when to quit, do you?"

She gave him a sloppy smile as she feathered her tongue around him. She dragged his pants down and scraped her nails down his sensitive buttocks. He bucked, and she took all of him.

"Fuck, I can't."

He shoved her backward. She landed on her back and spread her arms on the thick carpet as if she were about to make a snow angel. She sighed as he spread her legs and filled her. He braced his arms on either side of her with her skirts floating around them.

She knew it was going to be rough, and she wasn't wrong. She cried out as he pounded her into the floor, which was definitely not as soft as the bed. He pulled out so only the tip was in, and then used his full weight to slam back home. He grabbed the lace neckline of her gown and yanked until he could get at her breasts. His arms hooked under her knees, changing the sensation.

"Come," he said as he bit her nipple.

She wrapped herself around him and slid around on her skirts until he was fucking her just right, every thrust sending bolts of lightning through her. She bit his neck as she came, clawing and fighting the excruciating wave. Roth pinned her to the carpet and fucked her hard enough to make her contemplate tapping out. When he came, he balled her beneath him, keeping her ass tipped up as he spilled.

When he collapsed on top of her, she let out a pitiful moan. He buried his face in her hair spread over the carpet.

"You shouldn't test me," he panted.

"I can take it."

His fingers slipped over her swollen mouth. "Tell me."

She knew what he was asking. Still, she resisted. He lifted his head. His expression was as gentle as it was ever going to be when he had the weathered features of a pirate.

"Jasmine."

She stared at him and said nothing.

"You're mine." His hand went to her hand and brushed over the ring. "Legally, you're bound to me. Sexually, you can't resist."

"Emotionally? You have no power," she hissed.

His expression hardened. "I'm going to break you."

"Not if I break you first."

His lips curved in a cruel smile. "I'm looking forward to it."

He rose. She closed her eyes and clamped her shaking legs together. She heard the sound of running water and then Roth was back. He brushed her legs apart and ran a warm, damp cloth over her. She lay there and allowed him to do whatever he wanted as she floated. Four times he traveled to and from the bathroom, rinsing the rag before he came back. She hissed when he tried to clean her face with baby wipes.

"Roth! Makeup wipes!"

"Where?"

She gave him instructions, and when he brought them to her, she slapped his hand away when he tugged on her fake eyelashes.

"Dai's going to freak out if she knows what you did to this dress," she said as she brushed her hand over the ripped bodice.

"I paid for it. I can do whatever I want."

He scooped her up and placed her in bed. When she tried to pull the dress down, he stopped her.

"I haven't gotten my money's worth yet."

He stretched out beside her, wrapped a layer of satin around his cock, and closed her hand around him. She tipped on her side and got comfortable as she stroked him. His eyes roved over her face, assessing and cataloging. When she couldn't stand his appraisal another second, she slid down and used her mouth on him again. This time, when he came, he aimed at her snow-white skirts. She made a face as his eyes closed.

"Aren't you going to help me out of this?"

He tucked her against his side. "Sleep in it."

"I can't sleep in this! It's tight and uncomfortable."

His hand brushed over the fluffy skirts. "Give me ten minutes. I want to fuck you one more time in it. Then you can sleep."

CHAPTER 21

*W*hen she woke, the room was still dark. The fire had long since died, leaving a chill in the air. She rolled away from Roth who was facedown and snoring lightly. She winced as she straightened. He had put her through her paces last night. She stepped over the ripped and soiled gown on her way to the bathroom and showered before she crept downstairs. The house was quiet. She couldn't have gotten more than four hours of sleep, but her mind was wide-awake. She made herself a cup of coffee and went to her sanctuary. She paused in front of her father's desk and gave him a silent good morning before she built a fire in the library. She settled on the couch with her notebook and listened to the pleasant crackle and pop.

Kaia's words still floated around in her mind, but she couldn't dwell on them. It was done. She married him. Roth could be a merciless asshole, but a monster? Although he would spend millions in the name of revenge, she didn't think he needed to be institutionalized. Her father could be classified in the same category as Roth. Men like them didn't recognize the word no and never forgot a slight. That was what drove them to be the best and succeed in a world that wanted to keep them down. They were fighters.

"Miss?"

She turned and saw Thea hovering near the doorway. "What are you doing here so early?"

"I came to make breakfast. I was hoping to catch you alone." Thea advanced into the room with her hands behind her back. "I tried to speak to you yesterday, but I was the last to know."

"What are you talking about?"

Thea held up an envelope. "This is from your father."

Her heart soared. She leaped to her feet and rushed toward her. "I have a letter? Why did you wait so long to give it to me?"

She took the heavy envelope, which had her name on it in her father's bold scrawl.

"I had orders."

"What orders?" she asked as she broke the seal on the envelope.

"I was instructed to give this to you only if you became involved with…" Thea looked back at the door before she whispered, "Mr. Roth."

When she froze, Thea nodded vigorously.

"He told me to give it to you directly and not to trust anyone with it. I tried to give it to you before the wedding, but I couldn't get you alone. I'm so sorry."

"I don't understand," she said.

"Me either, miss. I hope… I hope it's not too late."

She reached into the envelope and pulled out her father's personal stationery and a disc. She unfolded the letter.

JASMINE,

If you're reading this, you've broken your promise to me, and James Roth is back in your life. Don't let him in. He'll take what he wants from you and leave you with nothing. He's not the kind of man you need. He—

"MISS!"

Thea's panicked hiss broke her concentration. She raised her head to find that Roth had entered the library. She hid the disc and letter behind her back as he cupped her face.

"You're not supposed to leave the bed before me," he said before he gave her a deep kiss.

She couldn't participate when her heart was in her throat.

He pulled away and cocked his head. "What's wrong?"

"Nothing."

His hand went behind her back and brushed against the letter. She stumbled back.

"I'll meet you in the kitchen," she said with a brilliant smile.

His eyes narrowed into slits. "What's going on?"

"Nothing. Just let me—"

He grabbed her arm and forced it around. He ripped the letter from her grasp and held it aloft when she leaped for it.

"Roth! That isn't for you!" she shouted.

"This is your father's handwriting," he said quietly.

"Give it to me!"

He turned from her and began to scan the letter. She went cold with panic and saw Thea watching with her hands over her mouth. Jasmine tucked the disc into the back of her pants, and started after Roth who paced toward the window as he read. She ran toward him and made a dive for the letter.

"Roth, give it to me!"

He grabbed her flailing wrist and twisted her arm, forcing her to drop to her knees or risk breaking it.

"Roth!" she screeched.

"Miss!" Thea cried and rushed toward them.

"Where the fuck is that disc?" he snarled.

She looked up through watery eyes. His mask was missing. Whatever her father had written in the letter had shoved him into a black rage. The grip on her arm wasn't a threat, it was a promise. The man she tempted and teased throughout the night was gone. She was looking at a stranger capable of anything.

He released her as Thea reached them. She cradled her throbbing shoulder as tears of pain streamed down her face. She saw him stop in front of the fire and make a flicking motion.

"*No!*"

She stumbled toward the fireplace and dropped to her knees in front of it. The letter perched on a log. When she reached into the flames, he hauled her back.

"Let me go! That's the last thing I have from him!" she screamed.

She watched with horrified eyes as the flames licked the corner of the letter. Orange ripped through the thin pages. She saw the ink bleed a moment before black scorched them, her father's words disappearing forever in the blink of an eye. When he released her, she knelt on her hands and knees, staring at the last message from her father turned to ash. She couldn't breathe.

She felt her sweater ride up, and a moment later, the disc was pulled from the back of her pants. She whirled as Roth strode to her father's desk. She lurched to her feet as he grabbed a gold statue and brought it down on the disc.

"Roth, *stop!*"

She raced across the office as he brought the statue down three more times. By the time she wrenched the damaged statue from his hands, the disc was shattered. Roth grabbed the pieces and went back to the fireplace and threw the shards in before he turned back to her.

"Where the fuck did that letter come from?" he asked softly.

She opened her mouth, but no lie came to mind. He turned toward Thea, who had her hands over her mouth. He started toward the older woman with a purposeful stride. The housekeeper backed away, hands raised to protect herself from a blow.

"Roth, no!"

He grabbed Thea by the throat. Even across the distance, she saw Thea's eyes bulge with terror as she wrapped her hands around his wrist.

"Did he give you anything else?" He shook her like a rag doll. "Answer me!"

Jasmine slammed into him. "Roth, let her go!"

He ignored her and tipped Thea's head at an angle that made her freeze.

"Holy shit, Roth, you're going to kill her!"

"Tell me if there's more and tell the truth before I snap your fucking neck," he said in a voice she had never heard before.

"No," Thea said hoarsely. "No more."

"What the fuck is going on here?"

Roth released Thea who crumpled to the ground, wheezing and choking, as her family clustered in the doorway. Jasmine dropped to her knees beside Thea as Lyle advanced into the room.

"What the fuck, Roth?" Lyle roared.

Polara began to cry, forcing Colette to retreat. Ariana herded Kye and Bailey backward as they stared at her with puffy eyes the size of saucers.

"Thea, are you okay?" Jasmine whispered as panicked tears slipped down her face. "I'm so sorry."

"What happened? Do you—" Rami dropped to his knees beside them and spotted the marks on Thea's throat. He shot Jasmine a stunned look. "What's going on here?"

She ignored him. "Thea, should I call an ambulance? Can you talk? Is there damage? I—"

Thea squeezed her hand and shook her head as her trembling hand brushed over her throat.

"You can't talk," she realized. "Rami—"

"Roth, tell me what the fuck is going on, or I'm calling the cops," Lyle shouted.

Roth stood in front of the fire, hands in his pockets. As Lyle came close, he turned. It was clear that Roth was ready for a physical altercation. She knew Lyle could hold his own, but there was something about Roth... He didn't play fair, and he didn't care who his opponent was. Case in point, he had just attacked an elderly woman without hesitation. Kaia's words drifted through her mind as she climbed to her feet. *The psychologist says he lacks empathy. It allows him to focus on his goals without letting emotion get in his way.* Roth's eyes flicked to her.

It was a clear warning to stay back. She ignored the warning. This was her family he was attacking.

"Roth, don't!"

"Explain what the hell is going on here, Roth," Lyle ordered.

"The housekeeper gave Jasmine something from her father," Roth said.

"And what was that?" Lyle demanded.

Roth's gaze skewered her. "Blackmail."

She felt the bottom drop out of her stomach. Behind her, she could hear voices and movement, but she couldn't move. She was welded to the spot.

"Maximus blackmailed me. He told me he would destroy the evidence if I agreed to his terms. He double-crossed me."

"And he gave the evidence to his housekeeper?" Lyle asked, trying to follow the logic.

There were five beats of silence before it clicked.

"He gave it to her for safe keeping, in case you came back into the picture," Lyle surmised.

Roth looked back at him without expression.

Lyle turned to her. "Where is it?"

"He destroyed it," she whispered.

"Did you see it?"

She shook her head.

Lyle turned back to Roth. "It didn't even take twenty-four hours for you to fuck up. We're out of here. Let's go, Minnie."

"She isn't going anywhere," Roth said.

"I'm not leaving her with you," Lyle snarled as he reached for her arm.

"Touch her, and I'll deck you."

"I'd like to see you try."

"Lyle, stop!" She pressed a hand against his heaving chest. "You... you should leave."

"You're not staying here."

She gripped his arm. "You need to go."

"I'm not—"

"I'm okay," she said in a dead voice.

"You're not okay. I'm not going to let him abuse you."

"He doesn't," she lied as her shoulder throbbed. "Please, Lyle. Just go."

"I can get you out of this," he said. "You don't have to put up with him. If he's using you in some way—"

"He isn't," she ground out and pushed against his chest. "Please."

Lyle stared at her for a long minute before he shot Roth a murderous look. "If I find one bruise on her, I'm going to do what Maximus should have done and call a hit on your ass." He kissed her temple. "Promise me you'll call."

"I will," she said instantly.

"We'll take Thea."

"Yes, please get her checked out. Make sure she's okay," she said hoarsely.

Lyle gave Roth one more fuming look before he stalked out of the library. She stared straight ahead as she listened to the sounds of her family's departure. When the front door slammed, and the sound of cars careening down the driveway left them in buzzing silence, she finally looked at him. He had resumed his stance in front of the fire. His mask was back in place, and he looked unfazed by what had transpired. The wrath that exploded out of him had disappeared as if it had never been. The only sign of destruction was the broken statue and fresh gouges on her father's desk.

"What have you done?" she whispered.

He said nothing.

"You went through all this trouble to convince my family we're doing things right this time around, and then you fuck it up. What the hell is wrong with you?"

"That was unfortunate."

"Unfortunate," she repeated and then shouted, *"Are you fucking serious?"*

She ran across the library. He turned as she stopped beside him. Her hand stung as she smacked him with every ounce of strength she had. His head snapped to the side. When she tried to hit him again, he grabbed her wrists and held her still as she fought him like a wild thing.

"You vile, disgusting pig! You destroyed the last thing my father ever gave me. You hurt *Thea*! How could you do that? What the fuck is wrong with you?"

"Calm down."

"Fuck calm! What did he blackmail you about, Roth?"

His gaze sharpened. "You didn't read the letter."

"I didn't have time to read more than a few lines before you came in! Let me go. I don't want you touching me."

He released her, and she paced away, arms wrapped around her middle as bile rose. She felt as if a bomb went off in her face. She was dazed and still trying to process the chaos. She stopped in front of the massive windows and looked out at the lake. The sun had risen, spreading light over the beautiful, tranquil scene. Everything looked as it should, but her world felt as if it had been turned upside down. Something ugly and evil had erupted in her sanctuary, and she didn't know what to do about it.

If you're reading this, you've broken your promise to me, and James Roth is back in your life.

She clapped a hand over her mouth to smother a sob. If her father could see her now, he would lose his fucking mind. But what choice did she have? If she hadn't... Several things collided in her mind and her blood ran cold. She turned and found him standing nearby, watching her intently, waiting.

"You came back after he died," she said numbly.

His neutral expression didn't change. There was no emotion in his eyes; they were a matte black that revealed nothing.

"That's why you're back in the States." She wrapped her hand around her throat as it began to swell. "If he was alive, you wouldn't be able to come near me."

The silence made her skin crawl.

"I'm right, aren't I?" she whispered.

After seeing him in action, his motionlessness made the hair on her nape rise.

She took a step back. "He blackmailed you to sign the divorce papers."

Like he had in that empty hospital corridor in Colorado, he moved with her, blocking the exit.

"You gave Maximus a reason to dig and uncover something that should have stayed buried," he said quietly.

Terror ripped through her. She held up a hand as she retreated. "Back off, Roth. This was a mistake."

"I'm not going to hurt you."

She let out a raspy laugh that made her eyes fill with tears. "You expect me to believe that after what you did to Thea? After you nearly broke my arm?"

He held out his hand. "Let me ice it."

"Fuck you. Stay away from me."

His expression hardened. "This changes nothing."

She halted in her tracks. "How can you say that? It changes *every-thing*. First your mother and now my dad sent a warning from the grave." A thought slipped through her mind, and she tensed. "Do they both know the same secret?"

He stopped stalking and came at her with purpose. She froze at the sight of him stampeding toward her and pivoted at the last second, darting past him and streaking toward the exit. She didn't hear any sound behind her. She was so close to the door. Maybe Mo or Johan could—

An arm banded around her middle, yanking her to a halt with such force that she thought she was going to puke. He pulled her back against him and buried his face in her hair.

"Don't you fucking run from me."

She was so freaked out that she didn't move, barely even breathed. He grabbed her arm and led her out of the library. She followed in a stupefied daze as he walked into the kitchen and rummaged in the freezer for ice. He boosted her onto the wood island and kept an eye on her as he wrapped a dishcloth around a bag of frozen vegetables. When he prodded her shoulder, she let out a painful hiss. A muscle tensed in his jaw as he draped the bag on her shoulder.

"I'm sorry."

She kept her eyes downcast, unable to look at him. All she could think of was Thea's terrified expression. He had been seconds from—

When he cupped her chin, she almost toppled face first off the island in an effort to get away from him. He let out a low growl as he placed her where he wanted her and stepped between her knees, boxing her in.

"Now you're afraid of me?" he hissed.

"I'd be a fool not to be."

She chanced a look at his face. He was scowling, and as she briefly met his eyes, saw that savage rage was still there, just banked. She looked away.

Neither of them said a word as he adjusted the ice pack on her shoulder. The clock on the wall ticked away as questions tumbled through her mind. When she couldn't stand the silence any longer, she spoke.

"What did you do that was so horrible that you would kill to keep that secret?" she whispered.

She looked up and saw he was staring out the window at the lake.

"Are you in the mafia?" she asked, watching for a reaction.

No response.

"Did you steal from someone?"

Nothing.

"Murder?" she whispered hoarsely.

He turned back to her, face expressionless. "You'll never know."

She shook her head. "I can't do this."

"You will."

She stared at him. "You can't be serious."

"One year, Jasmine."

"But…"

"I hoped we could be civil this time around, but Maximus interfered again." His eyes skewered hers. "But he's too late."

"You think my family's not going to fight you after they saw you attack a defenseless woman? When they know Dad blackmailed you about something?"

"I don't need your family's approval. It would have made things easier, but it wasn't necessary."

"This isn't going to work!"

"It will."

What the hell had she gotten herself into? "What are you going to do to me, Roth?"

"Nothing." He brushed a hand down her cheek and locked his jaw when she jerked away. "I'm not going to hurt you."

Her gaze dropped to the ice pack he was holding against her shoulder. "You already have."

He stared at her for a long moment before he confessed, "I've done much worse."

Ice spread through her chest as he confirmed what she already knew. "You really are a monster."

"I am," he agreed. "And now you have to live with it."

AUTHOR'S NOTE

Hey everyone,

I know. I KNOW. Don't kill me. I tried to make this book a stand-alone. I really did! 75% in I was like, "Oh, shit." I considered stuffing everything into one book and not exploring the dark corners, but it would have been a disservice to the characters and once the door closes, it can never be reopened. So, I left the door open.

This book was really out of my comfort zone. I had vague ideas of the beginning—exes getting stuck in a cabin in the middle of a snowstorm, but I didn't realize their world would be so intricate and vast. I didn't realize their history would be so complicated or that I would connect so strongly with them. I hope you enjoyed them as much as I did!

If you have a chance to leave a review or recommend my books, please do so! It helps me out so much! Make sure you sign up to my newsletter (https://www.subscribepage.com/MKNewReleases) to stay informed.

Sincerely,

Mia

Sneak peek of the next book in series, Bitter Secrets, at end of book!

BOOKS BY MIA KNIGHT

Crime Lord Series:

Crime Lord's Captive

Recaptured by the Crime Lord

Once A Crime Lord

Awakened by Sin

Crime Lord's Paradise

Singed Series:

Bitter Heat

Bitter Secrets

ABOUT THE AUTHOR

Mia Knight is the author of the Crime Lord and Singed Series. She writes dark, contemporary romances that make you question your beliefs and leave you feeling drained and emotionally bereft. If you like your men dark with questionable morals and a possessive edge, you may have come to the right place.

When Mia isn't writing, she's on the road in her RV. She loves coffee, daydreaming, road trips to nowhere, and the sound of rain storms. She is constantly shadowed by her dogs who don't judge her when she laughs and cries with the voices in her head. Mia's also a notorious hermit so please be patient if she doesn't get back to you promptly.

Website: https://miaknight.com/
Newsletter: https://www.subscribepage.com/MKNewReleases

g goodreads.com/authormiaknight
BB bookbub.com/profile/mia-knight
instagram.com/authormiaknight
f facebook.com/miaknightauthor
twitter.com/authormiaknight

SNEAK PEEK

BITTER SECRETS, BOOK 2

Jasmine stared out of the floor-to ceiling-windows, blind to the multimillion dollar view of New York City spread out before her. The state-of-the-art kitchen was filled with golden light, giving the impression all was well in the world, when nothing could be further from the truth. Wracked with indecision, she wrapped her arms around herself and bit her lip. She wasn't sure how she should handle this, but it couldn't be put off any longer. She had to say *something*...

She snatched up her phone, dialed, and paced around the island. She jumped when an impatient, masculine voice barked in her ear, "It's been three fucking days."

"I know, Lyle. I'm sorry." She rubbed the throbbing space between her brows. "I told you, we've been trying to sort things out."

"Are you hurt? Did he touch you?"

"Of course not," Jasmine said even as she rotated her bruised shoulder, which no longer ached.

He exhaled loudly. She could imagine her brother-in-law pinching the bridge of his nose as he prayed for patience. Under other circumstances, she would have been amused, but there was nothing funny about this, and they both knew it.

"So," he bit out. "What's the verdict?"

She opened her mouth, but no sound emerged. Her hand fluttered to her throat as panic took hold. Could she do this? Did she have a choice?

"Minnie."

Lyle's clipped tone warned her he was out of patience, not that he had much of that virtue on the best of days. He left her with Roth against his better judgment and would have returned for her if she hadn't convinced him to stay away, so she and Roth could figure out how they would proceed in their relationship.

That was a lie.

Her father's damning letter made no difference to Roth. He was holding her to their original agreement. She drew diagrams and made lists, hoping for a solution to magically appear on the page, but no matter how she looked at her situation, there was no way out. Roth demanded recompense for the hell her father put him through. Either she would pay in the privacy of their marriage, or her family would pay publicly.

She could disappear; her family couldn't. Roth inhabited the same world they did. Their every move was observed by tens of thousands —employees, business associates, reporters, Wall Street. If Roth and her family clashed, the consequences would be devastating. Even if her sisters sold off their shares in Hennessy and Co, Roth wouldn't stop. She had no doubt he would go after her brothers-in-law. There was no limit to how far he would go in his quest for revenge.

The ease with which Roth orchestrated his takeover proved that he had been strategizing behind the scenes for years. Her father taught him a valuable lesson when he ran him out of the country. Roth spent the intervening years fortifying himself so no one could best him this time around. If she tried to back out of their deal, she could only imagine the hell he would unleash. The best way forward was to keep the charade intact and play the part of a fool in love, willing to overlook all the red flags, and give him another shot.

"We…" She swallowed hastily to coat her dry throat. "We're going to work it out."

"What the hell does that mean?"

She straightened her spine and tried to sound sure of herself as she declared, "It means I'm staying."

Available on all retailers!

Made in the USA
Middletown, DE
03 February 2023

23850763R00179